A PETE BROWN MYSTERY

Murder in the Mangroves

ANGIE ROSS

MURDER IN THE MANGROVES

Book One of the Pete Brown Mysteries

All rights reserved. The content contained within this book may not be reproduced, duplicated, or transmitted without direct written permission from the author or the publisher.

This book is copyright protected.

This book is only for personal use. You cannot amend, distribute, sell, use, quote or paraphrase any part, or the content within this book, without the consent of the author or publisher. Under no circumstances will any blame or legal responsibility be held against the publisher, or author, for any damages, reparation, or monetary loss due to the information contained within this book. Either directly or indirectly. You are responsible for your own choices, actions, and results.

This is a work of fiction. Names, characters, business, events and incidents are the products of the author's imagination. Any resemblance to actual persons, living or dead, or actual events is purely coincidental.

Printed in the United States of America

Copyright © 2023 Angie Ross

All rights reserved.

ISBN: 979-8-9900567-1-8

For Jesse

I am full of love tonight
Come look into my eyes, and let's go off
Sailing, my dear, on a long ocean ride.
This world will not touch you,
I will keep you snug upon my seat.
Let's plot
To make the moon jealous
With a radiance leaping from your cheek.

-Hafiz

PROLOGUE

"Alright people," Shae said as she handed a life jacket to each of her guests. "I know many of you are up way past your bedtime, but I don't want anyone sleeping with the fishes, if you know what I mean."

Light laughter ensued among the guests.

Her skin was getting sticky with sweat under the blue long-sleeved SPF hoodie and leggings but she knew she'd cool off once they got on the water. And sweat was better than getting eaten alive by the mosquitoes. Shae tucked a lone dread back up under her baseball hat.

"It's very important you all wear your life vests the entire time. In the unlikely event we get separated, you also have an emergency kit in your boat with a flashlight. But it's super important you don't use any light during the tour. The organisms are very sensitive to light and we want to respect the natural ecosystem. Any disruption can cause major damage and we want to leave their habitat as we found it."

Shae knew it was an impossible request. Someone would continue the day drinking they'd started at the beach and toss the evidence right into the river. And without fail, some older couple would have no idea how to use their camera and blast the beautiful darkness with their flash.

But it was important to aim for an aura of seriousness. People wanted to feel like they were getting ready to hike Mt. Everest. The comb jellies and dinoflagellates were beautiful but not the 'underwater shooting stars' as she had seen some guides market them. Sadly, the internet had done people a major disservice in setting expectations for a bioluminescent tour. They were miracles of nature, yet the photoshopped images led to most people feeling disappointed rather than awe-struck.

The experience of lighting up the water in the black depth of a mangrove tunnel was magical if you had the right attitude. Shae knew it was up to her to create the kind of environment where people would still feel they had seen something important—beautiful. Perception was everything, after all.

That was easier said than done when leading eight boats out on the water in the Endless Islands at night. The channels were narrow and it was difficult to give her tour spiel without yelling so everyone could hear, which really killed the vibe.

But Shae was stepping into her own and getting skilled at moving alongside the boats, softly back paddling so each boat would get one-on-one attention. This also had an effect like the police presence at a stadium. People tended to be less unruly when she might show up alongside them at any moment.

"Okay, boats in the water." Shae's voice was hardly above a whisper.

"And remember, this is the trickiest part of the whole night—one foot, 2', and then shimmy." Gracelessly but without incident, all 16 people were on the water. Shae breathed out; she always held her breath for this part.

The group glided through the neighborhood, a little taste of Venice as they oohed and aahed at the massive waterfront houses. The bungalow in Tropical Orange with the old-school slide into the 40' long pool. The two-story painted in Venezuelan Sea blue with coordinating striped chaise lounges and a resort-style cabana poolside. A Moorish mansion in classic off-white Seapearl, contrasted by the Spanish tile roof and the bright green Sabal Palms. Soon, they would hit the river and enter the Endless Islands. Shae smiled in anticipation of the group's reaction; the view never failed to disappoint.

The group turned east from the beautiful houses and the collective gasp was audible. Shae loved this part. The constant hum of landscaping and traffic disappeared and the operational sounds of nature took over. A mullet jumped out of the water and an osprey swooped in for the catch. Multi-story condominiums that had loomed large on land were eclipsed by the marsh.

Other than the occasional plane far above, there were no visible markers of modern life. The June sky maintained a hint of the blue; it looked almost smoky. The dusky sky added a certain haunting beauty and created the illusion that the Endless Islands were, in fact, endless.

Shae knew dusk also ignited primal fear in many guests—something about being out in the water wilderness at night. It wasn't like the forest, where you might retrace your steps if you got lost. The water erased your trail as quickly as you made it. A little bit of fear heightened the senses and would make the bioluminescence that much more powerful. Shae remained purposely silent to deepen this moment.

Shae understood, however, that too much fear would create a panic. And really, they were in Mother Nature's backyard and she didn't take kindly to hubris. So, Shae began to tell her story about her childhood in the Endless Islands. She talked about her work to get this area declared an official Florida sanctuary and talked through the many birds and animals that called the islands home.

The guests, inevitably amazed she was able to make sense of the unique trees and islands, released some of the tension. They were grateful to give their survival to someone else. Someone with a 5-star rating on Google must be good enough to keep you alive.

Soon the group would enter deep into the islands where the creatures shined the brightest. Shae discovered this little cove years ago and had a sort of unspoken dibs on it, in large part because it was almost impossible to find.

The cove was unique because of a sandbar big enough for the group to disembark on and take pictures from the island. It was always a big hit to take pictures of the guests with the glowing water in the background—even if the photos were somewhat disappointing. She'd have a tiny bonfire ready for s'mores. Although the tour was only a few miles round-trip, a little snack always helped people get through with less complaining.

"Oh my goodness, look at the bright pink!" one of the women in the front boat gasped.

They were almost to the hidden entrance to her island. Shae was towards the back and was mildly annoyed as she tried to ease through the narrow canal to the front. Shae liked to be the one to announce the colors but had gotten stuck in the back with a talkative couple from Milwaukee.

"It's such a bright pink—almost magenta!" the other woman shouted.

Shae frowned as she continued to maneuver to the front of the group. The creatures were almost never pink. The guests were all fumbling with their wet bags to grab their phones. The boats were bumping, making it nearly impossible to pass and putting more than a few guests dangerously close to falling in the water.

It was shallow enough to be safe, but a wet customer became a cranky customer. Shae felt a vague sense of panic growing inside her chest as she struggled to maintain calm. Panicking was the worst thing you could do out on the water.

"Wait, what is that?" More frantic searching for phones; people were desperate to capture something on camera. "Shae, what is that?"

Shae sensed doubt in the voice, doubt they were safe after-all. "Is that...is that..." And then a scream pierced the darkness. It was a shrill noise that was incongruent to the natural beauty around them, better fit for a horror movie.

Shae closed her eyes and turned her head upward as if pleading with the heavens. In that moment, still stuck in the middle of the group, Shae knew exactly what they saw.

"Please, people! Put the cameras away!" Shae hated how her voice sounded, whiny and begging. Not at all like the authority she rightfully had as the captain.

The group made it to the sandbed. The two women that had been up front were huddled together, sobbing, while the older couple from Milwaukee regaled them with a story about how they had once seen a deadly car accident and been the first to call the police. But most of the group were taking pictures. Some took stills, some narrated the scene on video. As if trying to reenact their favorite true crime podcast.

Shae felt her knees buckle in fear but tried to maintain control of the situation. Her mind was reeling, but Shae did her best to put out an image of calm. "Everyone, I know this is unexpected and very distressing. But the best thing we can do is calmly return back to the main shore so we can contact the proper authorities and also get you back home safely."

This last line shifted the mood as the guests begrudgingly acknowledged their own mortality. They quietly stepped into their boats and awaited Shae to lead them to safety. Shae took one last look at the body, unable to look at the face. The expensive lowlights were now matted with conch sand. The vibrant pink bikini hung loosely off Emily's shoulders, the strings extending out in the water like tiny jellyfish.

1

Finding a dead body should be the worst part of someone's month, but no such luck for Shae Brunell.

'Unimaginable that anyone would support this business. The owner is just a bad person. ONE STAR!'

'Perfect if you want your life to be in peril on your family vacation. Otherwise, skip this one. One star.'

Shae's chest tightened as she thumbed through the never-ending page of reviews. Every single day, there were more. Her perfect 5-star rating from 82 reviews had dropped to 1.2 with over 2,000 reviews. She knew she should be more focused on the fact that someone died—the bloated body flashed in her mind and her stomach lurched—but she'd worked so hard. Her reviews represented five years of hard work with hundreds and hundreds of happy customers.

Shae dropped her hand to pet River's head as she tried to push away the petty thought. She hated how much online reviews mattered in her business. Those 82 reviews were hard won at the expense of years of hustling, pleading, giving her all on every single tour no matter how she felt. Instead of late nights partying, Shae gave the better part of her 20s and now 30s to building a business that was being destroyed in a matter of weeks. Shae wanted to cry but her whole body was still stuck in disbelief, even over a month later.

Vaguely, she sensed her pulse pounding in her chest. She'd grown used to ignoring the panic signals from her body. There was no way to process through the stress at this point. She knew she shouldn't, but she found herself clicking over to Twitter. River gave a sigh and turned circles at her feet.

The hashtag #watergate still sat at the top of the trending list. As if the reviews weren't enough, Twitter users were losing their minds because the local police had suggested Emily's death was an accidental drowning.

An accidental drowning wasn't exciting enough for the crowd; they were insisting some kind of foul play. Don't do it, don't do it. But Shae was subject to the same rubbernecking urge as everyone else. She clicked.

There is no way Emily accidentally drowned in 2' of water. Her course on SUP yoga was the BEST. Something fishy is going on. #watergate

I still can't believe there has been no justice for Emily. Still can't believe our podcast was her last interview. DM me for link. #watergate #livinglovelypodcast

We are so saddened by the loss of a legend. We had just signed a brand deal with Emily and are devastated by this loss. #watergate #glowyourboattours

This last one was from another local tour company. She noticed a pang of jealousy. Why had Emily picked them instead of a female-owned company like Shae's? So much for girl power. She kept doom-scrolling.

Does anyone think Sheriff Carter looks just like Stewey from Family Guy? No wonder he can't get this right—he's a baby! #watergate

Me when my boomer boss asks me to make a PDF. #watergate #funny. An animated gif of Shae with block letters, 'Don't be a noob,' flashing over her face served as the punchline.

Shae closed her eyes and drifted back to that awful interview. The tour had barely pulled back on land, but the news vultures were already there with their bright lights and news vans. Someone must have tipped them off.

Shae hadn't begun to process what had happened when a mic was shoved in her face and the camera light blinded her. The boats were slamming against each other as people clumsily rushed on shore. One little girl wouldn't stop sobbing while the mother glared at Shae as if it was her fault.

In her effort to maintain authority, she'd come across completely cold on the carefully edited broadcast. She had learned from her life-guarding years that you had to convey authority, even if you were scared as shit. People needed to believe you could save them or they'd panic and bring you down with them. This was all the more necessary as a woman in a male-dominated industry.

She didn't even cry. Cold-hearted bitch. #cancelislandguy

More heat spread across her chest as the memory sharpened in focus. She'd said something about the importance of going out with a guide and how this was an example of why noobs shouldn't go out at night alone. Of course, it made her seem heartless and worse, self-promoting. People made comparisons to her saying Emily was asking for it.

Shae's case wasn't being helped by the internet detectives who'd scoured Emily's social media to find a confrontation in the comments of one of Emily's posts. Emily had posted a picture of herself releasing flower petals into the canal and Shae had made a simple comment that the flowers weren't good for the local wildlife. Emily had defended the picture, saying it was a memorial for her grandmother. Shae hadn't seen how that changed anything and said as much.

With Emily showing up dead, people were insinuating Shae's comments had been more sinister. That it had been jealousy; people didn't hesitate to point out how much prettier Emily was than Shae. She mindlessly brushed her fingertips along her bicep and frowned. Shae hadn't struggled with body image before but all the comments about her 'man arms' were getting to her.

The now-familiar burn of bile hit the back of her throat. The viral 'noob' comment was nothing more than a clumsy statement in a moment of panic blown way out of proportion. Why did these people—people who had never set foot on her island—have so much power over her? Her chest tightened through alternating waves of anger and despair. She clicked back over to the review tab but nothing changed in the last five minutes.

She pushed out of the hammock chair and stood up. River raised an eyebrow but remained sprawled on the worn wooden floors. Shae felt trapped in some bizarre nightmare. She knew she should feel badly about the girl being dead. Emily was young. And she really was very pretty. Did that somehow make it worse? Shae shuddered with disgust at herself and the world.

Shae fiddled with the small gold hoop in her right nostril, a new nervous habit that was verging on a tic. The isolation of being a social outcast was so painful, it was almost physical. How had her mom and brother endured it for so long? Shae felt guilty for all the times she had secretly judged her own family. She'd tried so hard to outrun their legacy, make something more of herself. Guess she hadn't outrun anything.

She looked out the window to see the blue-gray sky. Shae would be meeting up with her group by now. Giving the life jacket spiel about how even though it was nighttime she didn't want anyone to 'sleep with the fishes.' God, have to scratch that joke now. If she ever got the chance to give a tour again.

She glanced over the scheduling notebook lying open on her dresser. Nothing. Shae ran her hands through her hair and sighed. The main season was almost over. She'd done better than expected in the early season, thanks to some networking with the local Airbnb owner's group, but it wouldn't carry her through.

And through to what? No one would book with her with a 1-star review. Her body let out an involuntary whimper as she collapsed onto the bed, her dreads sprawling across the pillow.

She pleaded with the ceiling. Was this karma? Maybe. A young woman was dead. And she knew more than anyone else that it wasn't an accident. More heat in her chest as her stomach tightened. But at the same time, self-preservation flared up inside her. Why should two lives be ruined?

Rent for the boat storage was already overdue. Along with the payment on the new kayaks and custom Continental eight-boat trailer she'd bought in a flash of optimism after a particularly strong May. How foolish we are, thinking we know what lies ahead.

She considered selling them but she'd only get a fraction of what she paid, though they were essentially brand new. It wouldn't even cover the remaining balance of the loan. What else did she have to sell? A kidney? Shae felt desperate for someone to make this go away, to fix this for her.

There was nothing more to do for tonight. Her hand instinctively reached for her phone to refresh the reviews but she paused. How many more nights could she repeat this cycle? How many nights already had her eyes gone blurry reading the posts, googling her name, wishing none of this had ever happened? She wasn't getting anywhere and time was running out.

Shae needed to face this and stop wishing it away. Tomorrow, she thought. Tomorrow she would try something new. But for tonight, she pulled the glowing screen of her phone to her face and hit refresh.

2

After a week of living in the 'cone of uncertainty,' Pete Brown was ready to get out of the house. Pete loved everything about island life except for these weeks. He wasn't scared of hurricanes—it was the people. Pete was a people person as a rule, but the uninformed mass panic made this rule difficult. All the endless small talk where everyone predicted the direction of the storm made him crazy. Pete had historically been traveling during the worst of the summer storms, thus dodging the chaos.

Pete finished his ashwagandha and mango smoothie and walked out to the lanai, stretching in the chair so only his feet were warmed by the sun. The sun created flecks of gold out on the water as a manatee slowly poked his snout up out of the canal. Rubai-yacht seemed to stare at him forlornly from the lift. Pete was as ready to take her out as she was. Pete hated locking up and closing down his boat more than anything else about the storms.

Her name had come from the poem Rubaiyat, a pun on the crimson red stripe along the hull. The cloth-covered copy of the poem, sent by a friend after Pete's accident, was now well-worn. Pete opened up his website on his laptop and reviewed the day's booking.

Scanning through the notes, it looked like another girls' trip. Easy money. There would be no need to set up the fishing equipment or the full bar. As long as Pete hit all the best backdrops for a 'gram worthy' post, the ladies were generally content to relax with Prosecco on the deck. The trip would cover his outings for a month.

Pete's accountant was always mortified by this attitude of Pete's, not to mention a little annoyed by the task of accurately reporting earnings from things like 'gas trips.' Chris never tired of reminding Pete how he was 'more than prepared' to simply buy himself gas and enjoy his early retirement. Pete had invested his winnings well and still earned significant royalties from his collaborations with PB Boardshorts and Reefer sunscreen. Not to mention his second home in Kahuku that now functioned as a vacation rental. The board lights he'd invented for night surfing failed to perform but you couldn't win 'em all.

Someone in a white collar couldn't seem to understand that it had nothing to do with the money and everything to do with the joy of the game. Plus, Pete would go crazy if he sat around all day, doing nothing. He loved the challenge of making himself earn his rewards. Pete sent a quick reminder to Shae on the time and headed to the dock.

Two hours later, Shae was helping Pete with the final prep. Pete didn't normally allow friends or family on a paid trip, but he figured Shae must be feeling pretty low since finding that drowned girl. He hadn't really talked to her since the first couple days after it all happened.

Retired or not, Pete still considered himself an athlete and his strict health regimen rarely allowed for alcohol. Raki happy hour was the one exception. Uncle (as they affectionately called the Turkish owner) had been in rare form, keeping the Raki flowing while regaling them with stories of his homeland. Pete had grown nostalgic for his own childhood and sent an uncharacteristically vulnerable text to Shae saying he missed her. Within minutes, she'd agreed to join him on the trip.

Pete walked into the air-conditioned galley where the girls had gathered. "Welcome to Rubai-yacht. You've got a wonderful crew aboard to help you out today. Your captain, Pete, your engineer Pete, your deckhand Pete, and your cruise director—you guessed it, also Pete."

The girls gave a laugh, harder than the corny joke deserved, either because Pete was good-looking or because they were rowdy from the idea of spending the day drinking on a proper yacht. A blonde with a fresh blowout gave him a wink. This would be the one to keep an eye on. Was it Pete's imagination or did she give Shae a dirty look?

Pete gave them a quick tour, showed them the bar, and then headed back up to shove off. The girls were already busy splitting into factions, some taking pictures of each other posing on the bow of the boat and the others getting settled in the sun. Blondie was, of course, popping the Prosecco and filling glasses.

"I'm not going to make it, man," Shae finally said as they moved out of the canals to the open river. "Like, I don't think I can do this."

Pete was surprised Shae had jumped right into it, but he had lived through enough of his own dark days to know to be quiet for a minute. Shae continued, "They're roasting me. I'm down to a 1-star and I'm the joke of Twitter. It's bullshit. I don't understand what this has to do with me!"

Pete wasn't sure how to respond. He'd assumed Shae was upset about finding the body but he nodded solemnly anyway. At this point in his life, Pete was used to armchair haters and he didn't understand being upset about a bunch of randos on the internet. Still, he offered some token support. "You can't let them win and get to you like that. This is your business and your life we're talking about."

"Look, I don't want to give up! I've poured everything into this business. But I'm out of options. And what are they trying to accomplish? Sorry to be cold, but what does some tourist drowning have to do with me?" Shae bitterly shook her head.

At the same moment, Blondie blew a kiss to Pete from the bow and the group dissolved into laughter. Pete gave a small half-wave and kept driving.

"People have been trolling me half my life at this point." Pete gave the captain's wheel a gentle turn to move to the deeper part of the canal.

Shae rolled her eyes. "God, Pete. It's not a competition."

"Everything's a competition." Pete lifted an eyebrow and side-eyed Shae.

Shae rolled her eyes again, but said nothing.

Pete shook his head. Why was Shae so willing to let a few Twitter posts ruin her life? It didn't make any sense. He knew she was tougher than this. "Why don't you fight fire with fire?" Pete asked. Shae stared at Pete, so he continued, "They are using words to paint a certain image of you, first of all. So you can do that, too. You can use words—or public relations—to manage your image online. They hid all their flaws while blasting yours. It's like modern *Art of War*. So you start calling out some of their bullshit directly. You build up your image while taking their image down."

Shae nodded slowly. "Okay, but like how. My life is the outdoors, I was never good at writing essays. And you saw my interview. I don't think I'm a great spokesperson for myself. I'm afraid they are going to use anything I say against me."

Pete shrugged. He didn't want to make Shae feel worse, but there was no denying the interview was a train wreck. Maybe she'd be easier to manage online.

Pete had learned a lot from the people out at Dimension Four, the talent firm that managed his publicity. He'd never forget the way @petebrownofficial had posted the news about the break-up with Jenna. Wordsmithed by four different writers, the post embodied the perfect balance of male accountability and heartbreak. Just as they'd promised, his 'brand awareness' and 'market trust' had increased by 10 points. Pete knew it was part of the game, but he took no pride in that part of his fame.

"I'll help. I'm helping out Billy B with some boards this week, but after that, I've got time." Pete was going to deliver some custom boards to Jax Beach in exchange for a seriously discounted shortboard from his favorite local shaper.

Shae looked like she might cry. "Are you serious? You would do that? You have no idea how alone I feel. Funny how people are your friends when you're doing well, but when the shit hits the fan, they're nowhere to be found." Pete sensed the bitterness radiating off of her. It was uncomfortable.

"I'm not making any promises. I'm just saying there are some basic things you can do. And yeah, I don't mind helping. This will blow over soon. You'll see." Pete wasn't sure this was true, but it felt like the thing to say to move on.

Shae looked like she wanted to say something else, but remained silent. She stared off towards the deep tangle of salt marsh and mangrove tunnels.

Pete gently pulled Rubai-yacht next to the swing rope, always a great hit with the guests as it provided shade, great photo ops, and some play. He took a sideways glance at Shae, noticing for the first time the gray in her dirty blonde hair and a new sharpness to her features. Were they really this old now? Pete hated cliches, but it truly did feel like yesterday he and Shae were sneaking booze and swinging this same rope into the water.

Island living had been so easy, now it often felt like a fight against rising costs from West Coasters eager to take advantage of their hidden gem. And even though he thought Shae was overreacting, there was no denying the unwelcome attention from this recent drowning was adding to the sense of disorder on the island. Things shouldn't be this hard here. It should be easy.

Suddenly, Pete jumped up and shimmied down the ladder. Within moments, he was off the boat and at the base of the swing. He belted out a yell and flung himself out into the water. The water was cold from the recent storm and took his breath away. He gasped and then a huge smile cracked over his face. When was the last time he had done this?

Shae looked down and Pete's heart stopped; the shade was turning Shae's bitter face into something downright sinister. After a heartbeat, Shae flashed her own huge smile and ran down to swing into the water with Pete.

Peace washed over Pete as he brought his feet up to float in the water. He wasn't sure what was ahead, but for this moment, they were okay. Pete had learned to let go of fighting for the future. These moments were all you could live for, and Pete mumbled to himself, "If this isn't nice, I don't know what is."

3

Humid air and pop punk filled the truck cabin as Shae tried to shake off the mortification of the day. She'd finally made it out of orientation and had her first full day on the job. Although she was grateful for a job, it had been humiliating to have the peppy resort manager—at least 10 years younger than her—walk her through their activities section, 'teaching' her about the different types of kayaks. He'd given her a bright smile and pointed her toward the staff locker room to change into her uniform. As if Shae wasn't able to get there with her eyes closed. She felt like she was working for the enemy, but she was desperate.

Four weeks ago, she'd gone up to her building to find a new lock on the door with a note from the landlord. Shae was 60 days late on rent and Ray had locked her out with all her boats and equipment inside. If Shae didn't come up with at least one month's worth of rent ASAP, Ray said he'd confiscate her stuff. The building held at least 10-grand's worth of top-of-the-line kayaking equipment, well over the measly $1400 she owed him.

So she'd gone, tail between legs, back to the resort where she'd gotten her start as a teenager all those years ago. Where she'd worked her way up from a lifeguard to an activities director. She'd first cut her teeth giving a tour there, practicing how to keep people entertained while also educating them.

She'd left on good terms and so the general manager was willing to give her a job, though Shae hoped against hope that it was only until this all died down. He'd been nice enough, but she could tell Mike had his own misgivings about hiring her with all the negative press she was getting.

Shae hated mass tourism like this. It was an all-inclusive resort where activities were included. In Shae's experience, this meant people couldn't care less about the nature or the tours. They were here to get their money's worth and check something off a list. It was the antithesis of what Shae tried to create at Island Guy Tours.

Shae needed to at least get enough to get her boats out. She had no idea what she'd do with them once she got them out, but that was a problem for tomorrow. For today, she'd had to face buttoning up the hideous Hawaiian shirt with a fake-ass smile. She tried to remind herself it was worth the feeling of handing Ray the cash and getting a new key to her unit.

Shae knew she should be grateful. It was tough to find work at the end of season like this and doing something outside was hard to find. The island had no shortage of the laid-back outdoorsy type competing for jobs like this and Mike was putting himself on the line for her. Still, Shae struggled to be happy about making minimum wage to put on a cheesy performance for what she thought were a bunch of spoiled guests.

Even with the gig, Shae would be scraping by. The tours were only an hour and she could only book so many tours in one day. Mike said Shae might be able to pick up a few bartending shifts if she wanted. What Shae wanted was irrelevant at that point; she was in survival mode. She caught her reflection in the rearview mirror.

The pixie cut was cute enough, but the loss of her signature blonde dreads—because they didn't fit the corporate dress code—felt shameful. She'd started the dreads right after leaving her resort job as a sign of her freedom, only to cut them in a reverse ritual of servitude.

Bright pink Hawaiian shirt, pleated khaki shorts, and bright white sneakers. She fidgeted with her shirt until the collar covered up the line-drawn feather tattoo above her heart, a reminder to hope after losing her mother.

Shae frowned and shook her head. It might as well have been a clown costume. She gave a slow smile until she creeped herself out. She looked like the Joker, smiling at herself all scary-like. She flashed a bright smile and gave her reflection an over-exaggerated thumbs up. As was always the case now, the pink in her shirt triggered her mind to replay that awful night.

At least Pete agreed to help. Everything Pete touched turned golden; it had been that way since they were kids. Shae was never jealous like some of the other people they had known growing up. Pete was a nice guy and while Shae wasn't sure whether people deserved anything—good or bad—she'd never be mad about a guy like Pete having the luck he did.

Shae saw how hard Pete worked, even though he made things look easy. It wasn't luck alone. Pete may have had more opportunities than other people, but he'd also met all of them with a lot of hard work. Shae was confident, if there was any opportunity for this to go away, Pete would be the best guy for the job.

And if nothing else, it was good to have a friend in all this. She wished she would have thought to call Pete from the start. She'd been so trapped in her own shame spiral that she felt paralyzed. Things were going to change; she just knew it. She gave herself another thumbs up and this time it felt real. Shae could do this.

Shae was busy drumming along to the music and failed to see the police cruiser parked outside the storage unit as she pulled into the parking lot. Her heart felt as if it was swelling to the music, full of the knowledge that she was about to open up the storage and see her boats. She had just cut the engine off when she heard her name. On instinct at the deep male voice, Shae mentally prepared her body for defensive fighting and turned around.

The air became still at the sight of the uniform and badge. Her surroundings became preternaturally bright as time slowed. Shae attempted a neutral face as she faced the officers. "How can I help you?"

"Shae Brunell, we need you to come to the station with us."

Shae thought about running, but where would she go? She gave a quick glance at the locked garage door. She was desperate to see her boats, but couldn't risk letting the police in the storage unit. She was exhausted, yet did her best to muster a friendly smile.

Neither officer returned the smile as the younger one motioned a hand to the squad car. Shae was mortified by the idea of riding with them, but wanted to seem cooperative. She gave another bright smile and slid silently into the back of the car.

4

Across town, Pete grabbed the flyers out of his canvas satchel and started walking south on the main strip of downtown. It was the second Monday of the month, which meant it was advertising day. This month would be the south downtown shops and businesses. Pete created a whole system so as not to bombard people while staying top of mind.

He took a last look at his new flyers. He had to admit they looked pretty slick with the new color scheme and custom sans serif font. It wasn't over- or under-designed, but right on point. You had to be careful with that around here; the locals wanted to know they could trust you, but did not like sales pitches. Pete made these flyers himself after taking a free webinar on graphic design and was pretty happy with the results.

Pete walked into Sea Grapes & Stems, narrowly avoiding a collision with a woman holding a bouquet of ranunculus and zinnias so large it covered her face. The bell on the door jingled and Mary walked to the front, drying her hands on her apron.

She gave a slight smile to Pete as her graying braids fell over her shoulder. Mary did most of the arrangements for his dad's church and Pete knew her well. She had yet to advertise with the radio station Pete bought back in February, though it didn't stop Pete from trying. She'd been a sucker for all the school fundraisers he'd done as a kid and he had a feeling she'd buy an ad eventually. Plus, he liked to visit with her. Mary glanced at her blooms of the month calendar and gave a laugh.

"Can't believe I'm due for a pitch already," she teased good-naturedly.

Pete handed her an updated flyer with the latest statistics on the growing audience at his public access channel.

"Sea, Salt, & Air Waves is the top choice for local weather and to find local businesses. You can get a commercial every two hours for less than a Facebook ad." Pete knew Mary wouldn't buy today. But every pitch moved him closer to someone who would. He only needed a few more advertisers before he would break even on the station.

"You know I don't do those either, Pete. I have more than I can handle from word of mouth," Mary motioned to all the arrangements in progress around her. "I should be retired as it is, not taking these orders in."

Mary tried to sound annoyed, but even at 76, she loved her work too much to retire. The locals depended on her and Pete knew she'd do this until the day she died; maybe making her own funeral arrangement.

"Try one of these new fancy bars, with their custom ice cubes and lavender syrup. They'll buy anything." Mary pointed across the street and rolled her eyes. Mary preferred an iced cold beer and, like many of the old-timers here, had a strong distrust for fancy cocktails. Especially when mixed by young men with tattoos and elaborate mustaches.

It didn't help that more and more of those who had established the downtown many decades ago were being pushed out by the newcomers. Pete looked at the animated neon sign on the other side of the road. An old-fashioned finger pointed down to a gothic-style font reading, 'Speakeasy Here.' It was a little too on the nose for his taste, but he didn't want to disparage a potential customer, so he kept quiet.

"I wouldn't bother with Miss America's shop next door, though, the one with the fancy clothes. They like to stay on the down low." It was rumored that the owner was a former beauty pageant winner. Beauty pageants could also be found on the long list of things locals were suspicious about.

Pete continued to say nothing. He didn't like to encourage gossip, but he wasn't going to shut down perfectly good information either. Mary was happy to continue, "No way she does enough business to pay the rent there selling fancy clothes here. Word is the husband is a private pilot who happens to make a lot of trips to El Salvador, if you know what I'm saying."

Pete really didn't know what she was saying and again stayed quiet. Mary continued. "I heard the husband runs drugs and Ali uses the store to clean the money. That's how they have a Bugatti."

Pete responded with a noncommittal shrug. He'd heard so many wild stories about the people on this island that nothing phased him anymore. Less than 20% were likely to be true, but then Pete knew some were true stories that were so outlandish that maybe they were all true. Pete wondered if all beach towns were a little weird or if there was something special about their island that seemed to attract the most outlandish people.

As if on cue, a shirtless man rode a three-wheeler down the road with a stack of chairs in the back basket and a sign plastered to the front that read, 'FOR HIRE: UPRISINGS QUELLED...SALOONS EMPTIED... BEACH CHAIRS...'

"Anyway, good luck today." Abruptly, Mary was done with the conversation and shooing Pete out the door.

An hour later, Pete slid back in the driver's seat with a sense of satisfaction. He'd not only met his goal to break even, but he'd exceeded it when a local interior designer heard him talking to one of the real estate agents. Pete's stomach grumbled and he checked his phone. Dinnertime.

The smell of fried fish emanating from the many nearby seafood spots pulled on Pete, but he'd bought a ton of fresh produce from the local farmers' market this past weekend. He knew it would go bad if he didn't cook it tonight. His papaya tree was also heavy with ripe fruit. Pete walked over to the fresh seafood counter at The Fish House and got a filet of grouper brought in earlier in the morning.

Next, he hit Bubbles + Casks, the independent wine shop. He grabbed a non-alcoholic wine to go with the grouper and chili lime salad he planned on making. While tucking the cash back in his wallet, his phone rang: someone from the police station. It was probably Dave. Pete considered answering and inviting the mystery caller over for dinner.

Then again, after a long day out doing sales, a night alone sounded pretty amazing. While Pete had been contemplating, the call had stopped ringing and the caller hadn't left a voice mail. Pete shrugged: *decision made.* The message bubble on his phone reminded Pete he was due to work on Shae's project. He'd left her on delivered since yesterday, not wanting to admit he hadn't done anything yet. He was pretty spent and had another long day planned for tomorrow. He'd get to Shae soon, but for tonight, Pete wanted to enjoy his dinner.

He clicked the icon to read the new message.

Might need to do some damage control. Sponsors are getting antsy. Let's chat tomorrow. His agent, Sydney, included a link to a headline.

Pete was not in the habit of reading headlines about himself, but he couldn't remember the last time he'd done something to make his sponsors 'antsy.' He sucked in a breath and clicked through. Almost immediately, he let out a laugh.

Pro-surfer cruises Florida's canals with suspected killer and potential sweetheart Shae Brunell.

It was so over the top that Pete was shocked Sydney had even sent it. Skimming through, it was factually incorrect on so many levels. Was this a joke? Sydney was whip-smart with nerves of steel and almost devoid of a sense of humor. If she said sponsors were getting nervous, then Pete had no choice but to pay attention.

5

Pete stretched his back and sat down in the stiff leather office chair at his desk. He'd spent the day driving back from Miami to pick up an Airstream he planned to refinish and either sell or turn into a rental. He was tired from the four-hour drive, but he really needed to get some work done for Shae. Somehow, more than a week had passed since they had been out on Rubai-yacht together.

The office felt foreign to him. He looked at the black and white prints of surfboards and palm tree fronds as if seeing them for the first time. The boards in the picture were Padillacs, made for big wave surfing, not the beach break waves found at Beach Island, the ones that had made him famous. Pete hadn't wanted to be picky, and technically, he had won The Eddie on a Padillac, so it was fine.

The wall color was a pale teal called Vibes and came from a Brooklyn-based paint company. Pete remembered because they had charged $95 per gallon. He couldn't understand how it could be that much better than the paint from his local big box store, but the interior designer had won out.

Pete was not a sit-at-a-desk kind of person and didn't visit the room often. He'd only added the office at the insistence of Kelli, the interior designer. She'd done a great job on the space, that wasn't the problem. School had been one detention after another because he couldn't stand to sit still when there was so much to do outside, and even today, Pete was more likely to do any admin type work out at the lanai rather than in this room. The custom balsa desk—another 'suggestion' from Kelli with an eye-watering price tag—was beautiful but Pete hated desks in general.

Pete cracked his knuckles. "So…" he said to no one. Minutes passed. He nodded and shook out his fingers. Pete was not often clueless, but he wasn't sure what he had agreed to anymore. The urge to get up and leave was almost physically uncomfortable. He opened up the search bar and looked for information on the story. Nothing jumped out at him. The majority of the headlines talked about the tragic accidental drowning of a young girl in the Florida waters. Skimming through, he saw images of Sheriff Carter looking somber at the scene. A few images of Shae popped up, but nothing too drastic. Maybe Shae was overreacting.

Shae had mentioned people were posting online, so Pete decided to try Twitter. He'd expected to take some time finding these posts and was caught off guard to see #justiceforemily as a top trending topic. He clicked through to see thousands of posts, many blasting Shae.

@rain_5: Nasty troll of a girl that was obviously jealous of Emily. She should go kill herself.

@mike5587: White trash whore. Glad Florida still uses the electric chair can't wait to watch her burn.

@therussbus: Can we end this trending so I can stop seeing this bitch in a bathing suit? Looks like a 12-year-old boy. Talk about a crime against humanity. Attached was a still from the news interview with Shae.

The posts were pretty vicious and Pete felt bad he had been so clueless this was going on. The timber was a stark contrast to the news stories he had skimmed. No wonder Shae was so upset. Governments had done away with the public square because it was deemed too cruel. Those medieval stocks had nothing on the world of Twitter. The sheer amount of anger in these posts was kind of overwhelming.

@dhughes6765430: This is what the feminist agenda gets you.

@gh33f00: She says Island Guy was to give her more power. Looking at her, pretty sure she's just actually a guy. Pass.

@mary_mary: I hope she drowns. I hope her family suffers like Emily's.

Pete was more stuck than before. Again, the urge to get up and leave was powerful. A post trashing the local police caught his attention and he knew he should do something. Locals were weary of strangers. He doubted Sheriff Carter knew about the Twitter storm brewing. Pete hadn't been aware of just how much was being posted about the island. Pete wasn't sure it would blow over in a few days.

A thought occurred to him. He opened a new tab and searched, 'Marie Benson in New Hampshire.' The image results turned Pete's stomach and he quickly scrolled down to the article in *The Atlantic*. It had started the same way, a tiny beach village with what was originally labeled as an accidental death. Somebody made up their mind that something was off. *Track a Murder*, Apple's top-ranked crime podcast, had gotten involved. He'd come across the town during a surfing shoot and the heavy energy had haunted him the entire trip.

The internet had gotten hooked on the story early on and soon it went national, until millions were glued to the gory trial for months. Of course, in that case, one might argue the internet crusaders had helped bring justice about for the victim, but still. What about the quiet coastal town? No longer a little main street with taffy shops and seafood straight from the ocean. Now it was home to a disgusting tourist attraction with the option to spend the night in the home where the gruesome murder had taken place. The recent throwback on the *Track a Murder* podcast had reignited public interest. A newer search result headline read, 'Angels & Demons: Inside the Mind of New Hampshire's Crucifix Killer.' Ten years and the little village was still in the thick of it.

"Okay. Okay let's make a plan." He knew from a cursory review @bugcatcher was one of the most vocal posters about Shae and the island's handling of the accidental drowning. Pete bristled at the idea of some anonymous, random dude dragging his friend and hometown through the coals from the comfort of his own home. Pete was getting pumped up to argue with this guy, but first he would have to create a new account.

He thought about using his blue check account, but then he'd have to vet everything through his social media manager, Lizzy. He could already hear her talking about content consistency and algorithms. No, it would be easier to create a new account not tied to his public image. Pete had to smirk at his own hypocrisy; he was about to be some random dude on the internet roasting someone else from the comfort of his own home. Well, when in Rome.

After all the necessary passwords and validation steps and proving he was not a robot, Pete was in. He searched again for #justiceforemily and thousands upon thousands of tweets pulled up. He skimmed for the most liked and retweeted. Here he was—@bugcatcher.

How did Emily manage to surf the gnarly waves at Trestles yet drowned in 3' of calm freshwater?? #justiceforemily #watergate

Pete rolled his eyes. Trestles was not gnarly by any measure, but whatever. He wasn't here to argue tough surfing spots. He skimmed through several similar posts. Pete knew better than anyone, Mother Nature had her own ways, no matter how good you felt in the water. Pete responded with a similar sentiment, balancing enough snark to get retweeted with an appropriate level of concern for Emily. He didn't want to look insensitive like Shae had. He was getting on a roll responding to several other tweets when one of @bugcatcher's earlier posts stopped him.

If it was an accident, why did Emily post a picture of the Endless Islands with the caption, 'Help,' right before she died? #justiceforemily #impeachthepolice

An image was attached. The photo was dark and almost grainy, but Pete recognized the Endless Islands immediately. Pete clicked over to Emily's Instagram account and the photo stuck out like a sore thumb. Every other photo was beautiful, her feed was expertly curated. Lizzy would be proud. This photo was ominous in its darkness when compared with the golden light of the rest of the feed.

Huh. This was a pretty compelling point. Pete stared at the screen, waiting for some kind of quippy response to write, but he had nothing. Why *did* she put that post up? If the death had been ruled suicide, maybe.

What were the odds that a person whose whole life seemed to be dedicated to this space of squares put up something so random, so ugly. Did the police see this post? Pete clicked on one of the responses from @freefrominfluence—he'd seen a lot of posts from this user, too.

Oh please. Emily was KNOWN for being a hack. Girl never had an original idea in her life. Go look at @shadesofbrown and tell me she wasn't copying her latest gothic photos. #justiceforemily #givemeabreak

And then:

Who would possibly post on Instagram instead of calling for help? Doesn't even make sense. Y'all are a bunch of morons. #justiceforemily #givemeabreak

Pete wasn't convinced. He hated to admit it, but @bugcatcher had raised a pretty good point. Why was Emily posting help from the island hours before her death and then found dead, floating in the water? The picture didn't seem gothic to him, just creepy. Pete wondered why the police were ruling it accidental so quickly when she had made a post like this. He made a mental note to reach out to his friends at the sheriff's office to get some facts.

Pete's phone dinged. 'Been trying to reach you where RU??' Pete checked his phone to be sure. No missed calls from Shae.

'Wdym. When? What's up?' Pete pecked out on his keyboard.

'Police picked me up from the garage. Acted like I was super sus but FINALLY let me go.' Shae attached a GIF of Joey from *Friends* shrugging.

Pete understood they needed to talk to Shae, but what about the unofficial trial that was happening online? Did they even know?

6

Pete flipped his hat backwards to prevent losing it during the short scooter ride from his house to the police station at city hall. Parking was difficult downtown and, as it was every day here, the weather was perfect for the electric scooter. Warm and salty with the coolest hint of ocean breeze. He had originally bought the scooter for easily touring the Bahamas during his bi-annual boating trips, but found it worked just as well on the island. Besides, the station was barely more than a mile away. In less time than it would have taken him to find parking among all the tourists, he was folding up the scooter and carrying it through the front doors.

After pounding his head against the problem the night before and then the escalation of Shae going to the station, Pete realized it would be a whole heck of a lot easier to talk to Dave and Nate. They'd have more knowledge of the situation, and from there, he could get back to writing snarky tweets. Pete wouldn't admit this to anyone but himself, but it was kind of fun coming up with the perfect set of 144 characters to shoot somebody down. It was like a haiku, except you felt both better and worse after writing it.

The sliding doors of city hall creaked open as a blast of cold air hit Pete. Small town living meant the two-story city hall was home to the mayor's office, the central library, the senior center, and the police station. Pete had no need to consult the small map on the coral-colored wall and headed straight for the small group of desks housing the town sheriff's office.

"Excuse me. Sir. Excuse me! SIR!"

Pete startled as an elderly secretary stood up and pointed towards the door angrily. He looked around to see where her bony finger was directed.

Behind him, a long-haired man hung his head sheepishly and walked over to the corner, his bare feet making a swishing sound across the terrazzo floor. He grabbed a pair of flip-flops from the bin underneath the SHOES REQUIRED sign by the door. The bin was full of flip-flops leftover from surf sample sales or donated from local surf shops. The man made an exaggerated show of putting a pair of bright blue slides on and the secretary nodded curtly before returning to her work.

Pete gave a shrug of solidarity to the man and continued to the police station.

"Nate, buddy! How's it going? What about those swells today?" Pete fist-bumped Officer Nate Tybe as he entered the station.

"The pier was sick, bro. Dude, I love hurricanes!" Nate's surfer brogue was a strange juxtaposition to the crisp police uniform.

Pete remembered the days of Nate hosting the biggest (and most illegal) beach bonfires back in the day. Once again, Pete was reminded of how old they were all getting.

Pete nodded in agreement. Summer and fall were flat as a lake and they'd all go crazy waiting on those dogs of winter if not for the storms. Of course, Pete usually got in a couple of surfing trips during this time, but local surfing was always his preference. No need to haul a bunch of gear and he'd have the pick among his large collection of boards instead of the one or two that would fit on an airplane. "So, hey man," Pete scanned the office, "is Dave around?"

Nate glanced down the hall. "Let me check... Yeah, Sheriff Carter should be back in his office. Y'all making more off-roading plans?" Nate gave the slightest conspiratorial wink.

Only two months ago, Pete had gotten a late night call to bring Sarg out to the Swamps to tow in Dave Carter and his buddy. They had gone off-roading in their Chevys and gotten stuck on one of the mud cliffs. Pete was sure the mass of empty Coors Light in the backseat might have contributed to the situation, but he never said a word.

Pete wasn't sure how much Nate knew, so he just gave a light laugh. "Not today. Helping out a buddy and have a question for him. Shouldn't take too long."

"Head on back—I'm sure he'll be glad to see you. See you on the outside, Cat!" Pete gave a fist bump and walked to the back office. He never knew how to feel hearing his old nickname. He'd earned the name El Gato early on in his surfing days from legend Gabe DeSouza. Pete rode so many waves to the shore that Gabe said he was like a cat that hates water and El Gato was born. Later on, with Pete's love of Converse, it morphed into his unofficial surfing name. Pete found the nickname a bit silly, but he'd learned to laugh it off. Another part of the surfer image was showing you didn't take things too seriously.

"Pete, man! So good to see you!" Sheriff Dave Carter gave Pete a tight hug and a hearty slap on the back. "How's it hanging today?" Dave gave an awkward shaka sign with his meaty hand.

"Life is good, can't complain. How's Joyce and the kids?"

"Still in the doghouse." Dave laughed heartily. "Boy, the missus won't be letting me out to play anytime soon! Her 2500 needs a new transmission." He shook his head pitifully.

Pete laughed and shook his head. "Probably a good thing! So, listen, I'm helping out a buddy of mine and wanted to see if I might run something by you."

"Of course—anything for you!" Dave sat down at his desk and motioned for Pete to do the same. He sipped coffee from a mug that read, 'I can't stop STUPID but I can CUFF it!'

"Shae Brunell is getting hammered out there. The whole Twitter army is really having a field day taking her down for the drowning. It's crazy."

Dave's jaw tightened and the mood in the room instantly shifted. "Is that so? Yet another reason I stay off the internets. I'm busy enough keeping this town safe, don't have time for that social media garbage. So why come here, son?" Dave leaned back in his chair and cracked his knuckles.

Pete was struck by how drastically Dave's tone had changed. He was also surprised that Carter appeared unaware of the online storm taking place; although Sheriff Carter was known for being old-school, he assumed he at least checked in with major stories like this. Pete stared at the massive computer screen on Carter's desk. It was more suited for the Oregon Trail than a modern day police force. Perhaps Carter didn't know how bad it was out there. He tried again, "Shae's not the most computer literate. I mean, me neither—I much prefer person to person over screen to screen." Pete gestured his hand between them, perhaps in a desperate attempt to rebuild the connection between them. "But people are using the internet to do some damage to her reputation. So I said I would kinda do some research, you know? Answer some of the online stuff out there and try to get rid of these reviews. The whole situation is a mob mentality joke, but it's really killing her business. Poor girl."

Sheriff Carter gave a terse nod, as if telling Pete to go on. No doubt about it, he was now talking not to his buddy, but Sheriff Dave Carter. Pete cleared his throat. He wasn't great in these situations, people being angry. Pete was a chill dude and wanted to keep the peace. And he had no clue what he had done to change the vibe.

He went on, though unsure, "Uh well, it seems pretty simple to me. We all know this is a bunch of internet losers playing detective. I thought if I got more information from you guys, maybe I can sorta shoot down these conspiracy theories." What had seemed like an easy ask of a fellow islander now felt like a crime.

"No, Pete. No, that's not going to happen. The case is being closed next week and we won't be responding to any online comments. This is a clear case of a tourist making the senseless mistake of going out in the water alone. I'm proud to have kept Beach Island crime free for the last eight years and I didn't accomplish that by pandering to a bunch of outsiders." Sheriff Carter was firm and direct, ringing ever so slightly of his ongoing campaign for reelection. "Do I make myself understood?"

Pete nodded again and again, as if to say alright, alright, even though he disagreed. The grainy image of the island was burned into his mind. "Ok. Yeah. Makes sense. I trust you guys know what you are doing. I guess I was just thinking that addressing some of these crazy theories with some facts might sorta take the steam out of them, you know?"

"It's not been my experience in this line of work that people want facts." Carter stood up to put some papers in the trash. He sounded almost bitter at this point. "It's a tough break for your friend, but they'll find a new victim to troll soon enough. I'd suggest you leave this alone and tell Miss Brunell to lay low for the next few weeks and let this blow over. Leave this to the Authority. I'm pretty surprised you would get involved in this. You've got a reputation to protect."

Was that a threat?

"Pete, you don't want to associate yourself with these crackpots spinning their conspiracy theories. Besides, the Board of Commissioners' Bravely End All Crime Here task force has already completed its review of this case. They are unanimous that the best course is to rule it accidental and close it as quickly as possible."

While admittedly Pete knew very little about police procedure, it was bizarre to him that the city commissioners—made up of locals who had lived there forever and thus were nominated more on popularity than knowledge—would have any idea of what was best when it came to a death in the city.

He'd always thought when Carter had established The Life's a Beach & Then You Die squad (as the task force was called unofficially), it was a ploy to keep bored retired people entertained. He had no idea they had actual influence over police affairs. Also, he was really feeling how inappropriate the task force nickname was—he'd have to stop using it. He did his best to mirror the statement back to Carter without any emotion or inflection: "The city commissioners decided this was accidental?"

Carter's face reddened, but he kept his expression neutral. "Pete, this situation is under the jurisdiction of the police and is being handled accordingly. Given the magnitude of attention this case has already received, the local citizens have a right to become involved. And these aren't just city commissioners. This is a specialized task force. And we all agree the best course of action is to close this as quickly as possible. And since you enjoy a certain amount of *privilege* here, if it were me, I wouldn't want to find myself on the other side of... Well, the other side." Here, Carter attempted a laugh, but Pete noted the vague implication of a threat.

Pete had never seen Dave so serious. Sheriff Carter was known as a larger than life character with a wicked sense of humor. A few years ago, Sheriff Carter had caught a group of freshmen smoking weed in the woods. Instead of arresting them, he'd made them pick up litter from the woods at night while still high as hell. Meanwhile, he had a few officers play frightening animal sounds over the patrol car PAs. Rumor was those kids never touched drugs again. As Pete reflected on the somber mood in the office, he felt both disappointment and shame for reasons he wasn't quite able to place. He couldn't think of a single thing to say and time seemed to drag on for an eternity.

Dave suddenly brightened and stood up. "Well, gotta get back to the grindstone! It was great seeing you, man. Glad it was under different circumstances than the last time!" He laughed deeply again and slapped him too hard on the back, as if they had spent the last several minutes catching up instead of talking about the drowning case that was going to take his best friend under. Pete had a sense of whiplash, but did his best to give a smile. He mumbled some kind of goodbye and received another backslapping hug.

He walked out through the lobby, blinking and dazed. His brain was racing to make sense of the awkward situation it had endured. Pete hadn't even asked about Emily's Instagram post; he'd been so flustered. Thoughts assaulted Pete—had he done something wrong? Why had he even involved himself in this? Why had Pete thought it would be appropriate for him to ask something like that?

"Yo, Pete!" Pete was jarred out of his thoughts and looked up to see Brody Jackson strolling by in a suit. City Commissioner Brody gave the kind of quick wave to create the feeling that while he was happy to see you, it wasn't happy enough to stop him from the important business he was on. Brody had always been good at using his signature side smile to make everyone feel like he cared about them while he was only ever talking about himself. That was unfair. Pete was in a dark mood now; he knew by his reaction to Brody. He gave a short nod and walked out.

7

Pete's mind raced the entire drive home and even the entire time he undocked Rubai-yacht. He was on autopilot all the way up until he was turning off his street's canal and pulling into the larger canal that would take him to his fortress of solitude. Just the sight of the mangroves and the knowledge that he would soon be out on more open water was a balm to his soul. He even gave a slight smile. The mangroves were the original island local, one of the few plants able to survive the punishing salty environment. They protected water and sky alike, providing shade for the tarpon and nesting space for the spoonbills.

The tension began melting away as he expertly navigated the shallow spots of the canal. He knew these waters like his own soul. Everyone had laughed at the idea of a yacht that size on the canal; they teased about how they'd be on call to come tow him off the sand bar. Pete knew you had to go slow and pay attention. Three years and he hadn't been stuck once.

Soon, he was deep in the Endless Islands, away from the sounds of traffic and lawnmowers. Pete killed the engine and dropped his anchor. He walked down to the lounging deck, kicked off his flip-flops, and lay on the cushions. He wasn't here to fish, or to do anything. Pete was here to be.

The first year without competitions, he literally thought he was going to go crazy. He had no idea what to do with himself. How much time had Pete spent out at this exact spot in the canals after his "retirement"? Healing, physically and emotionally. Weeks turned to months then months turned to years. He had finally reached a place of detachment and now was good with his carefree life. The aimlessness that had once bothered him was now a sort of living motto. But now it was like he had never spent a day on his journey. Was he really that close to a relapse? Could a single difficult conversation send him reeling? Pete searched the open sky for answers, seeing only the soundless cranes.

Out on the water, he had a little distance from his feelings. Still, he was stuck: didn't Dave care how much these internet wackos were hurting Shae and the island itself? Didn't Dave feel the need to protect this little slice of peace? Couldn't he see ignoring this wasn't the answer and, in fact, it was only bringing more attention and disgrace to the island—not to mention the horde of shock journalists. A sudden thrashing of the water near one of the islands caught Pete's eye: a dolphin out for a daily feeding.

Pete shuddered at the thought of what might happen to his beloved hometown. He was overwhelmed by the thought of someone burning this all down, with no skin in the game but their own entertainment. Pete's anger simmered—why were people so careless with other people's lives?

Where would he go if he couldn't be here? He knew Shae likely felt the same way. They had grown up here together in as idyllic a childhood as possible. Pete laughed out loud, remembering the time they had tried to ride a mattress down the canal Tom Sawyer style, slowly sinking as a neighbor watched dully while mowing his lawn. Pete had always dreamed of providing that kind of childhood to his own kids, if he ever had any. Of course, things had changed in high school. A pang of guilt stabbed his chest as he thought of how he was letting Shae down.

As he closed his eyes, Pete thought back to his first time meeting Shae. It was the summer before middle school when Shae brought her board to a stop and stared at Pete, who was trying to land an ollie with all the grace his 12-year-old body could muster. She'd been riding home from the park when she saw Pete and stopped to watch, oblivious to the reaction her presence was creating in this poor kid.

She'd raised an eyebrow, her face showing disapproval more strongly than her words ever would have. She blew a giant BUBBLE YUM bubble. "You're not getting enough air," she said pointedly. As if that wasn't completely obvious.

Pete's whole body was hot; he wasn't looking for some random girl to stop by and give him pointers. If fate hadn't brought Shae along right at that moment in Pete's already difficult life, they might have had a thing.

Pete should have had a crush on the cute skateboarding girl with an attitude and a Billabong jacket. Instead, Pete was highly annoyed. He was already struggling to feel cool and having a cute girl observe and critique him didn't exactly create feelings of romance.

"Do it like this," Shae said lazily, executing a perfect ollie like nothing was easier.

"My axle is loose anyway, so I think I'm done for the day. Thanks for the tips," Pete said, not meaning it.

Shae shrugged like nothing mattered less to her. "A bunch of us practice over at the ramps park if you ever want to come along. I'm Shae."

Pete shrugged back. "Okay, cool. Maybe I'll see you around there. I'm Pete." He walked through the house to the backyard where he continued working on his skills.

Pete spent almost all his waking hours over the next week perfecting his ollie enough to brave showing up at the park. Of course, that had to include making it look effortless. His heart was pounding as he rolled up to the skate park. The kids looked like something out of an MTV video; everyone looked so intimidating with their baggy jeans and long hair. He saw Shae standing by the rail, the only girl there to ride instead of standing around watching the guys. Pete took a breath and executed his new move.

When Shae saw him land it, she smiled and said, "Guess you got your axle fixed. Nice." She then took off to the half-pipe and did a perfect axle stall, winking at Pete.

Pete's competitive nature kicked in and he headed over to the half-pipe. For the rest of the summer, they'd take turns showing off new moves and coaching each other until they were the two best skaters at the park.

They ended up being in several classes together when the school year started and kept that dynamic all the way through middle school—always trying to one-up each other like siblings. The difference was that there was no parental attention to fight for and no real gain. They were two smart and competitive kids who needed to be challenged. They would explore the island until dark, always searching for a new adventure.

Shae's older brother was high school royalty because of his band, Big Wednesday, which made Shae a middle school princess. She generously used her popularity to help Pete through the roughest times of his dad's conversion to the Catholic priesthood. She couldn't totally protect him, but Shae's auspices went a long way.

Their families were opposites and secretly, neither had approved of the friendship. Shae's family struggled with poverty, and it was widely known that her mother struggled with drugs. Pete's parents worried about the influence she would have on him. Likewise, Shae's mother had a strong distrust of organized religion and worried about the influence Pete would have on Shae. To their credit, the parents mostly kept their opinions to themselves as it became clear the friendship was nothing but positive for them both.

In high school, it became the stuff of legends to get out to one of the secret island parties. Pete and Shae would be the ones out at the bonfire having intense philosophical debates—or at least as intense as stoned high school students can be. Their friends would tease them endlessly to 'get a room,' but it was never like that.

They never had to play down their ambition or their ideas with each other; together, they believed they could take over the world. They were each other's biggest cheerleaders; Shae was never jealous of Pete's huge success, unlike a lot of their other friends. Pete tried to repay their middle school days by endorsing Shae whenever possible. There was a lot of love between them, it just wasn't that kind of love. They were a safe space for each other—a space where it was good to be smart and curious instead of needing to play it cool.

Then, Blake Crowley died at one of the island parties during their junior year. Even though Pete and Shae had a strict 'no hard drugs' rule for their island parties, Blake had snuck in some oxycodone. Nobody found him until it was too late. Since they also had a 'no cellphone' rule (to prevent leaked photos of the island), Pete and Shae had to boat Blake's body to shore in Pete's skiff. The police got involved, but by this time, Pete was already making a name for himself in surfing and it got dropped. It was a traumatic event that brought Pete and Shae closer, even as it marked the last time they ever went to their hidden island.

Pete was the first one there when Shae's mom died of an overdose their senior year, and years later, Shae had spent all her money flying out to see Pete in the hospital after his accident. She visited every day for the first few months Pete was back home, not leaving until she got him to laugh at least once. Shae had a bawdy sense of humor and had no problem trying to shock Pete. He knew she was exhausted from trying to launch her new business and yet she never complained. She was always big on woo-woo and mindset and did her best to help Pete without being obnoxious about it. Shae had been the one to convince Pete to finally start going to therapy.

They stopped seeing each other as much once Shae's business picked up and Pete got a new routine of life on the island, but they always kept in contact. They'd usually meet up for drinks with friends or at least shoot each other a video chat, keeping each other updated. As close as he was to his family, Pete had been closer to Shae than his own siblings for most of his life. They had a lot more crazy stories together, most they'd sworn to take to their graves.

His phone buzzed and shook him out of his reverie. He looked down to see a text from Sydney, asking him to jump on a call with senior leadership at Dimension Four.

He noticed his heart begin to race again. Pete brought his hands to his heart and closed his eyes. *There is nowhere but here, there is nothing but now.* Deep breath in, breath out. Pete repeated this mantra until he was only thinking about the lapping of the waves, the smell of the salty freshwater, and the feeling of the sun warming his skin. *There is nowhere but here, there is nothing but now.*

8

Pete pulled Sarg into the narrow parking lot of The Jeweler's Shop. As popular as the place was, Pete never understood why Luke didn't buy the lot next door to better accommodate the constant flow of people coming into the shop. He was doing well enough. And paint the building, for that manner. The black exterior was a contrast to the artistic interior—Pete thought Luke was asking too much of people to get over the ugly outside and come inside to his beautiful world of jewelry.

Luke was so much more than a goldsmith. He was an artist at heart. On entering, one was swept through the epochs of jewelry history. There were jewelry art and history books everywhere, necessary to keep the line of loyal customers busy while they waited to see the one and only Luke. Luke had tried to hire help over the years, but everyone wanted to deal with him directly. Not only did he exude a true love for the language of jewelry, but he also gave a hell of a deal.

Pete had lucked out and found Luke alone, banging away at the goldsmith bench. At the door's chime, Luke glanced up—his visor making his eyes comically large as he peered at Pete. A huge smile broke out over his face as he recognized him. That was the other thing about Luke; he truly loved his customers. "What's going on, brother?" Luke jumped up and moved for a fist bump. "Are we buying or selling today?"

"Selling today. Some yard sale finds." Pete never ceased to be amazed at how people didn't seem to understand (or care, maybe) about the value of what they had. His ability to spot something real was like a sixth sense. "Whatcha working on?"

Luke wiped the rouge onto his leather apron and picked up the piece to show Pete. It was a stunning milky opal in the center of a dark, brushed gold bezel. Even unfinished, it was breathtaking. Again, Luke was a true artist. "It's for the Opal Queen herself, Ms. Catherine Mellon." Luke beamed with pride. He wasn't the falsely humble type and he knew it was a work of art. "Twenty-two-karat brushed gold and a 15-carat opal. Took some work to find that baby."

Pete whistled and gave the piece for Luke to place back on the bench. He wanted no risk of messing up this delicate opal if it belonged to Catherine. "Another masterpiece."

Luke accepted the compliment with a shrug.

"So, what have we got?" Luke motioned to the black velvet bag in Pete's hand and grabbed his scale.

As Pete handed the bag to Luke, the door chimed and Officer Nate walked in. "I know you're obsessed with me, man, but this is getting ridiculous." Nate flashed his goofy grin at Pete and went in for a hug. "You know, I'm playing. I'm here shopping for the wifey. Her birthday is tomorrow."

Nate gave an apologetic look to Luke.

Luke laughed. "At least you've given me 24 hours' notice this time! I think I've got something perfect for Jules. Let me finish this up and I'll grab it." Luke walked the bag and scales over to his bench as Nate grabbed the green cloth-covered *History in Jewels* and made himself comfortable in one of the plush velvet chairs. If customers had to wait, Luke was at least going to make sure they were comfortable.

"So, what happened the other day? Dave was in a mooood after you left, man." Nate shook his head, flipping through Cartier's panther period.

Pete cocked his head. "Huh. I have no idea, man. I was just trying to get some info to help Shae out; she's being buried alive out there. It was a weird conversation."

"Shit, man, that's right. We've been so focused on the stuff coming our way that I wasn't thinking about her. Boy, I bet she's hating life today." Nate shook his head.

Pete noticed a sense of foreboding creep into his chest. What had he missed? "What happened?"

"You didn't hear? We officially closed the case. Accidental drowning. I wish these tourists would take the water more seriously. Save us from a lot of trouble." A troubled look moved over Nate's face, likely from a happy-go-lucky guy being faced with far too many dead bodies over the years. "If you thought it was bad before, they are having a field day over on Twitter. Assholes. I mean, I assume at least. Dave's had the site blocked at work and has made it very clear we need to not go on there. I think some guy on parking duty tried to be a hero by responding and made a whole shitstorm out of it. Now the mayor's all pissed, too. And the commissioners." Nate rolled his eyes. "All from some bored people with nothing better to do than troll people who are actually doing a job for their money out there."

As much as he agreed with Nate's sentiment, Pete couldn't help but feel a little angry. "The case is closed? What about her last post? The one with the help sign? And the fact that the water was only about 4' deep? Didn't that seem a little weird?"

Nate straightened up, and his tone was cool. "I wasn't the lead on the case, but I'm sure we followed the leads and they were dead ends. Not everything is the conspiracy the internet wants it to be. I'm not saying everything was perfect, but I'm sure Dave knows what he's doing and it was the right call."

Luke glanced over with raised eyebrows. He had a sixth sense for tuning into the moods of others and conflict among customers was bad for business. "Thirty-five grams and it all tests, as you know."

Pete had his own scale and testing kit at home. He'd thought about getting his own refining license too, but it was easier to bring his finds to

Luke. Plus, as his dad would say, that way everybody eats. "Seven hundred dollars. Cash okay?"

Pete's mind was racing. He had so many questions, but he didn't want to create a scene at Luke's. And he knew Nate was a friend in a weird spot, too.

Pete forced a smile. "Tenfold profit from another garage sale. Not bad for 20 minutes' work. Cash is great, thanks." Pete sensed the collective relief from Nate and Luke that he was going along with the charade that there was no tension.

"It's too bad about that girl," Luke said, testing the waters and continuing only when he felt it was safe. "She came in here not long before she died, trading some jewelry for something new. I guess she got free gold and gemstones just for doing a single post?" Luke appeared baffled by the concept. Luke had been trying to get free jewelry his whole life. "Anyway, nice as can be although she seemed a little lonely."

All three got quiet and looked at the floor for a moment.

Pete took the money from Luke and turned to Nate, "Hey, tell Jules happy birthday, man. See you on the outside." The outside waves, the place that separated the tourists from the locals. The kids from the regulars. The insiders from the outsiders.

A strange look passed over Nate's face, almost like he wanted to tell Pete something. Instead, he put out for the fist bump. "See you on the outside, man." And with that, Luke began regaling Nate with the history of this perfect piece he had for Jules.

Pete sat in the front seat outside the shop. Was Pete imagining Nate's defensiveness? And what was that look? He was scared to check his phone to read the latest posts. He took a deep breath and clicked on the little blue bird.

This time, Pete didn't have to search the #watergate tag. #justiceforemily was the top Trending hashtag.

@funnygirl: Boycott Beach Island!

@slickrik: We're gonna need a bigger police force. A photo of a Great White was attached.

@meaty: This is an outrage. @cnn are you going to do some actual investigation? Clearly these yokels don't know what it means to actually solve a crime.

@badboileroi: Breaking: Florida Man solves crime by throwing it to an alligator.

@soledadsun: Accidental my ass. This poor girl was murdered. @trackamurder these hillbillies need you.

@earthfriend: This is why Florida is the armpit of the US. They don't give a shit what happens to you.

@dougmiller: Yet another example of Gonzalez's failed policies. Smaller government=rampant crime. #impeachgonzalez

@hellterkellter posted a meme of Sheriff Carter with the caption: Epic fail, try again

@westcoastflowerchild: We need @mariasabol stat! Get her and @investegativenow and we'll have #justiceforemily

@bugcatcher: The girl is found with bruises on her neck after posting help and these Floridiots are calling it accidental? Unbelievable. @fbi @nbc @camillaattorneyofficial @nancypaulson we need some help down here.

Pete stopped at this last one. This was the same user who had posted this same shot. What was he (she?) talking about, bruises? He pinched out the screenshot, squinting at where the guy (gal?) had finger-drawn messy arrows pointing at Emily's neck. Pete's heart skipped. Although it was grainy, it was hard to deny it looked like Emily had little marks on her neck.

Was this on the autopsy report? Did the police know? God, why wouldn't they read these? There are some pretty important questions being raised. Pete hated to admit it, even to himself. He felt like he was betraying the island.

@nancypaulsonofficial: @bugcatcher @soledadsun Something fishy going on down there, no pun intended. @michaelrawson what do you say? A little trip to Florida to @trackamurder?

Pete felt the world shift. Like he was stuck in a nightmare. *Track a Murder* was coming to his place, just as he feared. He looked up at Luke and Nate happily chatting at the counter inside as Luke wrapped Jules' gift. They had no idea that this was the before. This is the last of their simple little life in this gorgeous simple little town. He slammed his fist on the steering wheel. Sarg stayed firm, but forgave him. Why hadn't the police done some simple investigation? They'd have avoided this whole situation.

Disgusted, Pete finally tossed his phone into the center console. He was sick of reading these asinine posts. Responding wasn't going to help. The police weren't going to either. Pete had no idea what to do, but he was fuming and had the need to do something. He knew where to go—the only place he thought to go when he felt like this. Pete turned over the engine and backed out, carefully avoiding Nate's deputy's car. He knew he wouldn't get answers where he was going, but he'd at least get some better questions.

***

The swells were only seconds apart, but Pete paddled to the outside and dropped in again and again in an almost punishing rhythm. Out of the corner of his eye, he noticed people stopped on the shore watching but he ignored them. He threw a switchback, aggressively sending ocean spray feet into the air. It was the kind of move that would have taken him to the top of the heat, but Pete didn't notice.

Pete's mind raged as he caught wave after wave, his ankle aching badly. He knew he should back off, but he was too angry. The warning in his ankle increased, but Pete dug in with more determination. Finally, the tightness in his chest loosened ever so slightly. He looked at his Apple watch: he'd caught 15 waves in nearly as many minutes. His breathing was ragged and the pain emanated from his ribcage. His ankle continued to throb. He straddled his board and sat up tall, watching a pelican land on the water a few feet away.

He noticed his surroundings for the first time during the session. A cruise ship floated a mile in the distance. A gull floated above him, a single white dot among the wisps of cirrus clouds. Pete rose along with his board as a swell passed peacefully underneath him. Pete rode the next few waves, but with less fire; the crowd on the shore dispersed. Pete let the anger release further. He let out an audible exhale and caught the last wave in.

At home, Pete hosed off his board and his feet. He covered himself in a towel from the front porch, shimming his baggies off and hanging them next to the board rack. He grabbed his laptop and a coconut water from the mini-fridge and sat out on the lanai. With the anger out of the way, Pete was able to think more clearly. He stared at the fading wood pilings and retreated into his thoughts.

Neither of these situations was Pete's problem. He'd done what he could and there wasn't much else to do. He should have kept his mouth shut, but now he'd have to bow out gracefully. Which problem to tackle first? Pete had committed to Shae first so he would start there. The case was closed and Pete was sure the internet would find a new story soon enough. Shae would have to wait it out; she'd be fine. Pete rehearsed the text he'd send, but he still had a nagging feeling.

He sipped his coconut water and squinted out at the breaker pines just past the water, getting stuck at, *Hey, what's up?* in his head.

His heart stopped. "Oh shit." Pete jumped up, nearly dropping his towel. He ran inside, changed into dry baggies and grabbed his phone. Back on the lanai, Pete hunched over his phone, scrolling frantically. Pete shook his head slowly. "Oh shit. Shit." Pete spoke to himself quietly. He clicked on the zoomed-in photo of the alleged bruises on Emily's neck. It wasn't the bruises Pete was looking at. Now he knew why he had been struck by the picture. There, blurry in the background yet most definitely there, was a small fire in a fire pit. The exact fire pit he had sat at more times than he could remember.

How was it possible? This particular fire pit—painted back at one of the high school bonfires by someone Pete could no longer remember—was on an island that was secret, even among the locals. Its privacy protected by the blindfolds Pete used to insist on as the boats got closer. It was a move to ensure the girls had to cling tight to him, but it had paid off in keeping the island isolated. You had to know that the tiny canals leading there only looked closed off, but if you maneuvered carefully, you'd end up at this secret little shore that had the perfect space for a bonfire and the perfect clearing in the breaker pines to see the stars.

As far as he knew, only one other person had the knowledge and skill to navigate to that island. They'd been the ones to discover it together in what seemed like a lifetime ago. He thought they had promised never to return, but clearly, one of them hadn't kept their promise.

9

Pete pulled the new Hummer, Project X, up into the driveway of Shae's building. Shae's cobalt blue truck was in the driveway and the metal door was open. Pete had no idea what he was going to say as he neared the walkway. He planned to go to the front door, but something in the garage caught his attention.

A huge white chest freezer sat at the side of the garage; the kind his sister had to keep her massive family fed. Pete knew some of the local fishermen kept deep freezers, but Shae had never been into fishing. Pete ducked into the garage and opened the freezer: totally empty. As he opened the door, something slipped off the top to the back. Pete glanced behind the freezer: a pair of black gloves. Pete said out loud without helping it, "What the hell?"

Just then, Shae opened the door and jumped in surprise. "Holy shit. You scared the shit out of me." Shae put a protective hand to her chest and looked around nervously. "What's going on? Good news, I hope?" The freezer stood out like an elephant in the room.

"I mean, not really. This whole situation is kind of a hornet's nest. I was kind of hoping you would clear some stuff up for me, actually." Pete fumbled for his phone as he motioned to the freezer. "You're not storing dead bodies, are you?" Pete laughed nervously.

Shae laughed way too loudly and too quickly. "Ha ha, man. Very funny. Uh no, just you know...trying to find a new way to store concessions for the trips."

Pete thought this unlikely since it was empty and because she only brought small snacks on the tours, but he maintained focus on the task at hand.

"Anyway," Shae seemed eager to change the subject, "what did you want to ask me?"

Pete took a breath and gathered up his courage. "You see this picture?" Pete held his phone up close to Shae's face.

Pete could have sworn Shae blanched before she looked away. "I guess, I mean these sickos have posted a lot of shit. I kinda stopped looking at it."

Pete moved the phone back into Shae's line of vision. "Notice anything familiar about this?"

The energy shifted and Shae seemed to let out an exhale of relief. "Look, it's not what it looks like." Shae looked at Pete with pleading in her eyes.

"Okay...well, right now, it looks like you're the Island Strangler with your gloves and your fucking creepy freezer." Pete meant to make it sound like a joke, but his voice came out scared and questioning. Pete hadn't realized how afraid he was of Shae's answer. Pete was terrified to lose her.

Shae sat down on an overturned bucket, and put her hands in her face. The alternating sounds of deep throat breaths and whimpering filled the garage.

Pete was speechless and uncomfortable.

"Oh man, it's so bad. I fucked up so bad." Shae was sobbing.

Nausea filled his stomach, rising to his throat. Was one of his best friends a murderer? He had not signed up for this at all. "Uh, ok. Uh, maybe you should, like, call your dad? Or, like, a lawyer?" Pete didn't want to hear anything more, but to his dismay, Shae began to talk.

"I don't know what I was thinking. One thing led to another—I think I got so swept up in everything that I wasn't thinking at all."

Shae rambled on and on between sobs as Pete's horror grew. It was as if he was in a nightmare or a bad movie. Why wouldn't she stop talking?

"Shae, you really need to think before you talk here, even to me. You need to get a lawyer. You could get the death penalty in a case as visible as this!" At last, Pete seemed to have stopped the stream of words coming from Shae's mouth.

She stopped and stared at him, her mouth wide open. "What the fuck, Pete?! I didn't kill her."

Pete experienced both relief and embarrassment as she narrowed her eyes at him.

"I thought you of all people would know me better than that." Pete felt the sting of her judgment. She sighed. "But people are going to think I did." Shae looked at Pete, seeming to debate whether or not to continue.

Pete wished she wouldn't, but no such luck.

Shae mustered her courage with a big inhale. "I was setting up for the night's tour and I found her on my...our...island."

"What do you mean, you *found her*? You mean with the tour..." Pete had to interrupt. His brain wouldn't process her words.

"No," Shae's face was grim. "I mean that I found her when I was setting up. I always have a bonfire ready so people can take a break before paddling back. As I was getting ready to get the fire and snacks ready, I saw her." Here, Shae stopped and let out a guttural noise, reliving what had to be a horrifying moment.

Pete flinched. This was new information to him and not a particularly positive development. Pete was having trouble processing the information that Shae had been using their old island for her tours. How could she stand to go back after what had happened?

Shae took another deep breath in. "She was laid out next to the fire pit and I knew as soon as I saw her that she was dead." Shae swallowed hard, as if choking down vomit. "I...I was already set up for the group. I only had about 15, maybe 20, minutes to get back and start the tour. It was a full booking and it was one of the last nights of the season." Shae moved her hand as if to fidget with her dreads before remembering they were gone. She put her hands in her pockets.

"It was a perfect night with no moon. I couldn't afford to cancel the tour, so I moved her body to the back of the island. I kind of panicked. I know it's a shitty thing to do."

Shae was unable to look at Pete, which was probably good as his jaw was hanging wide open. There was no way for him to hide his shock that his friend was capable of such a thing.

"I don't know." Shae lifted her t-shirt to wipe snot off her face, leaving dark spots around the collar. "I panicked. Like I said, I was going to tell the police when I got back to the mainland, but the tour was so full. It was one of the last nights, and I don't know, I guess I figured it would be the same if I told them after the tour. What can I say? I freaked out. And if we go to the police now, I'm gonna look super guilty, but I swear she was dead when I found her. And, I think it wasn't an accidental death. I think she was..." Shae lowered her voice to a whisper, "murdered."

"Okay..." Pete spoke slowly and calmly, as if calming a child. "Okay. I can understand you freaked out." Pete did not actually understand but had no idea what else to say here. "What makes you say she was murdered?"

"Well, first of all, we both know there's no way she washed up on shore there. The mangroves are so thick around the island that there's just no way she floated there. She would have been caught in the mangroves. Plus it's true what they are saying, she did have bruises on her neck."

Pete nodded in agreement.

"And third of all..." Shae took another deep breath. "She had to have been alive when she got to the island." Pete's blood froze and he waited for Shae to go on. "Because the fire was already lit when I got there. So, it must have happened on the island. The island only you and I know about." A chill took over the warm garage.

"Why didn't you call the police? I don't think they'd have ruled it an accident if they had known this! And so what, a murderer is roaming free?" Pete's voice echoed against the concrete blocks.

A landscaper clipping a hibiscus plant across the street paused and glanced their way. After a brief pause, he returned to tending the plant.

Shae flinched. "I don't know. Again, I think I panicked. And I was thinking I would tell them in a day or two when the last of the tours were done. She was dead anyway. Then they started calling it an accident and I was so caught up with all the trolling online that a few days turned to weeks and it seemed too late. I just didn't have the emotional bandwidth. Ugh, I know how it sounds. I feel like a horrible person." Shae sounded miserable.

A day or TWO? Pete was angry. "Okay, well you should go to the police now." Pete's voice was firm.

Shae stared off catatonically. "Yeah. But now they closed the case," she said slowly, still not looking at Pete. "So, what would be the point? And there's more."

Pete audibly groaned at this point.

"I'd met with Emily a few weeks before about her promoting Island Guy. I turned her down because I didn't have the money and she wanted $6,000! For an endorsement! Then she signed with Glow Your Boat. I didn't know the last part until a few weeks ago. But between that and the argument on Instagram, it's going to look like I have a motive!"

Pete didn't know more shock was possible at this point and struggled for a coherent answer. He ended up making a noise that sounded like 'blargh.'

Shae's jaw tightened. "No, if I go to the police now, they're going to think it was me. We need to figure out what happened first. Because we agree with the internet on one thing—that was no accidental death. You know me, man. You know there is no way I killed her. But someone else did."

Something about Shae's voice had Pete convinced that, while she had done a really boneheaded thing in moving the body, Shae hadn't killed anyone. At least, so he hoped. He looked her over and considered her resemblance to her mother. No one thought she had been capable of what she'd done either. Looks could be deceiving.

Pete struggled to respond. Every fiber in his body screamed to convince Shae to go to the police, but then he thought about the cold response he had gotten from Sheriff Carter. And there would be no doubt of the mainstream press getting involved if word got out that Shae had been on the island with Emily's body. No, they would need to find a way to prove Shae's innocence before they went to the police about moving the body.

"And what about that thing?" Pete nodded towards the freezer.

Shae looked ashamed. "I was throwing ice out in the canal," she said, almost in a whisper.

Pete wanted to laugh at something so ridiculous, but Shae looked disgusted with herself as if she had admitted to a heinous murder, not tossing frozen water into not-frozen water. Didn't Shae know only a few minutes ago Pete thought she had actually committed a heinous murder? "Uh, ok. Weird, but not a big deal." Pete shrugged.

"Are you kidding me? It's a huge deal, Pete!" Shae's voice was raised in anger. "I was throwing ice in the water before my tours because it makes the phosphorescence brighter. It changes the salinity level. It's cheating, and worse, it's bad for the algae. I'm a fraud! I got so caught up in the competition and being the top-rated. I put my stupid reputation in front of what matters most to me."

Pete wanted to laugh in relief, then realized how much this all meant to Shae. It wasn't just a kayak tour or even a job. She loved this island so much and wanted to protect it. That made Pete want to protect her. He knew that meant not letting her off the hook, but at least acknowledging what she was confessing.

"That's not who you are, Shae. It was a dumb move, but we all know you've done more to create safe eco-tourism than anyone else around here. If it weren't for you, our little island might not even be there. You've done a lot of important work to keep the Endless Islands safe and it's not going to be erased by this. But let's toss this thing to the curb. Metaphorically speaking, of course. Let me sell it on the marketplace and we can split the money."

Shae gave a small laugh and agreed. It felt like a small, but important step back to herself. But for Pete, it was a step away from reality. He knew Shae was counting on him, but how would he tell Shae he had no idea what to do?

10

"Pete, darling! So good to see you!" Catherine Mellon fussed over Pete as he walked in. Catherine was a neighbor and longtime parishioner at his dad's church. She was also famous for establishing the Beach Island tradition called The Splash that Pete's family had been attending for years. By now, it had morphed into a ritual of the after-work drink on a boat or dock for most of the island residents.

Ever the traditionalist, Catherine still hosted a monthly formal Splash like they had back in the early days when the women would come donning a beehive and men in Guayaberas would smoke Cuban cigars out on the deck.

Catherine's family began visiting the island in the heydays of the 60s when the Pier still had a miniature Ferris wheel and there were more astronauts and engineers on the island than locals. Belly-dancing in the Torchlight Room of the Tiki Hotel was the top entertainment.

In the 70s, Catherine's parents finally turned the vacation getaway into their permanent home. By that time, the dirt side streets were paved and dozens of space-themed restaurants were peppered along State Highway A1A, none more famous than The Big Dipper where all the waitresses wore shiny silver miniskirts and fishnets.

The Mellons were well established as island royalty by the time Pete's family moved in a few streets down. Pete's dad had been assigned as the preacher of a church on Beach Island. And everyone knows a wealthy family must be in want of a charismatic preacher, so they'd been friends ever since.

Rumor was the Mellon's had lost all their wealth in the inflation crisis and had been forced to sell off all the other properties. Looking at Catherine tonight, Pete found it hard to believe she'd ever experienced a financial hardship in her life. Catherine was one of those women who exuded money and class, from her pronounced posture to the easy way she moved her hand while talking. She stretched her dewy glass of white wine out to the side as she gave the European double air kiss.

"Please, dear, you must try this single malt Teddy brought back from the Isles. It's over 100 years old and is to die for."

She waved him in as she trilled at the next set of guests coming in behind him: "Oh, Betsy, aren't you a doll! This looks like a vintage. I've been dying to try this!" Catherine's voice trailed into the background as Chet Baker crooning on the speaker came into the foreground.

Pete looked around at all the other royals deep in conversations about politics or golf or Botox. Phil Danning, owner of the largest dock builder in the state, was drawing large shapes with his hand in one political debate. His wife (the daughter of a newspaper magnate), Christine Lawton, kept a wary eye on the beer in his hand while sipping from the Riesling in her own. An older man whom Pete knew to be one of the most prominent engineers during the space race adjusted his glasses and gave a dismissive wave to Phil's animated speech. Without a doubt, Pete would be taking Catherine up on her offer of the whiskey.

Caramel, toffee, and peat burned Pete's nostrils in the best kind of way as he sat down out by the canal. Catherine had arguably one of the best views on the island. Her lot was angled in a way to give her a panoramic view of the street canal, the main outlet canal, and the river itself. A heron floated down on a Longleaf Pine on the island across the way. The golden hour was beginning and turned the bird into a kind of mythical Ibis.

"My favorite spot in the world. My little paradise." Catherine's voice had a dreamy quality to it as she sat next to him and stared off at the bird. "I still remember Mama giving me my first sip of Champagne in this very same spot. You know, Mama and Daddy were the first ones to throw a splash out on the island. Of course, now you see everyone out on their deck for the evening splash. But they were the originals." Her face was sad, like a little girl. "Just atrocious what is happening here." Catherine took a deep swill from her glass. "You'd think those of us that live here would have more rights!" Catherine's voice suddenly had a hard edge, and she motioned angrily next door.

Pete glanced over, unsure of the enemy he was seeking. The concrete pad surrounded by little wood sticks and pink flags stood out like a blot on the landscape. Pete looked back to Catherine for further clarification.

"Another one of these investors looking to make a quick buck with no care for people who actually live here. They bought it when George Granson died last year and are turning it into a vacation rental. As if that wasn't bad enough, the idea of us having to live with constant strangers coming in and out of our neighborhood. Throwing parties at all hours! No, now they're adding something called a tiny house to the backyard." Catherine's voice was vicious at this point. "And it's going to be right in front of my view!"

Pete thought to his own view of the canal at home—it was his morning and nighttime ritual to sit out there and enjoy the water. Pete understood why she was so angry.

"First, I tried going to the permits office but they were unbothered." Catherine walked to the outdoor fridge and refilled her glass. "They see some rich old White lady. I heard the girl at the desk call me a Karen. I looked it up, and it's offensive!" Catherine ran a hand down the bottom of her linen shirt dress to smooth the creases. "Then I tried talking to the new neighbor directly, which was a disaster. These people are just out for the money. They don't care at all about the people that live here. This is my family legacy we are talking about. There are over 60 years of our memories out here."

The fact this house was all she had left seemed implied. Pete had always enjoyed the company of her late husband, William. He'd never admitted it, but he had looked forward to the catechism classes he was forced to attend when they were led by Mr. Bill. He never dumbed things down for the kids. Mr. Bill's funeral Mass two years ago was the most heavily attended the church had ever seen.

Catherine sniffed. "They said there was nothing they could do, that they had pulled all the necessary paperwork. All this time, I've lived here and been a part of the community, and it comes to nothing."

While he didn't know exact figures, Pete knew from his experience with his dad's church that Catherine had been a generous patron of the Island's arts and culture. And she was the longest-serving member of the city commission council. One would think that kind of dedication to the city would mean something. No wonder she seemed so bitter.

"Did you try talking to the city manager about it? Justin is a decent guy, and I bet he'd help you. We go way back, and he's very committed to fighting for the locals."

Catherine looked at Pete with cautious hope in her eyes. "You'd talk to him?"

Pete had meant Catherine should talk to Justin, but he nodded.

"Oh darling, would you talk to him? I've tried talking to him and I can't bear to be dismissed again. Women of my age, no one sees us anymore. It's happening to me. I'm fading." The bitterness crept back into Catherine's voice.

Pete shifted uncomfortably, unsure of what to say.

"Now, you know you are still a beautiful woman," he reassured her. "But I'd be happy to talk to him. Anything for you." Pete laid it on thick; he couldn't imagine Catherine being invisible to anyone but gave the compliment just in case.

The memory of his meeting with Sheriff Carter flashed in his mind. "Speaking of the city, pretty crazy about the girl that died. Word is that it was accidental?" Pete tried to keep his voice light and uninterested, but he knew Catherine was on the task force and might have some insight.

"Oh, these tourists, absolutely dreadful." Catherine tittered. "They're as bad as the developers, if not worse. They come here acting like fools and get themselves killed. And we have to deal with the aftermath!" She shook her head disapprovingly, as if she were discussing a disobedient child and not a young woman who had died.

Pete sensed the same tone of finality he had at Sheriff Carter's office the day before, yet pushed ever so slightly. "You and the other commissioners don't think it needs more investigation?"

Catherine looked at him as if attempting to decode him, but Pete kept his face impartial, affecting the well-known surfer implacability.

"The sooner this goes away, the better for all," Catherine said decisively. Suddenly, Catherine jumped up out of the swing and clapped her hands, spilling the wine into the white rocks around the deck. "Now, Pete, you must come in and meet Mrs. Carrington's daughter, Kylie. She's such a doll. I think you two would get along famously."

Pete laughed and threw up a hand. "No, ma'am, you know how I feel about the church ladies' matchmaking. I'll sit out and enjoy your view, thank you very much."

Catherine narrowed her eyes at him and gave him a playful smirk. Catherine was not the kind of woman you said no to, but she was in a merciful mood with Pete tonight. She gave him another set of double air kisses and floated inside.

Just as Pete was settling into the warmth of his whiskey, the telltale white collar of a priest caught his attention.

"I guess they let anybody in here these days," came the familiar voice.

Pete shook his head with a laugh and stood to hug his dad.

It had been bad enough to be the son of a preacher, but at least they had been left to themselves both in and out of their tiny Anglican church. Then Pete's dad—and most of the congregation—had decided to convert to the Roman Catholic Church. That made Pete's dad a Roman Catholic priest, in spite of his wife and three kids. Pete was about 14 at the time, already navigating the brutal world of middle school.

Pete still remembered all the jokes about how his dad must be a pedophile, that he was going to rape little boys. As if being a priest on this island of Episcopalians and beach bums wasn't scandalous enough, Michael Brown was a priest with a family. It wasn't only the kids who were cruel about the situation—those who hadn't gone along with the conversion were as nasty and appeared to go out of their way to damage his father's reputation. But Pete's dad said he had landed on the truth and had the conviction of Simon Peter himself.

Pete didn't know whether to be angry at the Church for such a stupid loophole, his dad for putting him in that situation, or the kids for being idiots. Pete was angry, that's all he knew. His dad managed to keep a sense of humor—even when someone had bleached their garage door with the word HERATIC, his dad had joked about the quality of the local schools as he painted over the damage.

His brother and sister didn't seem to mind at all either. Thomas went on to be a full-blown muslin-wearing monk up in Kentucky with an oath of silence and everything. His sister, Becky, had what felt like a million kids out in the edges of DC where she worked at Catholic University. Of course, that was a good thing; her five kids were nothing but a source of joy to the family.

Pete felt like the character foil to his siblings. They never seemed to have a problem with the shift. For Pete, it was always complicated. He didn't know if it was because they were still in elementary school during the brunt of it and so weren't as jaded or if he was a jaded kind of person. His siblings had such genuine faith. Pete wasn't sure what he believed, especially over the last few years.

There was no denying, though, that the first person he turned to when he had a problem was his dad. His dad was an incredible man, both as priest and as a father. Pete had never met anyone else as committed to the truth, no matter the cost. Pete looked at his dad, noticing that he looked more tired than usual.

Pete experienced both an increased admiration and fear for his dad since his latest appointment from the Bishop. In a move that had shocked everyone, Bishop Kowalska had named Father Michael Brown as the Diocese's exorcist. They had laughed at first, who would need an exorcism on their tiny island? But his dad was expected to travel all throughout the large Diocese and the amount of requests was surprising, to say the least. This wasn't including the long stay in Rome during his apprenticeship. The appointment had only been eight months ago, but Pete worried the role was taking a toll on his dad.

"So you wanted to ask me about something? Must be serious if you decided to ask for help!" Rather than a dig, Pete sensed his dad's admiration at his independence. His parents had taught them logic using the Trivium and insisted on honing their critical thinking abilities above all.

Pete ran his fingers through his hair. "Yeah, I don't know. I just... I just feel kind of stuck. You've heard about all this Twitter drama about that influencer girl who drowned, right?"

His dad nodded slowly and waited silently for Pete to go on.

"Well, Shae—you remember Shae—good. Yeah, well, she was getting burned alive out there and was really freaking out. So, I said I would do some PR kinda stuff. To help her out, you know? But I was kind of running into some blocks with the stuff these people were putting out there."

Pete knew his dad's wheels were turning though he remained silent.

For some reason, Pete was afraid. "So, yeah, I went down to see Dave. And it was so weird. He was, like, maybe I was just reading into it, I don't know. But he was angry at me or something. And he said they're closing the case as an accidental death."

"You aren't convinced?" Pete's dad's face was neutral, no judgment in the question. The harsh scold of a scrub jay echoed across the canal.

"I don't know." Pete laughed nervously, shifting his gaze to the water to avoid eye contact. "I mean, I'm sure they did the right thing. I mean, those guys are good guys." Pete looked back to his dad, maybe searching for confirmation.

The impassiveness remained.

Jenny Cuthrow opened the door and gave a questioning holler for her husband, Matt. Pete shook his head in the negative and she closed the French doors behind her.

Pete sighed, "Okay, yeah. I'm not convinced. I don't feel like they did all the research they should have. Like there's this post on the internet right before she died. But you know how Carter is with technology. So, I feel like, yeah, maybe they missed some stuff. And something feels off about it." Again, the feeling of cold and fear filled the space around them. Pete had so much more to share, but he just wasn't ready.

His dad sighed and appeared to debate his words, which was unusual for his straight-shooter of a dad. "There are some mysteries to meditate on and there are some mysteries to try to solve. Try to love the questions." His father never seemed to tire of applying this pithy Rilke quote to every situation. "But, Pete, be careful. Sometimes, when things aren't as they seem, it's because they are covering something much worse. Stay alert and listen to your intuition." His dad was solemn. Maybe the new assignment was getting to him.

Pete shuddered to think of what his dad had seen in these last few months. Yet, the words resonated somewhere deep within.

Just as quickly as he had grown serious, Pete's dad shifted the mood with a smirk. "So, tell me about this latest refurb you have going on—Project X?"

Pete's eyes lit up, and happy for the diversion, he launched into the list of plans for his latest Army Hummer flip project.

11

Pete walked through the city hall doors as if for the first time. The now iconic image of him surfing Waimea, taken a year before his accident, hung poster-size on the wall. He'd grown to hate that picture despite the ongoing royalties. It was a constant reminder of what he'd never do again. The frangipani murals, although expertly air-brushed by a local muralist, were geographically incorrect. It was a pet peeve of Pete's how many Hawaiian references thrived on Beach Island. Why not use Florida's flora and fauna? He loved Hawaii, but he wanted Beach Island to celebrate its own wild beauty and not look like a cheap knock-off.

On his last visit, he had felt as if he was walking into an old friend's place but the outcome had left him unsettled. Pete and Justin went way back and he was confident Justin would be a friend in this situation, but the encounter with Sheriff Carter had left him doubtful. Though, to be fair, that involved life and death and this was only permits, he reasoned with himself.

And no matter what, he knew he'd rather have an uncomfortable meeting with Justin than face telling Catherine he hadn't come to city hall. There was plenty of island lore about Catherine's ability to hold a grudge and he didn't care to be numbered among those unfortunate souls. As he grabbed his visitor badge and walked back, Pete found himself adjusting his hat multiple times. He put his hands in his pockets to stop the nervous habit.

"What's good, man? Long time no see!" Justin jumped up for a half handshake, half hug, and Pete's nerves disappeared. Justin walked from around the desk to reveal flip-flops with his khakis and button-up. Some things about island life would never change. Justin took a seat back behind his mahogany desk. "What brings the Cat to these parts? You're not looking for another bronze statue, I hope? You gotta save some room for the rest of us!" Justin cracked himself up.

Pete gave a tight smile and did his best to seem good-humored; the two bronze statues of him marking the only entrances and exits to the island were not his favorite. Pete wanted to live a normal life but some of the local surfers, like Justin, treated him like a celebrity. Which he was, but still. It's not like he was walking the red carpet or anything. And he was still just Pete Brown.

"Yeah, I'm all good on statues, man. I'm trying to help out a lady in my dad's neighborhood—an old friend of the family. Uh, you know her, I'm sure: Catherine Mellon." The introduction was silly—everyone on Beach Island knew Catherine.

Justin groaned and looked up. His face was full of distaste as he regained eye contact with Pete. "I don't know that anyone can help that lady, but I'll do my best. What's up?"

Pete was momentarily thrown by Justin's response but pushed forward, "Uh, well, she's got this new neighbor. Another one of these flippers doing an Airbnb. And they're building a tiny house in the backyard."

Justin nodded, though not appearing to see any problem.

"Well, Catherine has this amazing view and the developer is putting the tiny house right smack in the middle of her view."

Justin waited for Pete to go on.

Pete thought the problem was very obvious by this point, but he continued: "I don't know, I guess I kinda assumed there are some code issues. It seems like you should have some kind of say if you've lived here for 50 years and then someone who isn't even a resident throws up a concrete building in your view."

"Look. Pete, I get it. I can't say I'd love it either. As I told Catherine, Ms. Finnegan has pulled all the necessary permits. At this time, her structure falls within the codes. I wish I had the power to do something but, technically speaking, Ms. Finnegan is going exactly by the book unless something changes at the next commissioner meeting."

Pete was confused. The island's codes were notoriously strict about buildings and add-ons; it was what kept the island from being some kind of little Miami. Justin was implying something had changed, but Pete was sure he would have heard about something that major.

Right at that moment, someone cleared their throat angrily in the doorway. "Well, speak of the devil: hey Ms. Finnegan. How can I help you?" Justin stood awkwardly behind his desk as Pete turned to see a petite brunette behind him. She wore a bright pink and aqua patterned mini dress, the brightness of which served as a stark contrast to the irritation painted on her face. Pete caught himself noticing the lack of tan lines under the tied straps on her shoulders and looked away.

"Ahh, an assertive woman must be a she-devil. How original. And I'm sorry, are you one of my neighbors? I thought this was a private meeting, so I'm a little unclear on what *this* is." Sam Finnegan made an aggressive move of her hands to indicate some kind of thing between Justin and Pete.

Pete threw his hands up in a mock surrender. "No, I dropped in on Justin. I had no idea he had an appointment. I'm here helping a friend out." Pete studied her face; something about her was familiar.

"What a small world it is on this island. Let me guess, your *friend*," Sam inserted air quote fingers here, "is Catherine Mellon?"

Pete did his best to do a chagrined shrug as Sam stared at him angrily.

"Maybe you can tell your *friend*," again, she used finger air quotes, "to stop leaving nasty notes and spreading rumors about me around the neighborhood. I've done everything legally so far and I have no problem addressing her harassing behavior to the full extent of the law."

Pete knew Catherine was a bit stubborn in her ways, but Sam's animosity seemed unfair given the fact she clearly had no regard for the people around her. "Well, Ms. Finnegan, I'm sure the fact she's a widow and is now losing her last bit of joy might make her slightly less than friendly." Pete surprised himself with the acidic venom of sarcasm.

Justin looked at him sharply and then at the floor.

Sam laughed bitterly. "Oh, Ms. Mellon is no victim. In fact, I don't know how she's made it this far in life without a major consequence. I don't know how things work around here, but I can assure you her behavior has no place in any kind of civilized world." The indictment of their small town, backward ways was loud and clear.

Justin cleared his voice. "Um, did you want to see me about something, Ms. Finnegan?"

Sam maintained fierce eye contact with Pete for another beat and then slowly looked to Justin. "I'm dropping off the final forms you asked for. Funny how you needed them since two of my neighbors were able to build sheds without them, but here they are all the same. I believe this means we're good to go?"

Justin nodded reluctantly. "So much for small-town hospitality," Sam muttered under breath. She gave a curt nod to both men and walked out briskly.

Justin once again shrugged at Pete, showing he was nothing but a middleman.

Pete opened his mouth to speak—he had so many questions—but the interaction had left him too angry to say anything coherent. He shrugged back and put out for a fist bump. "Thanks for the information, man. It was certainly...eye-opening."

"You're not here causing trouble again, are you? Sounded like you were giving my buddy Justin a hard time in there!" Sheriff Carter appeared suddenly and gave Pete the hard, back-slapping hug.

Pete tried to hide his grimace; he was still sore from the last "hug."

Carter gave a stiff laugh, but his words held more warning than humor.

Pete did his best to keep up the appearance of a joke, "Nah, just seeing an old friend. No trouble from me!" Once again, Pete threw up his hands in a mock show of innocence. The air was strained.

Sheriff Carter nodded in approval. "Good, you stay out of trouble."

Out in the main office, Officer Nate looked up from his desk. An indecipherable look crossed his face as he looked back and forth between Sheriff Carter and Pete.

Pete shifted the brim of his hat, removed it to smooth his hair, and pulled it back down tight onto his head. With a throw of his hand that he hoped passed as a wave, he walked out into the sunshine in slow motion.

Outside, Pete's mind was reeling as he sat hard on the front seat and then jumped up as he cursed. It was an art to get into an open-top vehicle in Florida without searing your skin off, but Pete hadn't been careful. He slammed the truck door. Since when had the city codes changed? Pete knew he would have heard about it—that was the kind of thing Pete paid attention to. Had the city commission passed them privately? Was such a thing even legal?

And what the hell was that with Carter—again? How many times had they drank beers together out at the Swamps, how many times had Pete pulled his ass out of the mud and not said a word? Now Dave was treating him like some kind of criminal or troublemaker. It made no sense at all.

Why had he gotten himself into either of these situations? He hated disappointing people and he was going to have to tell both Shae and Catherine that he'd not only made no progress but maybe made things worse. God, was it by arrogance that he did this? Did he buy into the statues and the blue checks and believe the hype?

12

The list of alerts had piled up on Pete's phone. Now they felt personal, as if there was a mob with pitchforks pounding on his front door. Each started as a ping on his phone and then a buzz on his watch followed by a second ping on his phone. The notifications might have been for something helpful, but he hated the idea of reading through more of the vitriol on the small chance of a new piece of information.

Yet another buzz on his wrist pushed him over the edge; he held down the little blue icon and moved it to the trash. Already, he felt lighter. He saw three missed calls from Shae and swiped those out of his view. He'd yet to respond to Sydney and she'd emailed him, this time copying the lead partners. A knot was forming in his ribcage as the anger threatened to take over. Pete wanted to throw his whole phone and its contents in the trash at this point. He tossed his phone on the counter and went to his workshop in the garage.

A four-wheeler still in need of tires, a Vespa needing a carburetor, a board that needed a few dings fixed before listing on the marketplace, and Project X. A long to-do list stared at him. As was often the habit with Pete, he walked towards the shiny new project and ignored the rest.

Pete put on the mask and turned up the volume of the speakers, hoping the heavy beats would drown out the thoughts in his head. They looped between the accusatory words of others and the ones in his thoughts. None of this was his problem! Pete remembered one of the posts showing Emily Larson as a little girl, a post by her best friend he thought. It was a sad situation, but you can't climb every mountain out there. He thought about his own best friend, Shae, and how scared she had looked yesterday.

He fluctuated between feeling sorry for Shae and being pissed at her for bringing him into this mess without telling him what she had done. Pete thought she should have given him a heads up when he'd offered to help. What kind of friend was Shae being, Pete thought angrily. What about his feelings? And how did Pete know if she was telling the truth? If Shae had hidden the fact that she moved the body, what else was she hiding?

Pete tried to imagine what it had been like to find the body and softened a little. Shae was pretty tough, but he had to admit that would be hard on anybody.

With that thought, Pete's anger shifted over to Sheriff Carter. He certainly wasn't any help either. Pete hated how the police were feeding into the provincial narrative so perfectly. Pete knew the guys downtown—it seemed impossible to him that they were so incompetent. These were smart guys with years of experience. And even if Sheriff Carter was old school, how had all the younger guys missed all of the online posts? It was all just too avoidable. And why was he the bad guy for pointing that out? None of it made sense.

Instead of using the electric sander, he worked off the loose paint chips with a sheet of sandpaper until his arms ached. Little bits of faded green filled the air, creating a haze that mimicked Pete's internal state. The hood was smoother, but he had barely made a dent in the thoughts in his head. Pete noticed a buzzing on his wrist; another call from Shae. Pete moved to the driver's side door and dug in even harder. Three hours later, Pete stood back to admire his work. His traps and lats ached as he stood straight, but at least the thoughts had finally subsided. He hadn't landed on any answers, he had simply worn himself out.

Project X was ready for the metallic gray paint, and soon she'd be ready to be listed on the market. Pete was going to miss her. He was filled with a longing to begin again on this project. Moving back here, this was all he wanted. A simple life with simple work. He sensed the pull back into the thought spiral so he grabbed the shop vac and began to clean the garage.

It was now very late and Pete debated jumping in the canal instead of showering. The storm surges had made it deep enough to jump in without risking his ankle. The surges also often brought unwelcome creatures into the canal. Pete looked up to the moon, so bright it was casting a reflection almost the entire width of the canal. A vision of Emily's bloated body floating in the canal intruded into Pete's mind; he thought better of his swim and took a long, hot shower instead.

***

A few blocks away, Sam stared at the same bright moon also unable to sleep. It was one of those nights when Sam thought her heart might break. She knew she should feel better by now, but no matter what she tried, she couldn't stop being so angry. Emily would have had the right words for Sam. Emily was always DMing her words of wisdom she found from the latest social media guru. Sam would usually roll her eyes while holding the heart emoji, but tonight she would love to read some woo-woo advice about how to heal.

They were supposed to be having the summer of their lives, or at least reliving the summer of their lives. They'd both been through so much and it had been like divine intervention when Emily had messaged her about visiting. Despite not keeping in touch for years, they had reconnected as if no time had passed at all. Sam missed Emily's witty replies and her ridiculous filters in their Snaps. Sam hadn't realized how much she had needed Emily back in her life and Emily had said pretty much the same.

It was so hard to make friends as you got older and good female friends were harder to find. They found each other again at exactly the right moment. Although Sam was thankful to be able to purchase her grandfather's house, she hadn't anticipated how painful it would be to tear down the outdated wallpaper or formica counters—they'd be tacky to a guest but, to Sam, they were the physical reminders of so many happy mornings with her grandparents. Sam's parents were distant at best and her grandparents more than filled the void with their love—both for Sam and for each other—over almost every summer of her youth. The pain forced its way out as a sigh; so much loss in such a short amount of time. Sam hadn't been much of a believer before all this, but now she was full of hate at a God or Universe or whatever that allowed things like this to happen.

Like every night since they'd found Emily, Sam walked through every decision she made leading up to that night. She knew by heart now all the things she could have done differently. Every bad choice she had made that led to Emily's death. She should have ended her trip earlier; she'd picked up the signs that Emily was getting lonely. She should have made Emily put the tracking app on her phone. Sam had been worried about some concerning texts from Emily's ex. Why hadn't she spoken up? As always, she'd been more worried about making things awkward than about speaking her truth. And now look what had happened. Sam wasn't sure it was murder—that was such a harsh reality to accept—but it was just as difficult to accept the idea that it was an accident.

Another sigh forced its way out of her body. It almost felt like someone else was there. They should be sitting out here together drinking rosé, but instead, Emily was gone. Forever. Sam hated herself and she hated the world. To her right, she saw the porch light flick on. Sam looked at her phone and rolled her eyes. Eight p.m. on the dot; Catherine would be coming out for her nightcap. Catherine's whole schedule was based on different times to drink: mimosas in the morning, white wine at lunch, a splash at 5 p.m. and a nightcap at eight. Sam felt nauseated at the thought of another argument with Catherine. God, she hated that woman. She knew she had as much a right to enjoy her back porch, but she didn't have it in her to get into it again tonight. She stubbed out the rest of her joint and went straight to bed.

13

"Honestly, Marc, it's like you are trying to get a bad angle." Emily Larson may not have been the most objectively beautiful influencer but she understood the power of angles. At the core, it was all about getting the right angle. She released a deep, annoyed sigh. She felt the pressure of the long line of people waiting to get their shot at this 'hidden gem.'

It would be much harder to get the shot herself but it would be faster. She wished Marc took her career more seriously. He loved the free products and discounted travel, but then had nothing but sarcasm when it came to putting in the work of taking the pictures that secured those deals. She snatched her phone from Marc and held her arm out and up at an angle. Too many chins. She shifted her head. Ugh, too many rolls. She arched her back a little more and then stared off slightly past the camera. She zoomed in and frowned. Did she have a crease on her arm? Were her freckles too close to mole color or were they on point? She would adjust those a bit with the filter. This would have to do.

Emily moved away from the moss-covered tree stump and gave the next couple in line a thin smile. The young woman's chestnut hair and ivory skin were going to contrast so nicely with the dark green moss Emily thought with dejection. Her own perfectly imperfect bronde and light tan were usually a point of pride, but it didn't match the vibe here in the forest. She'd have to make sure the next shots were either at the beach or desert—the California golden summer light always hit just right in those settings. Of course, Miss Perfect Fancy Brown Hair would be beautiful there, too. She glanced back and saw the light peeking through to highlight little flecks of honey in the woman's hair. A wave of despair crashed over Emily.

"Can we just go?" Emily snapped. "This is so stupidly crowded. It's not even that great of a spot." Her feet ached from the new boots. She arched on her toes to try and stretch, but the leather was so stiff she almost fell forward. She was supposed to believe some woman had hiked the entire Appalachian Trail in these? Emily was hardly able to finish the two-mile hike. She'd splurged almost $400 after seeing them in the movie—there was no denying the red laces against the deep leather had looked great on her in spite of the terrible REI store lighting. She thought they would add a certain credibility to her wooded shots, which were performing poorly. She wanted to complain a change in the algorithm was to blame, but she knew the content was not up to par. Forest baths were super in and she needed to figure out an angle. She didn't want to be one of those flat characters, a California babe only pretty on the beach. But here she was, hobbling along like a newborn horse. Her mood grew worse.

Marc looked at her through a cloud of cherry-scented smoke and shrugged. Emily closed her eyes and shook her head. How embarrassing to be vaping during a forest bath. And what was he wearing? A muscle shirt and Adidas? She had hoped to get a cute couple shot, but that was obviously out of the question. But that was Marc, irreverent and clueless. Actually, she fumed, he probably wore that outfit on purpose; he was always ready with a snide comment about her work. Although he never said it outright, he dropped enough hints implying his career as an engineer was more respectable—a 'real' career as he would call it. He always explained the 'real' world to her, like she was an idiot. Like they *both* hadn't earned a spot and then a degree at UCLA. Seneca Anderson was making six figures a MONTH as an influencer—Emily often challenged Marc to show her an engineer with the same results. He would only roll his eyes in a condescending way that said, "You're no Seneca." As if she didn't know it.

Emily looked up and was struck by the simple beauty of the treetops creating a natural lace over the sky. She was transported back to summers with her grandma, Bobbie, amazed by the hidden world created by the mangroves on the Endless Islands. In the very fiber of her being, Emily loved beauty. Her breath caught in her throat and she had an inexplicable need to cry. *Please, God, don't let this moment end.* Just as she tried to grasp the sense of peace, it began to float up and away. Yet, the smallest shift had happened. Emily brought her gaze back to Marc and knew she was done.

Emily was nothing if not determined once she made up her mind. By the end of the night, she had broken up with Marc by text. Predictably, he had not taken it well. Within 15 minutes, he had deleted every photo of them together on Instagram and changed his Snap. He sent text after text about what a mistake she was making; she was a wannabe influencer; she'd be back; no way she would find someone else to put up with her narcissistic shit.

She rolled her eyes and hit block. Marc wasn't the first angry ex and certainly wouldn't be the last. She had a life to manifest and Marc clearly wasn't going to be a part of that. Marc's horrible style proved a blessing as it meant there were fewer photos of him to delete from her account. After cleaning up her feeds, she decided to splurge and lit her Scentsami candle to celebrate. She took a deep inhale. She had never lit the candles before and the smell was intoxicating. And then, because she couldn't stand for it to go to waste, she took a few pictures to post later.

Thirty minutes later, and bored of journaling her feelings, Emily impulsively grabbed her phone and texted an old friend from her Florida summers. Emily did her best to drop hints about how great it would be to reconnect because she was desperate for an excuse to go back to Florida. She hadn't seen this girl in forever, but the memory from earlier in the day wouldn't leave her. She missed her grandmother so much and, in a way she couldn't quite articulate, she missed herself as well. The ache rose in her chest again and Emily was suddenly overcome by total loneliness as she waited for a response.

In what seemed a complete sign from the universe, Sam texted back almost immediately and shared she had recently purchased the old house on the water and was planning on flipping it for short-term rental. She was thrilled at the thought of Emily visiting and the two of them having sleepovers like the old days. They texted back and forth rapidly and what started as a hint was a firm plan with dates by the end of the night. Sam sent pictures and Emily was overjoyed to see how the house hadn't changed since their childhood. She loved the vintage vibe and it made her sad to change the place, but Emily promised to help Sam decorate in exchange for the free place to crash. It would give her some fun DIY content, a first for her since she'd always lived in apartments. And the canal would be the perfect blend of beach and woodsy for her feed.

The pure hope of it all made Emily giddy. It would be a real stretch to get the airfare since it was peak season, but Emily was confident she'd secure some good brand deals once she landed. The island was an actual hidden gem, not yet saturated with other influencers. And who knows, maybe she'd help raise the awareness of the place? Get more visitors and put Beach Island on the map. She'd be helping these small businesses—businesses like Grandma Bobbie's old boutique. Wasn't that why she'd started doing this, to make a difference? Emily let out a deep, contented sigh and fell asleep, visioning out all the cute shots she'd take at the airport.

14

Pete rubbed his hand up and down the stubble on his face. He hadn't slept well in a week, which was rare for him; sleep was a very big deal to Pete. He looked over at his phone: 10 a.m. Pete hadn't stayed in bed this late since the early days of his 'retirement.' Pete knew the warning signs: he was headed for depression if he didn't make some changes, and quickly. Of course, that was easier said than done. Once the fog started to take over, it became harder and harder to do the things he knew would fight off the darkness.

One little step. Just take one little step, Pete thought to himself. Pete tried to think through his self-survival list. A shower would be easiest. After that, he might have the energy to go through his problem-solving sheet. Pete tried to avoid thinking about steps after for fear the overwhelm would kick in and he wouldn't even be able to shower. "One step at a time, man." Pete slowly rolled to his side and got out of bed.

Pete did feel better after the shower—enough so that he put on some music, which carried him through fixing avocado toast. He'd reward these first small steps with a trip to the coffee shop in a few minutes. Even the stormy sky seemed a little less gray as he walked out to sit at the canal with his notebook. The fog lifted a little. That's all he needed—just enough to back away slowly from the cliff and he was good. Pete had started to write out his columns when his phone buzzed. Another text from Shae. The despair came back in full force. *Enough is enough,* Pete thought. Without thinking it through, Pete hit the phone icon and called Shae.

"Finally, dude! I thought you had fallen off the face of the earth!" Shae sounded both worried and a little angry. "I've been trying to get ahold of you forever. Any news?"

Pete registered his annoyance that Shae hadn't asked if he was okay, but decided to let it pass. He had more important issues to tackle. "Yeah, sorry. I've been really busy." A lie, since Pete was retired, but Pete wasn't sure how to say, 'I've been okay just completely ignoring you.' Instead, he said, "But I did want to talk to you."

Shae let out an audible sigh of relief. "I knew you'd figure something out. You were always the smart one! Okay, so what's the plan?"

"Shae, this is too big. I can't help with this. If you won't go to the police, then I am going to talk to Dave this afternoon." The line was silent. "You still there?"

Shae cleared her throat. "Pete, you know what will happen to a girl like me in this situation. Some rich White girl shows up dead and then it comes out I moved her body? No, *Darlene Brunell's daughter* moved the body. I will literally get executed, Pete. I know I fucked up, but they will kill me. I thought I could trust you!" Shae's voice was high and shaky, amplified by the tinny cell phone.

"Dave's a good guy and very fair. He's going to understand you made a mistake." Pete wished he felt more confident than he did, once again remembering how cold Dave was at that last meeting. The truth was, Pete wasn't sure how Dave would react. He had to have faith that there was a process in these things for a reason.

"Easy for you to say. Always the preacher's son. You have no idea what you're talking about. If you go to them with this and nothing else, I'm done. The internet is already blaming me—wait until this comes out. This whole time, I thought you were helping me." Shae's voice dropped a register, almost to a growl.

"Shae, you can always trust me. I will be here for you. But this is too much for me—for us, so we need to let this go through the proper channels and trust the process." Pete hated how pleading his voice sounded.

"Too much for YOU?! Wow. After all we've been through. I spent money I didn't have to fly out and see you after Waimea. And how long did you crash on my couch? And now I need you in a life-and-death situation and it's too much for you?" Pete could almost see Shae shaking her head.

Pete sensed his own anger rising; he hated owing anyone anything. The beauty of the water faded into the background as Pete stormed inside, the door catching wind and slamming twice behind him. "Sorry I was such a burden. And I never asked you to fly anywhere, so don't go throwing that in my face. This whole thing is a little more than crashing on someone's couch. Somebody died here." Pete paced his living room. The mailman caught sight of him and gave a friendly wave.

"Pete, you are signing my death warrant if you take this to the police. Please. Help me figure out what happened and then we go to the police. You're hella smart and I know we can do this." Shae's voice was tired and scared.

Pete thought back to how close he had been to the abyss this morning. He felt bad for Shae, but he had to look out for himself, too. "I've gotta go. I'm sorry, and I hope you can understand where I'm coming from at some point."

Shae's only response was the sound of the line going dead. Pete looked down at his problems and solutions sheet, unstarted. Well, he didn't need to finish it. He knew what he had to do. He had to go to the police before he changed his mind.

***

Pete pulled out of Bitchin' Brews more confused than ever. He'd gone in for coffee and had somehow ended up doing an impromptu Facebook Live with some local vlogger. He'd been so distracted the entire time; people would think he was stoned even though Pete hated weed. He'd barely slept the night before; his relentless mind wouldn't quit. His defenses had been down and the guy had roped him in before he knew what hit him; Sydney would not be happy.

Pete's only hope was the guy had no followers and no one would see it, though footage of Pete had always had a way of going viral—especially now that he spent most of his time under the radar. Pete bristled with irritation at himself for letting it happen, but he had bigger issues to contend with at the moment.

He knew the right thing to do was to go straight to the police. He also knew Shae had a point. Maybe they would only start investigating her and it would not look good at all. Then again, thinking of his last visit with Sheriff Carter, Pete realized they might not investigate at all. Pete wasn't sure which was worse at this point. Pete shook off the thought. The police would have to investigate with this new knowledge and Pete couldn't imagine Carter would be very happy to re-open a case he closed while in the middle of his re-election campaign. Nobody wants a pissed-off police force investigating.

God, why had Shae done that? Why hadn't she gone to the police immediately and then Pete wouldn't be in this situation? Pete's mind raced as he drove past all the little concrete beach houses, turning on backstreet after backstreet to avoid the tourist traffic on the main drag. Bright primary colors spelled HAPPY BIRTHDAY KATIE in front of a bright blue ranch-style house. Before he realized where he was going, he found himself in his parents' driveway instead of the police station parking lot like he had intended. It was like his conscience had directed him there without him realizing it.

"Hey buddy, what's going on?" His father's voice was full of kindness as he opened the door and Pete almost felt like a small child again.

"Dad, I need to talk to you. I need some advice."

Pete's dad's face immediately grew somber; it was rare for Pete to be serious. "Of course. Come into my study."

In the background, a reporter was talking about the newest tropical disturbance with all the excitement of winning the lottery; storms were big business for local news stations. Father Michael Brown's study was where he met with other church leaders and parishioners, but never with family. Pete wasn't sure whether he was talking to his dad or Father Brown the priest. Either way, Pete knew that he would have the man's full confidentiality.

"I don't want to get into all the details," Pete started with a sigh. "I've got a friend in a bad situation. He's in a lot of trouble, but I genuinely think he's innocent." Pete hoped to cover up that he was talking about Shae.

Father Brown let out an almost imperceptible sigh of relief and Pete wondered if he had believed he had done something wrong. This bothered him, but he tried to brush it off. "Okay. Why don't you go to the authorities and tell them?" A simple question with no simple answer.

"I don't know. I want to, but I'm afraid that's gonna lead to more trouble. I don't think they're gonna listen to him and give him a fair read." Pete was thinking back to the long history of Shae's family and local law enforcement. Although Shae had risen above it all and made a life for herself, her brother seemed intent on following in their mother's footsteps and had frequent, drug-related interactions with the cops. He wondered if Shae wouldn't be guilty by association.

Pete's dad nodded. Unfortunately, there was a reality about the legal system in America that it wasn't always equally blind and he knew some people were more likely to suffer than others. Pete always thought Shae's brother, Trevor, had gotten a bad rap because they were poor. He took a quick inhale as if to speak, then changed his mind.

"Okay, so what are you going to do? What are your options?" Pete's dad, ever ready with questions instead of answers.

Pete noticed a familiar annoyance, wishing his dad would just tell him what to do yet knowing he'd keep asking questions instead. Pete looked up to the ceiling as if he might find the answer there and leaned his head back with his hand in his hair. "At first, I thought that maybe if I found some, you know, convincing evidence, I might be able to show them he really is innocent." Pete felt silly admitting this. What kind of person plays detective instead of going to the police? He couldn't believe he was thinking this thought, let alone vocalizing it out loud.

If his dad had a judgment on Pete investigating, he was hiding it well. "That might be true," Father Michael spoke cautiously. "People don't always want to know the full truth. Sometimes they want to be ignorant. And sometimes, people will go to great lengths to avoid the truth."

"Yeah, I know. But didn't you always teach us the most important job of a human was to always look for the truth with a capital T?" Pete shot back.

Pete's dad smiled. "I didn't say *I* could live with blissful ignorance."

Pete laughed.

"I'm saying, sometimes, when you go around looking for the truth, other people aren't going to like what you find. Satan isn't going to like it."

Pete flinched at the religious reference. He still imagined the devil as a bright red cartoon with a pitchfork but held his tongue.

His dad continued without noticing, "The people that want things to stay the same feel that way because the system is set up to benefit them. Very few people willingly give up power. And you're going to meet resistance. There's more to life than what we can see with our own eyes. Whether you want to call it psychological or spiritual, those drives to avoid the truth can be quite powerful."

It sounded as if Pete's dad had learned this through personal experience and Pete realized how much there was he didn't know about the man in front of him. "So, you have to be sure you're committed to seeing this thing through." Pete wasn't sure if he was being chastised. Seeing things through wasn't necessarily Pete's best strong suit and he knew it. Seeming to read his mind, his dad continued, "If you decide to take this on, it won't be about you. When you battle for the truth, there's no turning back. You're stepping into something outside yourself. Those of us with some leverage within the system should use it to fight on behalf of those that don't. At least, that's what I always believed." It was uncharacteristic for Father Brown to be so direct with his opinion.

Pete let out a strained laugh as he waved the air seemingly absentmindedly. "I'm sure it'll be fine. I mean, these things always work themselves out." The unflappable surfer returned to the surface. "I appreciate the thoughts, dad. Shae's not super tech-savvy and I think if I give her a few pointers there, she'll be fine." Pete blanched as the name slipped out; if Father Michael heard, his face showed no acknowledgment. Pete instinctively held his breath and willed the moment to pass.

Again, Father Michael appeared ready to speak but changed his mind. Instead, he pulled out a silver necklace and charm from his desk. "I've been meaning to give this to you for a while but kept forgetting. I got it for you when I was over in Rome." Father Michael did not forget things as a rule, but Pete focused his attention on the pendant. It was an ornate saint medal with Michael the Archangel, a figure that more closely represented a bodybuilder than Pete's idea of an angel. Not Pete's traditional style, but he put it on to make his dad happy. Instead of looking pleased, worry creased his dad's face. He said nothing.

"Thanks. I appreciate it. And you talking to me. I'm sure it's all nothing." Pete stood to leave. He hated to see his dad worry after all they had been through and attempted a light laugh. "Gotta get back to the garage and put some time into Project X. Sarg is getting jealous so I gotta get her out of there." His voice sounded insincere and he knew it.

Pete's dad said nothing and gave him a tight hug. Pete thought he heard his dad whispering in Latin as he walked out of the house and his skin crawled as he walked out into the gray afternoon.

15

"Hey! HEY!" a woman's voice shouted behind him as Pete pushed his cart through the parking lot. He rolled his eyes. It was almost dinner time and he was not in the mood to see anyone.

He turned to see Catherine's neighbor—what was her name? *Ugh*, Pete groaned inwardly. He was not in the mood to be yelled at again, having no idea what he had done to piss her off so much. He affected his best aloof surfer smile, eyebrows raised.

She was winded as she jogged to catch up. She released the bottom of her yellow and lilac print maxi dress that she'd held to avoid tripping. She bent slightly for a moment, hand on her side as she caught her breath. The dress dipped to reveal a crochet bikini top.

Pete flushed slightly and looked off towards the back of the parking lot as she recovered.

"Hey, thanks for waiting up. I'm Sam... We met the other day up at city hall." She put her hand out and her face was uncomfortable.

Pete nodded in acknowledgment, but wasn't sure what to say, so he shook her hand and said, "Pete."

Sam stood up straighter and seemed all business. "Look, I'm sorry for coming in so hot the other day. I'm just, I'm just going through a lot and

I wasn't my best self. My best friend died recently, and my dad is sick back in New York, so I've been traveling like crazy; it's hard to keep up with work; my boyfriend dumped me because I'm gone so much; and then I've got all this bullshit with the city." Sam's eyes opened wide and she seemed mortified to have shared so much. "Wow, I am so sorry for that dump. Like you needed to know all that!" Red crept up her neck and face. She was clearly experiencing a sharing hangover.

Pete knew those well. He cleared his throat. "Sounds like a lot. That's more than understandable. I'm sorry you're going through so much. I'm so sorry about your best friend." Pete put his hand on Sam's shoulder gingerly, making eye contact before putting his hand back to his side. His baggies had no pockets so his hand hung awkwardly. Pete felt a pang of guilt realizing he had been ignoring Shae so much. It would break his heart if Shae died. In fact, Pete hadn't reached out to any of his friends lately. He made a mental note to send some check-in texts later when he got home.

"It doesn't help that it's the latest entertainment for the masses. Her name was Emily Larson. She was here visiting me." Pete realized why she had looked familiar the first time around; he recalled seeing a picture of them together on Emily's Instagram. The pain and guilt in her voice was clear as if she had somehow caused Emily's death. A perfectionist who took on the responsibility for everything—Pete knew a bit about that, too. If she was like Pete, then he knew she would disdain the idea of someone pitying her, so he stopped himself from going in for a hug.

"Damn, I'm so sorry. We're a tight-knit place here and I know a lot of people were hurt to hear the news. I can't imagine what it must feel like actually knowing her." For some strange reason, Pete refrained from bringing up Shae and all the heat she was taking. He'd have to investigate that later.

"I only got to see her one night. We were supposed to be reliving our glory days," Sam gave a rough laugh, "whatever that means. Lord knows the shit we used to do would kill me at my age! We got one night at my place before I had to head back to see Dad. I got home the night they found her. She had texted me, but I never got to respond because I didn't get it until I landed. I didn't even get to tell her goodbye." Sam looked miserable, appearing to use every ounce of willpower to not bawl in the grocery store parking lot in front of a guy she had yelled at only days before. A young man with Down Syndrome whistled a cheerful tune as he collected carts.

Pete blew out a deep breath. "Wow, that's heavy. What did she say?" Pete couldn't help his curiosity; he hadn't earned the name El Gato for surfing alone.

Sam appeared to debate sharing more but looked off and said, "She told me she was out on an island. And she said she needed to give me a heads-up before I got home. That was it."

"The island? Like where they found her?" Pete's senses were alert.

"I don't think so? Her grandmother lived here way back when and we hung out for a couple of visits during the summer. One summer, we built this ridiculous tree fort, if you could call it that. Out in the Islands. We had a garbage bag for a pool and a couple of shipping boxes for bedrooms." Sam laughed authentically now and it was a beautiful sound. Like wind chimes before a storm. "It's pretty close to my place now and I think she went there? I suppose it is a little weird, now that I think about it. But I think it was for one of her posts or something?" Sam sounded unsure. "I just wish she would have texted me earlier—she knows how long the flight is plus the drive back from the airport. It would have been super late for me to call her."

"What time did she text you?" Pete asked. It all sounded more suspicious than weird to Pete, but he didn't want to upset Sam any more than she already was.

"I don't know because I didn't get it until I turned my phone back on after the flight. Sometime during the evening while I was in the air. "Do you think she was waiting for me to call and drowned?" Sam asked this so quietly, Pete was sure she'd never dared to voice this worry to anyone else. Pete wasn't sure why she'd trusted him to ask, but he was honored.

"Do you think that?" Pete asked back cautiously. He wanted to tread carefully on this sacred ground.

Sam investigated the question fully. Finally, she shrugged a painful shrug. "I don't know. I mean, it's so hard to imagine her drowning since she was such a strong swimmer. Though she was drunk at the time, so it's possible. Which was also weird. I just don't know."

She really was drunk. Maybe the police were right to close the case, Pete reflected. Although Sam seemed reluctant to accept that. Pete was afraid to push such a sensitive issue.

"What did the police say about the message?" Pete so desperately wanted to relieve Sam of her self-induced guilt.

She looked at him quizzically. "They never saw it. I told the officer we'd been talking, but they said there was no need for me to open any wounds and read through all the texts. As if I don't do that every night. They were way more interested in my permits than anything else." She shook her head bitterly at the last part.

Pete nodded as if this made sense, but was shocked. They didn't talk to her best friend or look through the texts? And why had Emily told Sam to be careful? About what? Why did Sam feel it was strange for Emily to be drunk? But the last thing Pete wanted to do was upset her further, so he kept everything to himself.

Sam brought them both back to the moment with a shake of her head. A minivan pulled into the space next to them and a sun-burnt family clamored out. Plastic beach toys hit the parking lot with a thud and the mom gave an apologetic shrug to Pete and Sam as if aware her kids were interrupting. They smiled kindly and gave a wave to indicate all was okay.

"Anyway, I wanted to say I was sorry. I shouldn't have been so rude the other day and I wanted you to know it wasn't you; it was me." Pete was impressed by her humility—it was a rare virtue these days.

"No worries at all. I hadn't noticed," he winked. They both cracked up. "But seriously, don't worry about it. Here's my number, give me a call if you ever need anything." Pete handed her his card from the local TV station where he was part owner and an occasional host.

Sam smiled, and again, Pete had the urge to hug and protect her wash over him. But he knew most women didn't want to be touched by some guy they barely knew in a dark parking lot, so instead, he threw out a fist bump.

Sam looked startled but grinned and returned the fist bump before walking away to her car. Did she also look disappointed or was that just Pete projecting?

Pete paused in the parking lot and reflected on how little he had thought about Emily Larson and what her death had left behind. A best friend blaming herself. A family grieving, thinking she had been drunk and caused her own death. A public left wanting answers on this senseless death. He'd been so focused on Shae and Beach Island that he hadn't thought about Emily and her loved ones. They all deserved to be freed by the truth, too. If only he knew what the truth was.

16

Emily stretched out in the sand, her body pleasantly buzzing from a decent session out on the waves. The warm sand formed beneath her body and warmed her skin. The smell of salt and sea grapes was subtle but intoxicating. How long had companies attempted to bottle that luscious scent, but failed? She would have preferred surfing today, but it was too flat, so she'd settled for paddle boarding. She'd felt strong and steady as she paddled rhythmically, purposefully moving further and further out. The shore had looked a million miles away when she was out there; she'd even paddled past a pod of dolphins. Eventually, she'd lain out on the board and stared at the sky while the waves moved gently underneath.

The warm Atlantic waters were a nice change from the ice-cold waves she was used to and she loved the opportunity to show off her body in the bikini instead of being covered up in a wetsuit. Earlier in the week, she'd taken some super cute footage of herself that she would add to her paddleboarding course. Her course had paid for more than a few vacations and it was due for an update. The new footage would allow her to launch new ads and the new location might draw in more East Coast fans.

Emily felt good, here in this moment. She was more than good: she was happy for the first time in a long time. She hadn't brought her phone out with her on the board—unheard of for her. She'd planned some great shots of her meditating out on the board as more updated content and packed the phone mount for her board. Nothing but endless oceans, endless possibilities ahead. But when she pulled into the lot and saw the blue peeking over the wooden deck, she'd impulsively left her phone and walked towards the water as unencumbered as possible. It was like deep calling to deep. Emily couldn't remember the last time she'd been so free.

Her happiness faltered as she thought about her phone. The last few days, it had been dinging with unwelcome messages. She'd blocked Marc, but he'd started DMing her on Insta and then having friends of friends reach out after she'd blocked him on all the socials. He missed her, they'd said. They said he was packed and ready to fly down and see her and talk in person, that he would do anything for her. Some friends hinted he might be planning on popping 'the question.' They talked about how perfect they were for each other but she knew they meant she was good for him. As if her purpose was to be the yin to his yang in life. People had always talked about how she lightened him up and he helped her be more realistic.

Emily secretly fumed at these comments. People had no idea how deep she really was. Instead, she'd always given a cute smile and tilt of the head, playing with his hair to confirm she was light-hearted and playful, nothing more. It was easier to play the part she was given than to try and show people her true self.

Emily sighed. Just a month ago, she would have been over the moon at the idea of a proposal from Marc. She had thought she was in love at one point. How many times over the last year had she complained to her girlfriends saying he was dragging his feet? She'd already had a secret Pinterest board for her perfect boho wedding.

But she'd been so sure of her decision to leave on their last hike out. They were too different and she knew she needed a change. Marc had always been too serious, fully the engineer that he was. She knew he found her shallow instead of understanding that she had a deep aching for beauty deep inside. Being here only made her surer she had done the right thing.

Last night, Emily had caved and finally responded to Marc. She didn't want him flying all the way to Florida, and she knew he deserved at least some kind of answer from her. After all, they had been pretty serious. She'd patiently tried to explain they were too different, but Marc desperately kept insisting he knew her better than she thought and that he loved her exactly as she was.

He wouldn't take the hint and, finally, when he'd told her he had already bought a ticket for a flight out the next day, she'd let him know she already had plans. She told him she would be going out for drinks on a boat with someone else. Marc was heartbroken. He grew angry at the end of the conversation and then ghosted her the rest of the night. Emily didn't love it, but at least he wouldn't be traveling to see her anytime soon. She figured he was bluffing; Marc was far too practical to do such an impulsive thing as buying a plane ticket before talking to her. That's why they'd never work.

Of course, Emily never said she was going out with another guy. She'd strategically phrased everything to avoid lying and Marc, in his jealousy, was all too ready to hear what he was most afraid of hearing. Marc, the doom and gloom, glass-half-empty kind of guy. Well, look where it got him, she tsk'd in her mind. If he'd bothered to ask, she would have admitted she was going out with a woman in an attempt to make a new friend. But Marc never asked, so Emily never offered. Crazy how we fill in the blanks.

If she was honest with herself, Emily wasn't sure it wouldn't be more fun to hang out with Marc than this lady. She wasn't quite sure why she had agreed to the outing as this lady wasn't Emily's type. But Emily knew it was important to put herself out there and meet new people. And starting with easier outings like this were practice for the tough things like new friends and dating once she got back home.

Because after a few weeks here, Emily knew she wanted to go back to California earlier than planned. She'd tried to make friends and land new deals, but nothing was going as planned. Locals were weary of her because she was from California—like she was some kind of elitist or something. And she'd not had much luck with brand deals. People here were suspicious of social media and didn't understand the power of the internet. She was getting impatient to go home, but the lack of brand deals also meant the lack of travel funds. She had a place here for free for the time being, so she'd have to stay longer, whether she liked it or not. Hence, for tonight, she'd try to get out and get to know the locals in hopes that it would lead to something more.

17

Calypso music hummed faintly in the background as Catherine beamed at her dining partner. "Brendan, you're just a doll for humoring an old woman," Catherine demurred as she stirred overcooked grits around her plate. "How is your mother? I haven't seen her at tennis in ages!" Catherine much preferred the Eggs Benedict at the country club but Herbie's Diner was where locals gathered.

"Mom is great, staying busy with the grandkids. Her knees are bothering her, so we felt it wasn't good for her to keep going with the tennis. But you know, she loves watching Riley." His mouth was full as he talked and Catherine bristled at the idea of her children thinking she would prefer being an unpaid nanny to her daily tennis. The arrogance of kids these days. Catherine did see her own grandchildren on occasion, but was quite clear she had her own life to live. God knows she had already raised kids and did *not* intend to do it again.

The waitress came over with a pot of coffee, "You two doing okay?"

Catherine scooted her cup for a refill. "Just wonderful, Patti. Thank you. How's Graham?"

Patti spent a few minutes sharing Graham's many health issues while Catherine nodded. If Patti noticed the disinterest in Catherine's eyes, it didn't deter her. The cook hit the bell for another order up and Patti shrugged her apology at being unable to share more.

Catherine took a hand to her forehead and then straightened her posture, returning her attention to Brendan with a smile.

"Oh, that must be delightful. How lucky for you both that she can be so involved." Catherine would rather impale herself with a tennis racket than watch a toddler all day, but she smiled brightly as she spoke, as if Brendan's mother Anne had won the life lottery. "Anyway, I was talking to Justin the other day and he mentioned you were thinking about running for the city commissioner opening. How very exciting!"

Brendan nodded in agreement that it was indeed. Kids these days found everything they did amazing. Just the thought of doing something was enough for them to pat themselves on the back, nevermind they were not likely to take the next step to actually do something. Catherine had to stop herself from rolling her eyes. But that's why she was here.

"Yeah, the wife thought it might be a good way for me to use my skills for the greater good. Plus, you know, she thinks it would look good at work."

Catherine looked at his pudgy face and wondered what possible skills he had. She simply nodded for him to continue.

Brendan smoothed out his shirt and took a sip of juice. "But, uh, I don't know. A buddy of mine says these races get kind of expensive. These days, all the developers are trying to find loopholes to find a candidate they can use. They've got the money to back the candidate they want. And I'm not sure I care that much." Brendan took another giant bite of hash browns and shrugged.

"Oh, but I agree with your wife! Think about what you could do to protect the island! If you aren't out there fighting the good fight, this island is going to be covered in high-rises and mega-resorts before we know it. And I, for one, would be willing to put my money where my mouth is!" Catherine set down her napkin with feeling.

At the mention of Catherine Mellon's money, Brendan finally paused his eating. Catherine went on, "It's terrible what these people are doing to our island. It's even happening in my own backyard—literally!"

Catherine did her best to look helpless, though she knew it lacked the effect it had when she was younger and prettier. "One of these developers bought the house next door and is building a second house right in the backyard! It's horrendous! I won't be able to see the river anymore." Catherine did her best to pout, but the Botox made her look disinterested.

Brendan was genuinely shocked. He'd never thought about someone blocking his own canal view. "How is that legal? Did you talk to Justin?"

"Of course I did! But he said his hands were tied, that it was up to the city commission board to vote on the codes. These developers are so sneaky. This woman, from California no less—" nothing was more offensive to locals than being from California— "figured out a loophole to get her permits through. Something about the codes expired while we're in between voting sessions. Now all the developers caught on and are trying to push through projects for approval. It's sick. The code is coming up for vote later this year after the vacant commissioner seats are filled. The meeting is months away! Justin is doing his best to delay permit approvals until the vote, but this woman is relentless. An absolute beast. And what if the new commissioner agrees with these people. Imagine if all these other projects go through. Oh, it makes me sick. I know keeping the codes the same is priceless to those of us that live here. We need someone with a voice to protect us." Catherine paused meaningfully.

Luckily, Brendan seemed to pick up on the meaning. Catherine saw his ambitions, previously vague, but now bankrolled, growing in his mind. He nodded with determination, "You're right. I have to fight for the voiceless. We can't have these blue state liberals, er outsiders, come in and change our way of life." Brendan was already practicing his campaign points. Catherine would need to hire him an image coach as Brendan did little to inspire confidence. She'd done more with less before and would do it again.

Catherine clapped her hands like a little girl. "You are going to be a hero to so many here!" Her face grew serious. "Thank you for being so selfless."

Brendan, like the baby politician he was, nodded magnanimously as if the fate of the world was on his shoulders. He took another giant bite of a biscuit and chewed thoughtfully. It looked like a biscuit eating a biscuit.

Catherine knew by the end of the week she'd see his face plastered throughout the neighborhood. He was already on his phone, likely spreading news of his campaign, obliviously forgetting the only person making his campaign possible.

Catherine leaned back and took a sip of coffee. Catherine Mellon may not have succeeded in the first battles of this war, but she did not give up easily. She'd tried dealing with the neighbor directly and it had not worked. She'd appealed to the commission and been rebuffed. Catherine rarely lost a fight in her life, and certainly not when money was involved. And of course, money was always involved.

She'd make sure her neighbor would become the poster child for the greedy carpetbaggers, coming in to destroy the home of a beloved widow. In the little she had talked to that young woman, she knew shame was the way to go. It would make the perfect platform for Brendan. The locals were already taking to social media to fume about the inconsiderate vacation rental owners taking over their neighborhoods. Brendan would be the match to light the tinderbox these people had already built. Now they would have a single face to unite against, a real person to channel all the built-up frustration towards. People felt helpless against faceless corporations, but they felt powerful as a group against a person. Yes, Sam Finnegan would make the perfect sacrificial lamb.

A memory of her neighbor, George, teaching young Sam to tend the garden entered Catherine's mind. He'd been such a nice man, she remembered. It was good he wasn't here to see what they'd all become. She exhaled, forcefully pushing out the memory. Nice man as he had been, Catherine would do whatever it took to protect her home.

She willfully replaced the memory with one of her mother tending to the oleander in the yard, wrestling it into an archway—still everyone's favorite shaded spot during the splashes. Little Catherine had pored through the pile of leftover lance-shaped leaves for nearly 30 minutes, making a bouquet from only the best blooms from the clusters of pink flowers. Her mother had dismissed it with barely a glance.

Catherine inspected the memory with clearer eyes, no longer clouded by the blissful ignorance of youth. Where she once saw a love of gardening, she now saw the delicate hands, inherited from generations of women with hired help to do this kind of work. But her mother Edith was resourceful—she'd keep up appearances if she had to do it with her own two hands. Catherine had learned so much from her. She'd had some inkling about the loss of the family fortune back then, but her mother had always made it seem insignificant. Like moving to Beach Island was the epitome of wealth instead of a last resort in a dire financial situation.

These days, beach living is a sign of wealth. But back then, before air conditioning, before the social dynamics had changed, they must have been seen as outsiders. Yankees. Her mother had created a new caste system on Beach Island, one where the Mellons were at the very top. This home had been the last hope for their very family name. Her family had been through so much to protect their home and she was not going to go down as the Mellon that lost it all.

18

Pete pulled into the city hall parking lot. He wrestled with the decision for days and hoped that someday Shae would understand where he was coming from. This was all too much for him and he knew Dave would understand why she hadn't come forward earlier. Dave would be able to help. The island was consistently voted one of the safest places in the United States for a reason. The police knew what they were doing here.

"Are we gonna have to start collecting a rent check from you or something? Maybe get you your own uniform?" Nate joked with Pete as he collected his stuff from the other side of the security checkpoint.

"This should be the last time for a while!" Pete laughed. "Can I see Dave? Shouldn't take too long."

Nate looked like he wanted to say something, but thought better of it. "Yep, he's back in his office. Go ahead." Nate nodded his head toward Dave's office and went back to work on his computer. Though, from the looks of it, Nate was surfing the internet instead of working—not that Pete would say anything. He imagined police work could get pretty boring here on the island.

Pete gave a soft knock on the door of Dave's office. Dave looked up and motioned him in with a big grin. He stayed seated this time; Pete was relieved not to have another back slap. "How can I help you today?"

"I have some pretty important information on the Emily Larson situation," Pete said hesitantly. He hadn't thought through how to say everything.

Dave put his arms akimbo. "That's a closed case. Not a situation, son."

"Yeah, I know. I thought you should know something. In case it changes anything. I think I told you how I was helping out Shae Brunell with some damage control. Well, it turns out she... She, uh, found the body on one of the Endless Islands earlier that evening and moved it... Her. And she thinks the girl might have been alive on the island and died there. Not in the water like it may have seemed. I think maybe there was foul play." God, it sounded so bad as he said it out loud. Shae probably had been right about keeping it to themselves, but there was no turning back now. Pete's heart raced with adrenaline.

Dave stared at Pete silently for a full beat.

Pete was certain at least a year of his life was carried away by the cortisol flowing through his bloodstream.

Finally, Dave spoke slowly and quietly, "I wish you hadn't told me that, Pete." Of all the things Pete might have expected to hear, that wasn't it. Dave got up and closed his office door. "You've put me in a bad situation here. And with Shae's family history and then y'all's history with the Endless Islands, it sure isn't going to be good." Dave let out a slow whistle. "Boy, this is some trouble."

Pete's heart raced faster, if it was even physically possible. It felt like each beat was doubled in his chest.

Dave seemed to contemplate the wall for a few minutes and then turned to Pete. "Pete, if we open this back up, we're gonna look even more like a laughingstock. And that ain't good for business. Murder is especially bad for business in a tourist town like ours. It's bad enough to have girls getting drunk and drowning. Makes us look like Daytona Beach. And if we open it back up and say we think there was—what did you call it?—foul play without a murderer already booked, it's gonna look real bad. Have you mentioned this to anyone else? How do you know Shae *didn't* have something to do with this? 'Cause she told you? The apple doesn't usually fall far from the tree, you know."

Shit. Shit! Pete was pretty sure he was having an actual panic attack now. Shae had predicted this. "I know moving the body was dumb—she knows that, too. But Shae would never hurt anyone. And no, I think I'm the only one who knows. Well, and you, of course."

"No, Pete. I don't know anything right now. You understand? We did an investigation and we closed the case. This is an unofficial conversation right now. And here's my unofficial advice: you either figure out yourselves a different chain of events from that night or you forget this ever happened. Because if we have to open this up right now, I can assure you your girlfriend is going to be public enemy number one. Nationwide. And I'm sure you don't want your reputation getting ruined over a piece of tail. Accomplice to murder doesn't sell bathing suits too well."

Pete bristled and had a brief surge of courage. "That's the thing, Dave. She already is. These people, on Twitter, they are raising some good points. And they are trying to get the media involved. I'm worried this is going to blow up."

"I'm not worried about some wannabe detectives online." Dave shrugged.

Pete wondered if Dave had ever even looked through what was being said online. He doubted Dave would be so careless if he had, but Dave wasn't the online type. He prided himself on his old-school ways like so many of the other islanders his age. The stack of printed emails on the desk caught Pete's judgment. Pete hated the whole social media thing too, but there was something to be said for at least staying in tune with what the world was saying. It was amazing how the internet both expanded and shrunk the world you lived in.

"If I don't say anything now and then somehow it comes out later I knew something, won't I be an accomplice?" Pete tapped his knees nervously.

Dave laughed. "First of all, that ain't gonna happen. And anyhow, you know we take care of our own around here."

Pete wondered if the same would apply to Shae as a woman. How had he ended up here, talking about covering up a crime with the head of police? Never in his life had he felt anything but safe on this island, now his whole world was tilting. Pete was sure he was having a panic attack at this point and needed to get out. "Okay, thanks for the...thoughts. I guess I'll see you around." Pete secretly pinched his arm, a reminder he was here despite the disassociated feeling taking over his body.

Dave squinted his eyes at Pete, but then made a shift to the lighthearted. "Don't know what you're talking about. You have yourself a great day, Pete. Thanks for visiting." With that, he opened his door and gave his hearty laugh as he motioned Pete out. As if they'd been shooting the breeze instead of talking about covering up murder.

Pete caught Nate looking at him with a strange look. Pete was sure he didn't look any better than he felt, but he threw up a peace sign to Nate and rushed out to the fresh air.

Once in his car, he flipped through his phone for his SOS meditation. He hated these panic attacks. It had been so long since he'd had one, but they used to torment him daily. At least he'd survived enough to know he wasn't going to die, no matter how much his brain tried to convince him otherwise. The calming voice flowed in through the phone speaker and Pete closed his eyes.

19

Pete's first panic attack had been at WSL finals. It had been his first time out on the water since losing the yellow jersey at Waimea. His therapist had warned him he might not be ready, but Pete had ignored her. He should have seen the warning signs when his stomach turned just at the sight of the waves. He chalked it up to nerves or adrenaline. He always had some contest day nerves, so he popped in his earbuds and cranked his ritual playlist. Another warning sign: the thrashing beats that usually got him pumped then scraped on every nerve in his body. Instead of gearing up, the fear grew with every beat. Jenna had been on her way to her own heat and didn't seem to notice the fear in his eyes; she flashed a hang ten and ran out to the water. He'd been sure to mention that a few times in the year after as their careers changed places.

His nerves had been so jacked that when his board hit his shin as he was getting out in the water, it sent excruciating pain up and down his leg. Pete had spent so long ignoring the pain in his body, and that day was no different. Until he got all the way out to the outside and it all hit him like a ton of bricks. The first swell passed and his throat was so tight he couldn't breathe. The next and he started shaking like he was freezing even though he was in a full wetsuit. He saw the other surfers looking at him in surprise; he'd earned the seniority to take these better waves, but he felt paralyzed out there. He wanted nothing more than to get back to shore—he sensed he was in mortal danger. He began to feel dizzy and then panicked, thinking he would faint out there and drown. This only led to more dizziness. Then he was certain he was having a heart attack.

Pete had never quit a heat, but finally, he couldn't take it anymore and he motioned to the medic on the jet ski to come get him. The guy towed him in and Pete faked a limp on his bad ankle, hoping to play it off that it was his injury flaring up and not a heart attack. After getting checked in the medic tent, the paramedic told him all his vitals were clear and that it was probably a panic attack. Pete wasn't a violent guy, but he was so embarrassed and pissed at the situation, he'd wanted to deck the guy. Even though he had been cleared to participate, Pete knew there was no way he would go back out there. So began Pete's retirement. How many people had congratulated him on being able to retire so early. If only they knew.

The woman's voice on his phone counted him through another set of box breaths and Pete finally felt himself coming back to the present moment. Although some of the panic had subsided, Pete didn't feel much better. What the hell had happened in there?

Was Dave corrupt? Or was he just trying to help Pete and Shae? It had to be the latter. Pete had heard of corrupt police, but that was for movies and big cities. Pete was struggling to make any sense of their conversation. Was Dave implying that Pete and Shae had something to do with Blake's death all those years ago? That was completely untrue! If anything, their rules had kept everyone safe. It wasn't their fault that Blake broke the rules.

And what would he tell Shae? How could he explain they either needed to take this to their graves or she would be the prime suspect in some bizarre sacrifice to the angry mob? But then, wasn't Shae already being thrown to the wolves? If the media did pick up the story, would it help or hurt Shae? Would it come out that Pete had talked to Dave? Was Pete supposed to pretend he didn't think that Emily Larson was murdered? For the rest of his life?

Sam's hollow look flashed in his memory. Didn't Emily's friends and family deserve to know the truth? How many other things had Dave decided didn't happen? He didn't act like a man carrying around the weight of secrets, but his perfect crime-free record started to seem less plausible.

There is a reason ordinary people aren't supposed to solve crimes—they aren't prepared for these kinds of questions. As the panic began to subside, Pete noticed anger rise in its place. This wasn't supposed to happen. He did the thing good citizens are supposed to do: he took the information and gave it to the police as if it were a box he could hand deliver onto their desk. They weren't supposed to send you back out to the world holding the box! His meditation ended and Pete stared out through the windshield.

What was he supposed to do now? Grocery shopping, coffee, surfing even—it all seemed so silly in the light of this new world he had unwillingly entered. Pete might have sat in the parking lot staring off all night if he hadn't heard the sing-song of his name being called out. He looked over and saw Catherine Mellon walking up to his truck.

Catherine was clueless about Pete's mental state as she marched up to his window. Pete forced a smile.

"Darling, your ears must have been burning. Justin and I were just chatting about you! I told him I thought you must be avoiding me!" Catherine smiled, but Pete sensed annoyance behind the smile. "Justin assured me you had come by to see him on my behalf, which I am so grateful for—even if nothing came of it and I never heard from you." Catherine tilted her head to the side and he noted the reprimand.

Disappointing people caused physical pain for Pete. "I'm sorry, Catherine. I did try talking to Justin, but his hands are tied here. And I meant to swing by to give you an update, but I've been... I've been busy with a few other things right now. I'm sorry." Pete was utterly exhausted. The truth was he hadn't thought anything about Catherine since his meeting with Justin.

"Oh, I know all about it," Catherine spoke in a hushed, conspiratorial tone. "It's shocking, really!" Pete's whole body went cold. Had Justin somehow overheard his conversation with Dave? He was only down the hall.

Catherine waved a hand dismissively. "I mean, he didn't come right out and say it. Justin made it quite clear this is bigger than all of us would have thought." She shook her head in disgust.

Pete felt the panic rise again; no, he had to stay grounded. Be here, now. Pete tried to take in a deep inhale to calm his nerves. "How so?" Pete asked casually.

Catherine smiled, thrilled to be goaded into the gossip. "Well, again, he didn't outright say it because you know what a good young man he is. Justin implied there is some big money behind this upcoming commissioner race. These codes have been in place for over 50 years and the big developers have been chomping at the bit to get a piece of our little island. It would be exciting if it weren't so disgusting!"

This was about city commissioners? Pete almost laughed out loud. Catherine had all the seriousness as if it was murder, but she was talking about city codes. As much as he loved the island, it seemed so silly in comparison to the lives that were at stake around Emily Larson. Pete was glad for the chance to think about something less heavy and he was sure Catherine had more to say on the subject, so he nodded her on.

Catherine almost clapped her hands together in joy, but likely sensing the impropriety, she smoothed out her silk paisley top instead. "I don't know who it is, but Justin distinctly gave the impression he believes at least one of the city commissioners is going to get a major kick-back in exchange for approving a new set of codes that will allow an increase in building height. That means they can build one of those mega resorts right on the oceanfront. It's tacky!" Catherine appeared personally offended by the idea.

She continued, "He's been doing his best to be slow on approving any new permits in the meantime, but it will only carry us through the vote. If the resolution gets passed, it's all over. Imagine these huge companies using their money to buy out a candidate. What happened to democracy?" Catherine lamented.

Pete tried to imagine all his favorite surf spots overshadowed by huge resorts. It was bad enough now, trying to look out for people swimming out too far and putting themselves right in his path. They had no idea how dangerous it was to be hit by a surfboard. Not to mention they were oblivious to the rip tide or sharks. Pete was amazed at how many people took their kids out with no flotation device, often outside of the lifeguard zone. So many people assumed they would be safe, having no idea how dangerous the world could really be. And it would mean more small developers building out on rooftops and in backyards, too. Every neighborhood would be like a tiny collection of resorts.

"So, what can we do?" Pete hated feeling helpless.

"I talked to Brendan Adams and he is going to run. He's exactly the kind of man we need running!" Catherine said excitedly. Pete remembered Brendan as the mild-mannered kid in his gifted classes. Smart, but hardly the guy Pete would put up against a soulless corporate machine. Maybe Catherine saw something Pete didn't. Either way, Pete was relieved to be off the hook with Catherine. She seemed content that Brendan was going to solve her problems and he had enough to worry about.

"Tell him he's got my vote." Pete had to admit he was disappointed about Brendan being in office. He was a nice enough guy, but Pete had a hard time envisioning him doing a whole heck of a lot for the island. But, Pete reasoned, sometimes you were just voting for the lesser of two evils. And Pete still preferred Brendan to whatever traitor was selling out their island.

"Oh yes, you must! There is nothing more important than keeping our island safe for the locals." Catherine looked seriously at Pete.

Pete couldn't think of anything else to say, so he nodded again. "Take care. I'm sure I'll see you around." Pete gave a small wave and turned over the engine in Sarg. The loud sound of the giant engine made Catherine jump. Her raised eyebrows told Pete she wasn't happy about him being the one to end the conversation; she was used to being in control. She gave a tight smile and walked over to her Mercedes. At least the talk with Catherine meant Pete finally would be able to cross something off his to do list. Now, if only he could figure out what to say to Shae.

20

Emily sat at the outside bar of The Mango Tree, enjoying the cool breeze and nursing her lychee-infused Old Fashioned. The bartender explained the lychee syrup and bitters were both crafted in-house while the bourbon was from a small batch distillery in rural Kentucky. The drink was sweet enough for Emily, but the bourbon was highlighted enough that she thought it would work as a man's drink as well. A sort of beachy folk music was playing in the background and Emily faintly heard the ocean, though it was too dark now to see the waves. It was muggy, but the bar had enough overhead fans that it was pleasant instead of oppressive. The walls had a gorgeous hand-painted mural of monsteras and mangoes; it wasn't the tacky kind of mural she often saw in beach towns but the work of a true artist. Emily was impressed; the vibe was spot on.

Emily didn't like to go to bars alone, but her Tinder date had canceled at the last minute and she didn't want to waste her makeup and cute outfit. She'd recorded a whole tutorial on her soft girl waves and she had to admit they had come out better than ever. She was glad she'd gone out because the bar was very hip and she'd gotten a super cute shot in front of the 'While we are young' neon sign. Emily had ordered a drink for the picture and in the hopes of meeting some people her age, but tonight, it was nearly all older people and couples. She was probably annoying the bartender by taking forever to finish her drink, but she didn't want to go back to her place quite yet. And really, she was pretty content. That was another rarity she couldn't let go to waste.

A middle-aged couple sat at the bar next to Emily and the husband commented on a piece of jewelry Emily was wearing. It was a cool lapis and 22k gold evil eye bracelet. She explained that she was an influencer and it was from an independent jewelry brand she was modeling for tonight. The owner was originally from Turkey and had relocated to NYC to try and make it in the US. Emily had a flush of pride as she remembered the enthusiastic text she had received from Alara gushing about the influx of sales she'd received after her latest post but kept that to herself. Emily might have been making a living putting her life on display, but it was important to keep some things just for herself.

The couple introduced themselves as Steve and Ali. Steve was a pilot and Ali owned a boutique shop a few streets over. At the mention of Instagram, Ali groaned and started sharing her frustration with social media. Emily was thrilled to provide some guidance, hoping it might lead to another brand deal. Plus, Steve had ordered her a second bourbon and it was making her chatty.

"I know social media gets a bad rap, but it's leveled the playing field for so many small businesses. Sure, bigger brands can do ads and it's possible to buy followers, but most people see right through that. Social media gives you direct access to your customers in an authentic way. You really do earn trust by putting out great content. Never before in history did small businesses have the ability to reach so many people for free like this." Emily knew people thought being an influencer was shallow, but she was passionate about helping local businesses.

She had come from a family of small business owners. Her grandmother had owned a boutique on Beach Island and her mom and dad owned a small sewing studio back in California. Probably the new boutique owner had never even heard of the studio. She knew firsthand how much work it was. She'd also seen how helping her parents with content had almost doubled their business by reaching an entirely new demographic of people her age who were into DIY.

Ali sipped her espresso martini and shook her head. "I hate it. I get so overwhelmed and I never know what to say. I know it would be good for the store but it kinda gets moved further and further down the to-do list because I get so stuck."

"I'd be happy to come by the shop and give you some pointers!" Emily usually charged for consultations like this, but she was feeling generous. She liked Steve and Ali. Plus, she rarely drank hard liquor and it was helping her feel even more generous.

"Would you really?" Ali's eyes lit up. "How about this? Steve's traveling next week and I'll be bored out of my mind. Why don't you come over to the house and I can take you out on the boat. I'd love to treat you to dinner out on the canals and you can give me some pointers! Maybe in the evening, when the shop is closed? It would be a girls' night out!" Ali looked at Emily with her palms pressed together in prayer form.

"Don't let her fool you into thinking she's cooking. It'll be catered from one of these places here," Steve motioned his hand as if sweeping the breadth of the oceanfront restaurants. All of which were delicious, Emily thought.

"Ali is a hell of a woman, but a cook she is not." Steve gave a wink to Emily.

Ali gave a tight laugh and Emily wasn't sure if the teasing was good-natured or not.

"He's not lying. I can cook, I simply choose not to. I always tell him we need another wife." Ali patted Steve on the knee. "So you just let me know if you have any dietary restrictions and I'll pick something up on my way home from the shop."

For a brief moment, Emily had the sensation Steve was looking at her for a beat too long. Ali must have felt the same because she cleared her throat and shifted on the bar stool, positioning herself between Steve's view of Emily.

"Sounds like a plan! And hey, I'm all for outsourcing!" Emily was relieved Steve would be out of town. She couldn't quite put her finger on it, but there was a vague tension between the two of them that was hard to be around. Still, Ali seemed nice enough and she had no good excuse not to go.

Emily hoped it would be fun and not awkward given that Ali was at least 20 years older than Emily. At this point, she was a little desperate to get out. Sam still hadn't been able to make it back to the new place and Emily needed to make friends. And, judging by the massive diamond on her hand, Ali did pretty well. She'd probably be more than willing to do a decent brand deal with Emily. Free dinner and she'd land another client, maybe a friend. Sounded like a win-win to Emily. She pulled out her phone, "Here's my Instagram. Send me a DM with when and where to meet. It's going to be so much fun!"

21

When Pete found himself outside the Jeweler's Shop, he knew he was in a place of avoidance. He'd convinced himself it was urgent to fix his pendant but he was just killing time instead of talking to Shae. Still, even with the self-awareness, Pete walked into the store all the same.

Luke looked up smiling at first, but then frowned immediately. "What's going on? No offense, but you look like shit." That was Luke for you, always willing to call it like he saw it.

Pete laughed. "You are too kind. Nah, I haven't been sleeping well. I'm good. Can you take a look at this? I feel like it's catching on everything." Pete slid his gold chain and gold surfboard up over his head.

He knew Luke loved this piece. It had been made by a jeweler up in South Carolina for one of the smaller surf contests he had done, back in the early days. Luke was the type not to be jealous of another artist and he had always loved this piece. There was no denying it was beautifully crafted. Pete had won bigger pots, but this handmade, one-of-a-kind 14K gold surfboard was still his favorite. They'd custom-made the alloy and carved the logo of his favorite shaper into the board. On the back, they had engraved, "El Gato #1." When Pete saw it, he felt like he had arrived.

Luke rubbed his thumb around the edges, both checking for damage and admiring the work. "Feels okay to me, but let me buff it a bit. It's dirty as hell, man. You should be taking this off when you get in the water." Luke shook his head, delivering his familiar lecture.

"I know, I know. The salt and chlorine can damage the integrity of the metal, blah blah blah." Pete finished the lecture for him, rolling his eyes. Pete did care about keeping it safe, but the board had become like a talisman for him and he hated to take it off. He had to trust it would stay safe.

Luke gave him a knowing laugh, his eyes crinkling at the edges. He also knew Pete would never take it off. "So, what's new?"

"Just working on a few new projects. Feeling a little in over my head, to be honest." Pete was surprised by his honesty. Like Pete's dad, Luke's expression had a way of setting him at ease. Plus, it was easier to talk to Luke as he sat sanding rhythmically at his bench.

Luke nodded, gently sanding the golden board with care as he did so. "It's like that sometimes. I think of it like arthritis or something. Sometimes, you're gonna get a flare-up of self-doubt. It won't last forever. You gotta get through it. Take the ibuprofen, get the rest, whatever it is. You just get through it. Think about when you first started surfing. You had hard times, but you took it as a chance to grow. Now no one can take that from you. Those experiences of overcoming, they are a part of you."

"At some point, you might actually be in over your head, right? How would you know the difference? I mean, doesn't protecting your own mental health mean something?"

Luke considered this for a moment and then admitted, "I suppose you don't really know. You're right that sometimes you need to push through and sometimes you need to quit. And unfortunately, no one can give you the answer. It's just something you have to figure out yourself. The figuring out. That is the answer."

Pete had a sense of hope for the first time in days. Luke continued, still not looking up from the bench. He hung the sander on a hook next to him and grabbed a metal file.

"You've been through some shit. Whatever this is, there is no one more capable of getting through it than you. You are smarter and tougher than anyone I know."

Pete thought back to the other day, panicking in the parking lot, and felt slightly ashamed. He doubted Luke would think he had courage if he had seen him.

Luke seemed to read his mind. "It's not about never feeling doubt or fear. It's not courage if you don't ever feel afraid, it's being fucking insane." Both Luke and Pete laughed, having known far too many people like that, growing up around surfers and skaters. "It's what you do in the face of doubt. Do you face it, take care of yourself, keep going? That's the journey, man."

Pete wanted to make a joke about Luke being like Yoda, but he didn't want to cheapen the moment. The fact was; it was exactly what Pete needed to hear right at that moment. So, instead, he simply said, "Thank you," with as much sincerity as he could muster.

Luke stood up and dusted off his apron. "Good as new! I used my Japanese blue compound—look at that shine. You can see your irises in the reflection!" Luke beamed with pride as he handed the necklace back to Pete. Pete was impressed. He pulled it close to his face and saw his blue eyes reflected in the board. It looked as good as, if not better, than the day he had won it.

Pete was brought back to that moment, dripping salt water up on the podium, grinning ear to ear in front of the crowd. He could hear the sponsor banners flapping in the wind. It had been a great day of surfing and Pete remembered feeling grateful to be alive. Here and now, placing the chain and board back over his neck, Pete felt a piece of that person come back to him for the first time since he had retired.

He still couldn't explain why he had gone in there, but he knew he had gotten something he needed. He held out a fist bump to Luke. "You're the best. What do I owe you?"

Luke shook his head and returned the fist bump. "Nothing at all. It was good to see you." Pete wished he could tell Luke how much the conversation had meant to him but he knew it would be like trying to describe the ocean. The words would feel empty and eventually cheap.

***

Pete was exhausted. He'd successfully delivered Project X to her new owner and he was happy to have the space back in his workshop, not to mention the big profit he'd made. He'd found a local shop to do some of the Airstream renovation for a decent price, so that project was moving along, too. No yacht bookings until next week—a bachelorette party, so another easy trip. He would usually feel good about having accomplished so much, but he was still reeling from the conversations over the last week. He felt raw from so much exposure; like he was on an emotional roller coaster.

Pete was having a hard time compartmentalizing everything that had happened. He was as uncomfortable with Luke's encouragement as he was with Dave's rejection, Shae's trust, Sam's pain, and Catherine's neediness. Sydney had mollified some of the sponsors, but they were still "uncomfortable." It was too much and he wished it would all just disappear. Or maybe he could disappear. He wanted nothing more than to veg on his couch, scrolling on his phone until the end of time. Or until his phone died, whichever came first. Pete plopped down on his couch, phone in hand.

Keith Lambert turns heads in Maui with barely-divorced (and barely-dressed!) supermodel Tabi Braxton. Pete couldn't help but click through; he didn't care about seeing a barely-dressed Tabi Braxton, but BeachBums was one of his guilty pleasures. It was like TMZ but for the surfing world, and they were the kings of the click-bait titles. Their over-the-top salacious writing was always good for a laugh. He'd been the subject of those headlines one too many times; he didn't miss that part of being out on the pro circuit. He was skimming the article when an ad caught his eye.

Become a Florida Private Investigator in 30 Days (or less!)

Pete was creeped out by the idea that big tech thought this was a necessary ad for him given his current situation, but intrigued nonetheless. The font was crappy and the color scheme was bright red so

Pete had doubts about the credibility of this school. Pete clicked on the ad anyway. **Sunshine State School of Investigation** boasted a questionable website with crappy pictures and terrible navigation, but according to the site, it was accredited by the Florida Commission for Independent Education.

His curiosity growing, Pete read through the requirements. According to the website, his AA in legal studies would apply to the license: a degree he'd earned through dual enrollment while in high school. It had seemed like the easiest to keep his parents appeased at a time when he had no thoughts of a future outside of pro surfing. He wondered if they still secretly harbored dreams of him becoming a lawyer. According to the website, he was allowed to skip the 40-hour class; Pete only needed to pay $200 and sit through an exam.

Pete was a pragmatist and didn't believe in fate, but this was more than a coincidence. He knew it was big tech listening, combined with some random choice he had made years ago. Still, it was hard to ignore the timing. Even harder to ignore was the feeling deep down inside pushing him towards pursuing this license. It didn't make any sense at all, yet, Pete couldn't shake the feeling propelling him forward.

Pete considered his options. On the one hand, he could try to ignore the situation until it went away, which it had to eventually. Or, Pete could try to do something about it. Pete argued with himself that he had already tried something to which he retorted back to himself hadn't worked, reminding him of Dave's complete lack of interest in helping. If he got his PI license, Pete wouldn't need to go through Dave. At least, not for everything. With his PI license, maybe he'd get the skills and access to the information he needed to clear Shae while finding true justice for Emily. It might even become another cool little side gig.

Pete was already drawing up a "Pete the PI" flyer in his mind. Pete pulled out his credit card and bought the course. He summarily approved a questioning text from his accountant. Chris was faster and better than his card's fraud detection department.

Just in the brief moments it took to get to the "order confirmed" screen, Pete was filled with waves of regret. This was probably a scam. And even if not, what in the world would he do with a PI license? He'd been imagining something cool like Rockford, but that was TV. He had no idea what a PI did. What would people think? He had no desire to go viral as the pro surfer turned wannabe detective. How embarrassing. What a waste of $200! His skin was growing hot.

Pete began to feel the negative self-talk start overwhelming him, but the same feeling he had felt pushing him forward a moment ago gave a firm "STOP" to the flow of voices inside of him. It was just like when doubt would creep up at entering a big wave barrel. Suddenly, Pete was not interested in any more negative self-talk. He'd had enough. He had a strength and determination he hadn't felt in a very long time.

Pete hated wasting money and the NO REFUNDS policy was loud and clear on the website. So, he made up his mind right then and there: he would get the license and get his money's worth. He would make sure he would use this license to make good on his promise to help Shae. Instead of focusing on his doubt, he would remember that he was working for the greater good. Pete was embarrassed by the realization that this was the first time in his life he'd decided to do something to help someone instead of for his own career or enjoyment. He shook off the thought: today was as good a day to start as any.

Pete had nothing on the agenda for the rest of the day, so he decided to get to work immediately. Skimming through the requirements, he saw he'd have to transfer over his transcripts and a few other things. Nothing Pete couldn't handle. So much for a day of rest.

22

Pete slid his latest custom shortboard out of Sarg's open back. The flatness of summer required only mid-length or longboards, but fall brought more rideable waves. Pete was stoked to see how this board would do. He admired the curves and the painted-on graffiti style Cat in Converse; it might have been Billy B's best work yet. He'd even shaped it slightly unevenly to counterbalance Pete's bad ankle. It was a work of art. The lot at third light was already almost full. Pete would usually be among the first here on a day like this, but he'd stayed up late working on his license. Pete knew he'd still get a prime spot in the line-up. Late or not, there was a very serious hierarchy in surf culture, and Pete had earned his spot. Of course, there could always be some kook, but that came with the locale.

Tropical Storm Valerie was creating some serious height out there; SurfGuru had predicted 8' or more. Pete was relieved to see only the regulars were out here today. He wanted to be able to get in the flow instead of having to worry about choosing between giving up a good shred or plowing down a tourist. He smiled at all the dots of humans. They wouldn't exist by the time he paddled to the outside. Today it would just be him and the waves.

Pete lost track of time. When he finally checked his watch, he saw he'd caught eight waves. Unreal—his ankle wasn't even hurting. Was it the new board? Or was it that Pete had somehow found himself back in the old flow? Maybe it had all been in his imagination.

The reason didn't matter—what mattered was Pete felt alive. It was more than that—Pete was having fun! And he knew the adage was true: no matter what moves you pulled, the best surfer out there was the one having the most fun. Pete couldn't remember the last time he'd had fun surfing. He looked up to see a dark cloud moving in, which would mean lightning soon. He also noticed he was pretty hungry. Pete hated to admit it, but it was time to head in. He looked out on the horizon to see if The Last Wave was out there, but the sea was becoming fairly flat. Pete decided he didn't need one last good wave—the whole session had been perfect and he was content to paddle back in.

Pete was rinsing his feet off at the shower when he heard someone calling his name. He looked up to see Nate jogging towards him, one hand holding his board and the other keeping his baggies from falling off. This crowd was notorious for low-hanging baggies that hit right at the hip bone. Good for looking hot on a board, bad for jogging without showing your whole bare ass. "Hell yeah, brother! You looked amazing out there today! Are you thinking about getting back on the circuit?" Nate looked at Pete in expectation.

Pete smiled and shook his head. "Loving life out there today. You pulled some sick moves out there yourself." Pete deflected to change the subject. "You off work today?"

Nate nodded. "I'm freaking starving now. You wanna hit up Sun City?"

Pete looked at his watch: it was 10:30 a.m. It was never too early for tacos after surfing. "No doubt. Throw your board in the back and I'll drive us."

Unsurprisingly, the tiny parking lot was full and Pete had to pull Sarg into the dirt lot behind the building. There was nothing better than Sun City after a set of waves and Pete was sure the entire crowd at third light had come straight here. Except for the few suckers that had to head to work. Pete and Nate found a tiny booth, and each ordered Cokes and the Big Kahuna plate of tacos.

After sharing stories about the morning's best waves in between bites of taco, Nate grew a little more serious. "I want to talk to you about something. As a friend, you understand?" Pete looked at Nate in his Volcolm shirt and baggies and intuitively understood Nate meant this conversation was outside of his standard uniform. Pete nodded.

"Look, I don't know all that went down when you met with Dave. And I don't know all that's going on. But, person to person," again, Nate gave the impression he was trying to emphasize that this was off the record, "I feel like there's some weird stuff going on lately. And I guess I thought you should know if you have questions and you aren't getting answers, Florida has very broad public record laws." Nate let his words sit and fill the air. There was no doubt Nate wanted Pete to pick up what he was dropping. Nate remained quiet, stirring part of a broken taco shell into his refried beans.

Pete tried to keep his face and voice neutral. "The case is closed because you guys didn't find anything. So I'm not sure what those records would show." Pete was working very hard not to make this statement sound like a question that Nate would have to answer.

Nate looked at him dead in the eyes. Finally, he shrugged. "Sometimes, when you do a job for a long time, you don't see things the way someone new might. Someone with a fresh set of eyes. Or maybe you get good at seeing what you want to see. So, if you have some ideas or want to look anything over, let me know and I'll do my best. Dave's pretty...busy...so ..." Nate looked both uncomfortable and determined. As if he'd crossed a point of no return. "Maybe come to me instead."

Pete debated telling Nate about the PI license but figured it would be best to wait until it came through. It felt like yet another sign from God, the universe, whatever. "Thanks, man. I appreciate it. I will be taking you up on that." With that, they both let the moment pass and they rejoined the world of surfers at Sun City, swapping tales of epic waves and wipeouts. Because even a wipeout made a great story.

***

After Pete dropped Nate off in the parking lot, he walked up the boardwalk and sat up on the wooden ledge overlooking the ocean. A toddler in a long-sleeved rashguard and bucket hat chased seagulls with a desperate outstretched hand. A lanky teenager rode a wave and then jumped sideways off the board into the rest of the wave. In the distance, a white and red tugboat pushed a massive black barge.

Reminiscing about some of his wilder surfing trips had left Pete feeling introspective and nostalgic. But did he miss it? Even if he hadn't had a career-ending injury, Pete knew he was too old for the antics they would get into and would most definitely not be able to hang today. Or even want to, if he was honest. Climbing up five-story mango trees, swimming out past the buoy and holding up an entire contest, drunk and naked surfing at midnight. And he'd spent almost no time at all at his house here on the island, being more of a tourist coming for the occasional week or two in between photo shoots, contests, and sponsored trips. It was easy to forget how exhausted he had been by it all and how homesick he often was. He loved now being a bike ride away from his parents; although they still had a while, they were getting older and Pete wanted to spend time with them while he could.

And having such a great session today was in stark contrast to the way surfing had felt then. The first couple of wins had been exciting, then the pressure to hold on to the lead mounted with every single win after. Soon, he was breaking records and the pressure was on to set new ones. He spent his long-haul flights out to Australia or Hawaii analyzing footage with his coach and finding all the mistakes he'd have to try not to make in the next contest.

Because every time Pete invented a new move, it meant all the younger guys would start practicing it. So Pete would practice twice as hard. Always aiming for perfection. No matter how close Pete's life got to the ideal, perfection always remained slightly out of reach. A near-perfect ride, but not quite. A near-perfect house, but he was never home. A near-perfect girlfriend, but they were always apart on different tours and timelines.

Pete's competitive nature had fueled him at first, but near the end, he was approaching burnout. Maybe that's what had led to the accident in the first place—he'd been tired and done poorly in his first heat. He speculated he was reaching too much to stay in first, causing him to make the mistake of taking the first wave. Looking back at the footage (which it had taken a whole year before Pete had been able to view it), it was so clearly a wave he should have passed on yet he'd paddled out and called it. He could have sworn he'd seen Filipe moving in for it and he was determined to get to it first. It was amazing how your whole life could be completely changed by a single split-second decision.

Today, something had shifted for Pete. Instead of feeling angry thinking about that day, he sensed something like peace. Pete had a good life, here and now. Maybe the ideal was just that—an idea. Pete's dad would always paraphrase St. Augustine and say we were restless because our hearts were longing for God. Maybe there was some truth that we were always trying to find an ideal not found here on Earth. And the closer you got to perfection, the worse you felt because it would feel so close yet so far away, like the imperfections got magnified the closer you felt to perfection.

Pete didn't want to be angry about how his career ended, because after it was all said and done, Pete was happy to be retired from pro surfing. And he was ready to move on. He was too young to live out all the rest of his days killing time. It was time to figure out what was next for his life. Pro surfing and surviving his accident had allowed Pete to see what he was made of and he was beginning to see he was made for more than being a beach bum. Even a rich one. He didn't know what that meant, exactly. He wasn't sure what was next, but he had the uncanny feeling he was being called to keep his eyes open and pay attention.

After this whole thing was over, maybe he'd get a life coach or something to figure out his next moves. For now, though, he'd finish up his license and finish this project for Shae. Pete might struggle with seeing things through, but he knew Shae was counting on him and he wanted to be the kind of guy people could count on. Pete was going to buckle down and give it the effort he knew he was capable of, for both Pete's and Shae's sake.

23

Emily took extra care with her makeup that night. She wanted to be sure she made Marc jealous. Although he had deleted her from all of his photos, she saw he was still watching every single one of her stories. She wanted him to clearly see that she had moved on. She applied extra highlighter to emphasize her cheeks out on the water; she always felt prettier by moonlight.

Emily wasn't sure why she was going. It sounded kind of boring to be honest, going out on a pontoon boat with some older lady. With Sam out of town, she didn't have many other options. The island had no nightlife, at least not compared to California. It was too flat here. Emily missed hiking the Sierra Nevadas. There weren't even hills here. Emily was growing homesick for California again and tried to push it out of her mind. She'd already decided she would fly back—maybe next week after Sam got back. The lady seemed pretty lonely. Emily had been in a charitable mood when the woman started chatting with her, a mood that unfortunately had not carried over to the night of the actual hangout.

She put on the second pair of false eyelashes and took a little selfie in the mirror, captioning it ready for a night out on the water! She tagged Seaside Designs, the local artist who'd hand tie-dyed the cover-up she was wearing. At least she'd scored a couple of new collabs while she was here.

She turned to the side—she wouldn't have picked pink and purple tie-dye herself, but she had to admit she looked super cute. Likes were already pouring in, confirming it was a good look for her. She hoped the colors would show up while out on the water. She sighed, lamenting that such a cute look was being wasted on such a boring night out. At least she would get some good photos from it.

An hour later, they were cruising through the canal. Emily oohed and aahed as if it were her first time and she hadn't been up and down this canal one thousand times since she was a kid. She didn't want to come across like one of those ungrateful Gen Y'ers the older people were always getting mad about. She sipped her drink with a smile—ugh, was it a screwdriver? Gross. She didn't know people still made those. Wow, this lady could mix a drink; it was hitting her hard. Maybe because Emily was used to White Claw on the rare occasions she had alcohol, not hard liquor. She felt a little sick. Emily needed to get off the boat.

"I'm so sorry. Do you think we could head back? I'm not feeling well," Emily called back, her weak voice carried away by the wind. Was it the new *poke* place she had been to? She thought the shrimp was local, but maybe it was off. Emily's whole chest was hot and tiny beads of sweat began to form on her chest. She was afraid she was going to throw up in front of this woman, or worse. Emily's breathing became so heavy, it started to sound like a wheeze—she wanted to get back into bed.

The woman slowed the boat to a troll and Emily became calmer. She suddenly had a grandmotherly look to her and Emily's mind was flooded with memories of boating with her grandmother, out in these same islands. Emily felt a sense of calm as the woman leaned over her. Emily thought she might put a cloth on her forehead just as her grandmother would do whenever she had a fever. But instead, the woman put her hands tightly around her neck.

Emily was so confused. She tried to scream, but her voice was thick in her throat. The woman's thumb was pressed deep into her trachea. The houses were so far away now; that they'd never hear her. Her breaths were so thin and the pressure was building just under her chin. Emily sensed herself drifting off when, all of a sudden, the adrenaline kicked in.

She remembered her self-defense training and she put her arms in between the woman's and pushed outward, breaking the chokehold. She then put her feet on the woman's chest and pushed back with all of her strength. Though it wasn't much by that point, it was still enough to shove the woman back. Emily grabbed her phone and, without thinking, jumped out into the water.

She expected it to be shallow as it had been when she was a kid, but the water was surprisingly deep and she kept feeling herself fall under. She tilted her head back in an attempt to float on her back and the first spattering of stars spun in the sky above. The roiling in her stomach returned and Emily pulled her head upright.

Emily swam desperately, trying to hide in the mangroves as the woman shined a flashlight from the deck of the boat. She was looking for Emily. There were banana spiders everywhere and Emily covered her mouth to keep from screaming. The branches were so dense that they gave the illusion of land. Emily needed to find an actual island so she could rest. Her arms and legs were so tired as she struggled to keep her head above water. Her body began to shiver and her teeth chattered as she noticed a small break in the salt marsh.

A tiny beach of sand was visible through the branches. She swam over as quietly as possible, pulling herself up on the sand. By a stroke of a miracle, there was a little stack of firewood set up for a bonfire. Must be a make-out spot for the local teenagers. Emily thought someone would maybe see the fire and send help. She couldn't admit to herself that it would be hard to see such a tiny fire from this deep in the tunnels. She had to maintain hope. If nothing else, maybe it would help dry her clothes.

Emily tried to strip off her dress, falling twice with the effort of it before she gave up. She continued to shiver despite the warm air. She struggled to hold the lighter on the wood long enough for it to catch. Everything was blurry, the pines seeming to multiply around her. Darkness rose from the brackish waters to the edge of the fire. The screaming *awk* of a heron pierced the silence. It was so hard to get a full breath and she heard a wheezing sound. Was her windpipe broken? She curled up next to the bonfire. More memories of her summer with her grandmother flashed into her head. "No, Emily," she commanded herself out loud. "Stay here."

In the near distance, she heard a young female voice yell flirtatiously, "Ethan, stop!" A peal of laughter was followed by a loud splash. A second splash—probably Ethan showing off with a flip off the boat. More laughter. They couldn't be more than a hundred yards away as the crow flies, but because they were on the other side of the thicket it might as well be miles. Emily made another effort to call for help, but her breath was as thick as sludge in her chest. Only the smallest groan escaped. A few moments later, she heard the loud rumble of the diesel boat engine starting. They were leaving.

She opened her eyes and tried to sit up when another wave of nausea hit her. Her phone. Maybe she could call for help. She picked up her phone and it was nearly dead: 1%. Emily couldn't think of anyone to call. She wasn't speaking to Marc. She started to text Sam but remembered she was probably still on a plane. Her parents would be at work and wouldn't answer. Her panic increased as she saw her phone dying faster as she lay there struggling to think of whom to call.

Emily had an idea. She took a picture, still lying in the sand with the island behind her. She would tag it and post it on Instagram. That way, she would reach thousands of people at once. Emily was relieved, knowing someone would help her and she could get some rest. Her phone seemed to take forever to upload the photo to Instagram and she tried to type her location. The warm summer days began to overtake her memory again. Instead of typing more, Emily accidentally hit the post button. Well, that would have to do. It was okay now. Someone would be here soon to help. Emily dropped her head down and sleep took her.

24

Pete woke up with a sense of determination and a fire in his belly. He'd been so focused on keeping the peace with Dave that he'd forgotten to get angry about it. A girl had definitely died, possibly died by murder. Which meant a killer was walking free. And Dave was worried about image? What about Shae's image? The more Pete thought about it, the more pissed he got. Pete got out of bed and did a half-kneeling flexor stretch on his seagrass mat. He walked out to the second-story balcony and looked at the water. How many secrets were hidden in those Endless Islands? Pete shuddered to think.

Pete's problem was that he had all this righteous anger and nowhere to direct it. He felt like he'd received sign after sign to look deeper into Emily's death, but he had no idea of what to do or where to start. How does one go about investigating a possible murder? Pete's surfing background wasn't any help. His degree certainly hadn't prepared him for this. It's not the kind of thing you call your friends up to ask or you search on Google. Pete remembered his PI class. The course was written by a former East LA police detective. Pete wasn't the classroom type, but maybe it was worth a shot to see if there was anything good in the course. Not to mention he'd sunk a couple hundred bucks into it, much to

Chris's dismay. Pete had no other ideas, so he walked downstairs to his office and pulled up the course.

The guy's bio was pretty impressive. Detective Gene Alexander had landed several high profile arrests, particularly among the drug gangs. The arrests had received so much coverage that he'd become a type of celebrity, even making a cameo on Saturday Night Live. Then he'd taken his fame and opened up a private PI practice, where he was instrumental in gathering the intel that led to the arrest of Cleveland Mayor Smith back in the 90s. He'd made a few other major busts as a PI before retiring to Boca and starting the Sunshine State School of Investigation. According to Gene Alexander's bio, the school was his 'magnum opus.' *Yikes*, Pete thought, as he once again mentally critiqued the website. Pete was pretty sure this guy's magnum opus had been bringing down drug lords not building a crappy website.

Pete clicked on the introduction and a video autoplayed. It was Gene, sitting at a very formal leather wingback chair with a mahogany desk behind him as he held a glass of what appeared to be whiskey. This couldn't be this guy's office, Pete hoped. Though, the idea it might be a set was worse. Pete did his best to pay attention as Gene waxed philosophical about the art of investigation, narrating the world's best detectives throughout history, both fictional and real. He talked about how his students would be joining the tradition of the greatest minds of history: Valentin, Clouseau, Guillaume, Holmes, Poirot, Columbo, and Drake. Pete only recognized a couple of the names on a list that seemed to go on forever; he was pretty sure he should know more of the names if they were the greatest sleuths in history. He changed the speed of the video to 1.5x as he downloaded the section's worksheet. It read:

THE 10 COMMANDMENTS OF CHASE

1. Thou shall not play God. Your job is to remain objective and consider all facts equally. As soon as you think you know everything, you will lose the chase.

2. Thou shall not place anyone or anything before the truth. Your job is to seek the truth, not play loyalties or please your clients. Review everyone and every fact with open eyes. You may upset a client here or

there, but in the end, your reputation will win you more business than you can handle.

3. Thou shall love your neighbor. Keep your enemies close, but your friends closer. Remember, you are playing the long game in this career. Don't burn your sources and don't burn any friends that would help you move a body. You're going to need good friends often in this career.

4. Thou shall not covet information you don't have. Don't waste time thinking about what information you wish you had. Squeeze every last drop out of the information you do have and the rest will come.

5. Thou shall not become a criminal. You're going to find yourself among a lot of nefarious people with a level of access that will be overwhelming at first. Never forget, you are a fighter for the truth and light. Know your values and stick to them. Check-in with those who keep you honest.

6. Thou shall rest. Rest is essential for the investigative mind. You'll be tempted by deadlines, money, and ego to keep pushing, but that's when your work gets messy. Take regular rest to allow the facts to percolate in your mind.

7. Thou shall do your job. Your job is to investigate, not wait around for a stroke of good luck. You will know the best tricks of the trade: use the tools at your disposal to win the chase.

8. Thou shall be free. You are not the police. They are limited by a political and bureaucratic system while you can roam free. Be creative and shrewd (but also, see #5).

9. Thou shall be quiet. Loose lips sink ships. Your job is to ask questions and allow silence. Most people hate silence and will overshare to fill the void. Don't be one of those people, and others will solve your cases for you. Talk too much and it will inevitably get back to your target.

10. Thou shall be organized, but cryptic. Keep notes, but keep everything secure using either encrypted technology or the Alexander Algorithm. By keeping notes and referring to them often, the patterns will show themselves.

It was hard not to cringe. Pete could have done without the fire and brimstone commandment motif. He was mildly embarrassed for the guy, but he had to admit the information was useful. And hadn't the guy earned the right to set some commandments? Pete was doing his best to get past the cheese factor because even now he sensed there was a lot of depth to what Alexander was saying. He took a deep breath, reminding himself of what was at stake. He settled in and clicked the forward arrow to learn more about the first commandment.

Pete mused on Alexander's list, starting at the top. Had Pete been playing God? Not literally, of course. Pete now saw he hadn't been objective. Thinking back to his conversations up to this point, Pete understood he had been clouded by how he thought he was being perceived or what he assumed others were thinking, even by his expectations of how the conversations should have gone. Instead of observing the conversations as they were, Pete had been both an actor and a writer. He'd allowed his anxiety or ego to color each conversation instead of being detached yet aware. Pete was frustrated: all that meditation for nothing. He'd have to work hard going forward to remain neutral in each situation.

Pete walked through his conversations with Shae. He did his best to pause the scene, walking around and looking at the details. Pete had been scared to see an unpleasant truth about Shae, but he knew he had to review every conversation with clear eyes. Then there was Alexander's second commandment; there was no getting around the fact that Shae had kept the information about moving the body secret for months. Shae had been at the island, which was possibly a murder scene. And Shae had been willing to act against her morals just to keep her tour business. What else was she capable of? He jotted a few notes in his notebook of follow-up questions for Shae.

Pete did his best to recollect his last conversation with Sheriff Carter. Pete had been so caught up in worrying about his future. He had been so incredibly afraid during their last conversation. Thinking back, Pete was angry about it now. He had done the right thing going to see Dave and he felt like he had been treated like a criminal. He knew that wasn't objective either, and so he did his best to allow the anger to give way to curiosity. Why hadn't Sheriff Carter been more open to the information

Pete was bringing? Had he been surprised by the information? Replaying the conversation in his head, Pete noted Dave hadn't seemed surprised at all by this information. He'd been more focused on telling Pete to stay out of it than asking questions about the situation. Interesting. Pete drummed his pencil on the desk, rocking to the tune of an Agent Orange song in his head.

Dave had reiterated it was a closed case. Was Dave more focused on what was good for the city than on what was true? Why? Pete had felt threatened at the time. Was Dave trying to threaten him? If so, why? Why had the police and the city agreed to close the case when there was so much talk about it on Twitter?

Sam Finnegan had mentioned Emily had been drunk at the time of her drowning. Sheriff Carter had also commented drunk girls drowning. Pete flipped back through his notes about the press conference the city had held. Nothing about her being drunk; they said it was a case of a tourist getting lost at night and dying from exposure. Had the police told Sam that Emily was drunk or did she know another way? If she was drunk, how did that happen? Did she get drunk before going to the island or did she get drunk there? Was there any proof she had been drunk? Pete made a note to review her Instagram again.

Who were the mysterious Twitter posters? Why were they so vested in Emily? Did they know her personally? Where did they live? Why were they so convinced there was a conspiracy? Pete's pencil moved across the page furiously. The page filled with connecting arrows, question marks, and his illegible handwriting.

What about Nate? Was Pete imagining that Nate was trying to encourage him to get involved? If Nate thought something was wrong, why didn't he say something to Dave or investigate it himself?

It was hard to stop his quick brain from making assumptions. Pete was in a lot of trouble if all the commandments were going to be as hard to follow as this simple one about being objective. Pete once again tried to channel a Buddha-like curiosity about each situation instead of jumping to answers. But he had to give Alexander credit—this exercise had raised many more questions for Pete to sort through. So, what next?

First, Pete thought about follow-up questions he might ask without raising any red flags with Sheriff Carter.

Nate had also mentioned Pete might be able to get information through the public records laws. Pete would need to conduct some research to see how that worked, again without tipping off Sheriff Carter.

Shae had mentioned the bonfire had already been lit when she got there. Pete wondered if there were any other clues on the island. Pete was beginning to feel a bit overwhelmed by his to-do list, unsure of where to start.

He glanced out his window to see a gray sky. Another storm was brewing in the Atlantic and it was predicted to be a big one. Pete wanted to get out there to look around before the storm hit and possibly covered up any clues. It had already been through one storm so it might already be too late. Mother Nature was prioritizing for him.

25

"Absolutely hideous!" Catherine slammed the front door behind her as she went out to have a word with her neighbor. "Is it really necessary for you to create such an eyesore?" Catherine asked, both hands on her hips.

Sam gave an exaggerated sigh and turned around, "Hello to you as well, Catherine. And in case you hadn't heard, there is another hurricane coming, and so yes, I do have to put this up," she motioned to the large slats of plywood that she was struggling to hang over the windows. She wiped away the sweat in an exaggerated motion in an attempt to curry some kind of compassion from her neighbor.

"It's very distasteful and," Catherine let out an exaggerated exhale. "Well, it's quite ugly."

"I will eventually have proper shutters, as I believe we have already discussed. The contractors all have a backlog and I wasn't able to get them on in time. And I don't believe this is violating any kind of code. Though I am sure you will address it if I somehow need to get a permit." The last sentence had a bit of sarcasm laced in.

"It might not be important to you, but those of us who have lived on the island for many years are a community. We care about our neighbors, people we have to see every day. I know this is just part of your portfolio, but it is my home! My family has owned this home since 1963—long before you were even born!" Catherine's voice was harsh and accusing.

Sam almost laughed out loud—her portfolio? She'd put everything she had into buying this place when her grandfather had died. And fine, she did intend to recoup some of the money by renting it out. It was also so she could preserve the memories she had of all her wonderful summers with her grandparents. Catherine acted as if she was nothing more than a soulless person chasing money above all. It was unfair and untrue. And Sam was so tired of the anti-outsiders crusade that Catherine was on. Maybe Sam didn't live here or grow up here, but the island was a big part of her memories. And she loved it here as much as anyone else.

Not like it would matter to say any of that to Catherine. She had tried to make friends, but Catherine shunned her at every single turn. She'd even gone so far as to put flyers in all the neighbors' mailboxes stating Sam had hired a known sex offender as a contractor. First of all, she'd hired a well-reviewed large company that had employed him. Was she supposed to do her background checks on every person working on the house? And second of all, she'd taken swift action as soon as she found out. Couldn't Catherine have come to her first before blasting her in front of the entire neighborhood? And how did Catherine even find out in the first place?

Sam was beginning to hate coming back to the house because she knew she'd have some kind of run-in with Catherine. This was one of Sam's happy places and she was determined not to let Catherine bully her. She had every right to finish the additions her grandfather had dreamed of, but never had the means to accomplish. Sam also had every right to make money by renting it. She would be very picky with her guests and she'd also stay there some of the year. Beach Island was full of people doing the same thing. Why was Sam the one catching such hell for it?

Sam did feel a little bad that the tiny house addition would change Catherine's view, but it's not like it was going to block it entirely. And, as Sam had tried to explain numerous times, if Catherine would move her sitting area a few feet, she'd still enjoy the same view she had always had.

Catherine had gone on and on about how selfish Sam was, how people like her were ruining the island, how her new renovations were 'ghastly' and 'gauche.' All of this animosity because Catherine wouldn't move her deck chairs a few feet. So, it was hard for Sam to feel bad about it anymore. Plus, it was her yard and she wasn't doing anything wrong. She wished she didn't feel so guilty, but that was life as a constant people-pleaser.

Sam finished hanging the last piece of plywood and went inside. She'd be heading back to Rhode Island after this storm passed. She had to get back to work there and it made her sad to be at the house right now. First, Emily's death and then all the harassment from Catherine. It was just too much. Sam was gutted by the unfulfilled plans with Emily. They'd had all these plans for painting nails, doing face masks, catching up on movies. They'd called it Sleepover Summer, but they'd both been so tired from traveling that they had a quick dinner of takeout before both going to bed, where they each stayed up too late on their phones.

They'd be talking shit about Catherine right now over a glass of wine if Emily was alive. Emily had texted Sam her first night here, saying, 'Sorry but the old lady next door needs to get laid or something. She is a real bitch and she is suuuuupppper pissed about the little house.'

Sam had bought the house from the estate a few months before and hadn't even met the neighbor yet. Sam had been mortified, hoping Emily hadn't added any fuel to Catherine's fire. Emily could be a little direct, at least compared to Sam.

Later, when she met Catherine, she had to agree about Catherine being a bitch. Sam had flown from Rhode Island to get Emily's stuff out of her house and mail it to Emily's family. She was an absolute mess, still sobbing as she went out to her car for packing tape. Catherine was out working in her garden and marched over to Sam. She started laying into Sam about the tiny house. Sam was flustered, still crying as she tried to explain that it wouldn't change the view much and also, "My best friend just died, so can we talk about this later?"

Catherine appeared unperturbed by Sam's grief. "Well, I'm sorry about your friend, but that's exactly what happens when you bring these people in who only want to get drunk and party. It's a liability to you and unsafe for the neighborhood! People are going to get hurt."

Sam had been stunned and nodded stupidly as she fumbled to get the tape and get back inside. Of course, now Sam had all the perfect comebacks as she replayed the conversation. She'd like to tell Catherine what a bitch she was and how everyone hated her. But she knew it wasn't true—she'd seen as much so far. Everywhere Sam turned, people knew Catherine and did her bidding. And they hated outsiders like Sam. It seemed so unfair, but it's how some small towns were. Sam had been naive to think her few summers here would have been enough. It was never enough for people like Catherine.

People like Catherine took power everywhere they could find it and there was power in being a local in a place like Beach Island, especially being a local who knew all the stories about how it was back in the day. Catherine's wealth only added to her legendary status as an island original. Locals loved playing the 'when did you move here' one-up game and Catherine would always be the winner. Sam was beginning to hate everything about Beach Island—the locals most of all.

The memory of Pete standing in the parking lot in his t-shirt and baggies came to mind, causing Sam to blush. Maybe all the locals weren't bad. He'd looked concerned for that day; for a brief moment, she thought (hoped?) he was going to hug her. He'd smelled amazing: like bergamot, lemon, and lavender. She felt bad for judging him so harshly at city hall. She'd assumed he was another person on Catherine's payroll. But he was so sweet in the grocery store parking lot. How was a guy like that working with a woman like Catherine? It made no sense. She'd hoped he'd maybe ask for her number or something, but no such luck. It wouldn't make sense with her spending most of her time in Rhode Island, but it would have been a welcome diversion. When Sam found herself thinking of Pete hanging the plywood for her, she knew it was time to get back to work.

26

Pete had a hard time getting to sleep the night before. His mind was racing with all the new information. Well, he had to acknowledge, he'd had the information but needed Gene Alexander's Commandments to process it. He had to admit he was enjoying giving his brain some problems to solve. It had been so long since he had done any problem-solving like this and he felt more alive, more himself. Pete did miss being out on his boat, but he was having fun (if it was okay to call it fun since it did involve someone's death). He hadn't challenged himself to learn something new in so long. Even though he didn't get a lot of sleep, he'd woken up fully energized and ready to get back to work.

'Think we should head out to the island soon b4 the bands hit. You down?' Pete texted Shae to try and get a trip scheduled as soon as possible. Looking at the weather forecast, they'd need to get out today or tomorrow before the conditions would be too unsafe for being out on the water, especially in kayaks.

While Pete was waiting on Shae's reply, he wanted to keep moving. He was still working through Alexander's course and he was getting into it. Each section went into more detail on the commandments and had great sample problems to solve and tips and tricks of the trade. He'd spent way too long modifying the Alexander Algorithm to make it his own. Whereas the algorithm used obscure terms from the game cricket, Pete made his own using surf contest lingo. The words were embedded so deep in his consciousness that it made writing his notes out much faster. Perhaps a bit paranoid, but he locked his decoding key in the safe behind the original Jeff Divine print in the guest bedroom.

It was like when Mrs. Hazel would give them cryptograms in Gifted class. He'd have to reach out when he was done and offer to help this guy with marketing. The website was crap, but the content was excellent. It was better than any class he'd taken in college, that was for sure. Although, the last time Pete had offered to help with marketing, he'd somehow ended up researching a possible murder, so maybe not. Which triggered the thought that this had all started with Twitter, but he hadn't been on there for a while. Maybe it would be good to check in and read through some of the old posts. Pete finished the section he was working on, took some notes, and then clicked over to Twitter.

Pete skimmed the app home page. #MoJo had overtaken #watergate as a top trending topic since the paparazzi had caught actress Moira Smith and NFL player John Needler at The Chelsea Hotel over the weekend. But #watergate was still getting a fair amount of traction. He scrolled through some of the recent posts while shoveling Kodiak Cakes and pure Vermont syrup into his mouth.

His heart stopped when he saw @trackamurder had tagged the official island account with the caption, '*Sunny skies and possible lies, we'll see you soon! We'll be recording from Florida all next week as we try to see what happened with Emily Larson.*'

Pete's fear was quickly replaced with the sensation of a ball growing inside his stomach, a feeling he recognized as his determination to win. "Bring it on," Pete whispered to himself.

Pete would have to work that much harder and that much faster if he was going to beat them to the answer to Emily's mysterious death. Sheriff Carter might not understand what they were up against, but Pete knew it would be much worse for business than Dave imagined if Nancy Paulson was the one to solve the crime. Instead of being an iconic beach town, they'd become a dark tourist attraction for the macabre. Nightly ghost kayak tours or private paranormal sleepovers where Emily had died.

And what if they somehow got to Shae? Shae had shown she was not good under pressure and not good in the spotlight. What if, somehow, they successfully implicated Shae in the murder of Emily? Although Pete still had some follow-up questions for her, he was pretty sure Shae hadn't murdered anyone.

But sometimes a strategic and compelling presentation of facts was all someone needed. *Track a Murder* was ongoing proof. It was great when people opened cold cases to get justice for the wrongly accused but it was dangerous for people to use their skills to find a murderer in the name of entertainment. Pete thought it was a conflict of interest.

His phone dinged. Shae gave a thumbs-up emoji to Pete's text.

'Tomorrow am?'

There was a long moment of typing bubbles before he received another thumbs-up emoji and nothing else.

Pete put the sticky plate in the left side of the sink while using his right hand to swipe open the Notes app. He would need all of today and tonight to work through Alexander's course and to make a plan of what they would need to look for on the island. He also wanted a chance to run by city hall before the trip out. Pete planned to ask if an autopsy had been performed on Emily as it was his understanding he could request results through Sunshine State laws if one was done at the request of the police.

He drummed mindlessly on the quartz counter while staring off. Pete had already felt under the gun, but having *Track a Murder* on his heels was putting the pressure on. Pete knew he could thrive under pressure, though. Years of surfing had taught him that he was ready for this and ready to focus. He'd finish the lesson on surveillance techniques and then head out to City Hall to see what there was to find in the police records.

***

Pete walked in through the familiar automatic doors and was relieved to see only the secretary at the front desk. He wanted to make this short and sweet and get out of there before he saw anyone he knew.

Pete put on his most professional smile and voice: "Hello, how are you today? I'd like to request to see the files on Emily Larson. I am invoking my rights as a citizen through the Sunshine State law." He gave another smile for good measure.

He'd upgraded his standard t-shirt and baggies uniform to a t-shirt and nice jeans. If Pete owned a suit, he hadn't been able to find it before heading up to city hall later in the day. He'd even busted out the Sun Bum hair paste in an attempt to tame his shaggy hair. He should probably book with Ben, his once-in-a-long-while barber, as soon as possible.

The secretary gave him a long, drawn-out look as if he was the stupidest man on the planet. "Police records aren't covered under the Sunshine State law." She sucked her teeth like she had plenty more to say, but instead went back to typing on her computer as if he wasn't there.

Pete had to laugh when he got back out to his truck. It sounded so obvious when she'd said it. Even he understood what a very stupid request it was—like criminal records would just be open to the public! If he'd been harboring the idea he was going to be some kind of slick PI, he was cured of those illusions of grandeur now!

Pete tried to regroup. Why had he gone in and asked for something so preposterous? Pete tried not to let the embarrassment cloud his thinking and instead tried to focus on staying objective about his original plan. He'd gone there because he had assumed Nate was dropping a hint at lunch. Pete replayed the scene in his mind. *Florida has very broad public records laws.*

Even on a second play-through, Pete believed Nate was making a knowing face and there was an urgency in his voice. Pete felt pretty sure Nate was telling him something by bringing up the public records request. And Nate would know Pete couldn't ask for the files on Emily, so it must be something else.

Pete pulled up an overview of the Sunshine State laws on his phone and skimmed through.

'All meetings of any board or commission of any state agency or authority or of any agency or authority of any county, municipal corporation, or political subdivision, except as otherwise provided in the Constitution, including meetings with or attended by any person elected to such board or commission, but who has not yet taken office, at which official acts are to be taken are declared to be public meetings open to the public at all times, and no resolution, rule, or formal action shall be considered binding except as taken or made at such meeting.'

From a glance, it looked like they mainly applied to public meetings. Pete clicked over to the city government site and skimmed past events; he found no public meetings related to the police force that he'd found. Was it something else? Pete thought about all the times he had received an email from the DMV, a school, or the tax collector: they all had the same language to the effect that Florida had broad public records laws and any email could be pulled under a Sunshine State request. Did Nate want him to request an email? Pete didn't feel he was allowed to ask for all the emails ever sent by any of the officers. Even if they would turn them over, he would never have the time to read them all. He'd have to narrow this down, but he had no idea what he was looking for. Pete was stuck; he decided to go to the ocean to clear his head.

Pete ran through the pieces of information he had so far and tried to create a mental timeline. He tried rearranging conversations and facts, but nothing stood out. Pete didn't want to get stuck on information he didn't have, so he decided to table this for now. As he prepared to turn around, scaffolding along the side of one of the beachfront hotels caught his attention. Probably repairing damage from the last storm, but Pete walked a little closer. A white plastic box on a wooden stake triggered something in his mind. It was a kind of box used for roofing permits. Pete paused and looked at the scaffolding, trying to let his mind play free association instead of forcing the idea.

Finally, the memory rose to the surface. Sam had commented that the police had been interested in her permits, not in talking about Emily.

'They were way more interested in my permits than anything else,' she'd said.

He'd been so focused on feeling bad for Sam that her words hadn't caught his attention, but his mind was finding something important about them now. Why would the police be interested in permits? Permits fell under the purview of code enforcement, not police. And hadn't Catherine implied there was 'big money' behind the permits? Alexander's course had mentioned more than once that following the money would almost always lead to the most crucial facts about a situation.

It seemed like a paranoid stretch, but Pete had an intuitive push to head back to city hall. Sarg sat humming in the parking lot as Pete ran another web search. He gave a light punch to the leather passenger seat. "Hell yeah!"

'Any agency or legislative entity that operates a website and uses electronic mail shall post the following statement in a conspicuous location on its website:

Under Florida law, e-mail addresses are public records. If you do not want your e-mail address released in response to a public records request, do not send electronic mail to this entity. Instead, contact this office by phone or in writing.'

Back inside city hall, Pete mustered a facade of confidence he didn't feel to face the secretary again. Great Whites, flesh-shearing coral, and big waves were friendlier than this small-town police secretary.

He approached cautiously as her back was turned, her brown curly hair fighting to escape the animal print claw clip as she typed furiously. Pete pulled himself as tall as his 5'10 frame would take him. "I'd like to request the email records of any officer related to permits."

She turned and gave him another long look. Pete readied himself for more of her curt dressing down. Instead, she said, "That's going to take me a few days because I'll need to do an agency-wide search function." She pulled out a form: "Put your name and contact information here and I'll let you know when it's ready."

Pete tried to hide his elation. He felt like fist-pumping as if he'd just won at Mavericks. Even if this was a wild goose chase, Pete felt a high from the process of chasing a lead. And from surviving an encounter with Secretary Standoffish. He filled out the form and left feeling like he was walking on air. As he was leaving, he saw Sheriff Carter walking in with someone in a suit. Judging by the wool material, it was a Northerner. Pete pulled his trucker hat down low and made a sharp turn towards the doors, narrowly avoiding a run-in. Though they went way back, Pete knew he didn't want to be there when Dave found out he'd put in a records request.

27

The weather was pretty rough for kayaking, but if he trusted anyone to take him out, it was Shae. It had been hard enough to find a time when Shae wasn't working and they really needed to get back out there to see if they might find anything. Pete studied Shae as she off-loaded the kayaks from the trailer and into the water in one continuous action, moving with the expertise of someone who'd been doing this for 20 years.

Shae looked better than the last time Pete saw her, but she still wasn't herself. Her hair was short like Winona Ryder in the 90s—probably from the new job—and her eyes still had much of that empty look. As she stepped into her boat, her face was in a grimace as if the pain was physical. At this point, it had been months since her last paid tour. Pete noticed Shae didn't take out her custom boat, but instead took out one of the boats reserved for her guests.

Pete couldn't remember the last time he'd been in a kayak. He was suspicious of every little ripple and bump in the water, sure it was a gator. Pete was used to being much higher on the water and on a much faster boat. From the corner of his eye, a 10-footer moved off the shore and into the water. Pete prepared his paddle for battle. On closer inspection, it was a piece of driftwood moved slightly by the small ripples hitting the shore. Pete paused to clean his sunglasses.

Pete tried to lighten the mood, in spite of the heavy reason for their trip. "Remember when we took your dad's shitty canoe out?"

Shae laughed, but it was polite, "Yeah, I remember when the banana spider jumped in the boat and you screamed so loudly I had to yell shut up right in your face so you didn't tip us!"

They both cracked up, genuinely this time. Pete had never been a fan of spiders. The mood was lifted, so Pete was content to paddle side-by-side in silence as they fought the wind out towards the island.

"You know, you could have come to me. That had to be really heavy to find a body and then keep it to yourself. And then all this shit after. I'd have listened," Pete said what had been on his mind for a while quietly.

Shae sighed, keeping her focus forward. "I was so depressed. I was so angry at myself and was constantly in a spiral. I felt like a burden. I didn't want to bring all my negativity to you."

Pete understood; he'd had those same thoughts after his accident. "It's not a burden. Letting your friends be there for you is a gift. It's like you're letting them see the real you, warts and all. Only a few people get that, so it's a gift to those who get it."

Shae gave Pete a long glance and nodded her head.

Pete saw Shae's eyes watering and knew he'd need to leave it there. Pete gave her an earnest nod and then changed the subject, asking about Shae's cousin and other generally safe topics. They chatted until they reached the island and the silence hit them once again. Because what was there to say when you were at a murder scene?

They pulled the boats on the sand and gazed around. Shae's eyes were clenched shut and her arms crossed her chest tightly. She took a breath and said, "This is rough for me. I'm feeling a lot of feelings being out here."

Pete was so grateful Shae was reaching out. He walked over and gave her a gentle pat on the back. "I hear you. I'm here with you. I don't know what happened, but I know you didn't murder anyone. And we are going to figure this out so you can get your life back. First, I need you to walk me through that night, step-by-step." Pete flashed his best let's do this look and Shae gave him a fist bump.

Shae gave Pete a walk-through of all her steps. Pete noticed Shae's hesitation in opening up and kept encouraging her.

"This is where she was lying in the sand when I got here."

Pete could barely hear her above a rising wind. The bonfire can was knocked over, leaving dark ash where Emily had died. He paused and gave a moment of silence in honor of Emily. He turned to Shae and asked as kindly as he could, "And where did you move her?"

She flinched, but motioned for him to follow as she walked him through a tiny clearing leading to the backside of the little island. That side of the island was more visible to the main river and heavily trafficked with motor boats. If Emily had made it to this side by herself, she might have been seen by someone.

Pete suggested they go back and try to recreate what might have happened to Emily. There was only one way to the island unless she had been out way deep in the river, which was unlikely. Plus, that would have made it almost impossible she would have seen the bonfire pit on the other side of the island. Pete used his kayak paddle to shift around the sand at the island opening but didn't see anything. They looked at the bonfire pit, carefully sorting through the ashes and the sand around but came up empty again.

The wind was whipping harder and a sharp whistling sound was moving through the pines.

"I think we're gonna have to call it a day, man. This is going to be a bitch to paddle back in. And we're not getting anywhere." Shae sounded dejected.

After another quick walk-through, Pete agreed it was getting too unsafe to stay and they started the trip back to shore. Pete was struggling to project positivity for Shae's sake, but he was feeling pretty discouraged as well. He was doing his best, but none of his ideas for leads were going anywhere. He felt way in over his head and yet like he had no choice but to keep trying. A heaviness settled in his chest as he realized Shae was likely having very similar thoughts about him. She'd put her faith in him, but so far it seemed frustratingly misplaced.

The water was choppy and sprayed over the front of the boats as they hit wave after wave. It was a struggle to paddle, so neither talked. The weather and the eerie feeling of being out on the island added a sense of panic as they paddled. Pete saw a strike of lightning hit out on the horizon. They'd ignored the warning of thunder for too long.

He glanced at Shae, who nodded in acknowledgment and they rowed until their arms were burning. Florida was the lightning capital of the world and it was more dangerous out on the water. Pete hoped they hadn't pushed their luck too far by going out there; the shore looked impossibly far at this point and the boats were so very slow. Although he was far outpacing Shae, Pete was used to his yacht and felt trapped by his lack of ability to make the kayak go as fast as he wanted. He was wasting energy while Shae, even in the rising waves, moved smoothly with ease. He cursed his TRX session with Mason the day before; his delts were burning, but he leaned in harder.

Finally, they were back on the shore, panting and loading the boats back on the trailer.

Rain pelted them as they loaded up the boats. As much as he had loved it as a kid, Pete never wanted to go back to that island again.

Soaked, they sat in the cab of Shae's truck and stared out the windshield until Shae began to cry.

Pete had no encouraging words to offer so he reached for her hand, holding it gently until Shae had cried herself out.

"You know, I'm almost okay sometimes. Like, I can get to a place where I can be at peace with this new life." Shae sniffed, using an old McDonald's napkin and the rearview mirror to wipe away the mascara rings. She shifted in her seat to look at Pete directly. "But then I start thinking about the future and all the what-ifs and I start freaking out again."

Pete nodded. "New beginnings are the hardest, especially when they're forced upon us. We like the feeling of control. But you know, it's all an illusion. Life is precious and precarious, and it's always at risk of falling apart. We think the plans we've made for ourselves are better, but we can't be sure. I know it seems hopeless, but you don't know what good lies on the other side of all this."

Pete hated how optimistic he sounded. He didn't want Shae to experience it as toxic positivity. He was keenly aware of the pain that came when your life fell apart. But he had also experienced the beauty of a rebirth of life in all its surprises. This very outing was proof of that. Above all, he knew the journey of the heart and mind was personal and private. He couldn't force Shae to think differently. She'd have to decide for herself whether or not to have faith in the future.

Pete had his own decisions to worry about.

***

Pete had the playback speed at 3x, his eyes dry and itchy as he struggled to finish up the section on courtroom demeanor when his phone dinged. He'd been at the computer for hours and was ready for a distraction. He stood up and stretched, clicking open the email app on his phone.

Your records request is ready.

The subject line stood out in Pete's inbox like it had its own spotlight. It had taken over a week and Pete was beginning to think he'd never hear back on the records request. Pete reminded himself to be happy for the progress. He read the email and learned he'd have to go read through the records at city hall or pay 10 cents per page for printed copies, which would also mean waiting there while they printed.

He glanced out the window: still gray and rainy. The necessity of going in person to get something currently in an electronic format rankled his anti-bureaucracy ways but he resigned himself to the truth of the situation: he'd have to go back to the police station. Pete wanted to lie low for the time being. His best hope was that the building would be empty like last time when he got there. Pete didn't want to wait any longer to get these emails.

Pete had no such luck this time. Sheriff Carter was out in the main lobby talking to the city manager right as Pete walked in. Dave bellowed

Pete's name and came over for a back slap. "What brings you here, buddy?" Dave asked good-naturedly.

Pete opened his mouth to answer when the secretary inserted herself into the conversation, "He's the one with the record request." Her tone was dry and vaguely accusing. She peered at him over her readers, holding eye contact like it was her Olympic sport. Pete thought there should be some privacy around his request, though he was aware of the irony in wanting a sunshine law request to be private. He returned his gaze to Dave.

Dave's smile faded and a concerned look came over his face. "You're the one looking through our emails? What the hell for?"

He'd been told by Dave to drop Emily's case, so he'd have to come up with something. He should have thought of this before coming up here. "Oh, I'm trying to help Catherine with something." He affected a casual shrug. "She's having trouble with a neighbor, something about permits. I told her I would see what I could do."

It was the first thing Pete thought of that was semi-plausible while also being somewhat true: he *had* told Catherine he'd help her out. Plus he was name-dropping—he knew Catherine was a regular funder of the local police association. Pete figured this would buy him some goodwill from Dave and throw off any suspicion.

But Pete didn't get the reaction he was planning on. If anything, Dave's face was darker than before. "Catherine put you up to this? This lady has some nerve," Dave muttered to himself and shook his head.

Pete was confused but maintained a neutral face. "Oh, I wouldn't say she put me up to it or anything. I'm only trying to do a favor. You know, see if there might be any last-ditch efforts for her." Why would Dave be upset about Catherine? Pete was starting to wonder if Dave had issues with all women or just the two Pete had asked him about.

Even with that passing thought, Dave seemed to become a different person in front of Pete's eyes. Local legends about him started to seem less funny and more problematic. Pete stood a little taller, marking the full four inches he had over Carter.

Dave looked at Pete, narrowing his eyes. "You sure do a lot of research these days. What's the saying about curiosity and The Cat?" Dave gave a mirthless laugh.

Pete checked his watch to see his pulse at 57. Good. This was the second time Dave Carter had said something vaguely threatening and he wanted to be alert, not clouded by emotions as before.

Pete gave a slight smile and decided to test the waters, "Can't say I've heard that one. I know you and Catherine go back a ways, so I'm sure you'd like to help out, too. Can I come to you with any questions once I get through these emails?"

Dave gave a tight smile. "I can't imagine anything more pointless than reading about code enforcement, but knock yourself out. I've got a bunch of closed cases that need to be alphabetized too if you're looking for community service. Or a way to fall asleep at night." Another empty laugh from Dave.

Was it a reference to Emily's case or just a joke? Pete didn't want to overanalyze everything, but it was hard not to with the vibe Dave was putting out. Pete simply waited.

Breaking the awkward silence, Dave finally offered, "Not sure what help I would be, but by all means, you have my number." With that, Dave gave Pete a curt nod and headed back to his office, closing the door behind him.

Through the glass insert in the door, Pete saw Dave picking up the phone to make a call.

Meanwhile, the secretary had been watching the whole exchange as if binging her favorite show. If she had set out to start some drama, it had worked spectacularly.

Pete flashed his best magazine-cover smile, "Can you print those records for me, please? I need to get going. Here's a check. You can fill in the amount when we count the copies."

At this, she frowned. No doubt she was disappointed he wouldn't be staying around to read them, denying her the opportunity to stage any more chats with her boss. For today, her show would be ending on a cliffhanger. Secretary Standoffish pushed back from her desk with a huff and walked back to the printer.

A few minutes later, Pete had a sizeable stack of warm, freshly printed emails. "I love the smell of printer paper in the morning," he cracked to himself as he walked towards the sliding doors.

If Dave's reaction was any indication, Pete's instinct to ask about permits was at least getting close to something important. But what about Dave's reaction to Catherine? He took out his notebook and made a note to come back to that later. He needed to stay focused on the task at hand, which was now making sense of these emails. He put the papers in his satchel and headed up to Bitchin' Brews for a coffee to go. He had a feeling he'd need some caffeine to get through all this.

28

It was 10 a.m. but it looked like night. Main Street had been emptied except for a few shop owners making last-minute adjustments to the straps on their marquee signs and moving outdoor chairs inside. Most buildings were already shuttered, a few sporting plywood boards with graffiti messages like, 'C U Later AL E Gator,' and 'This too AL pass.'

Pete made it to Bitchin' Brews just in time. The winds were gaining speed and Erin was almost done closing down the cafe early to prep for the storm. Pete grabbed his coffee and Erin gave him a paper bag full of several slices of vegan chocolate chip pumpkin bread for free since they were going to get tossed. Pete hugged her, told her to be safe, and headed home.

As soon as Pete walked into his house, the rain pelted the metal roof. The metal always made the rain sound worse than it was, but there was no denying this was a downpour. He flipped on the local news and tried to sort through the drama for an actual forecast of the storm. It was too early for semi-famed meteorologist Rick Precano, the gem in the news station's crown. Clips from his hurricane reporting were guaranteed to go viral due to his blend of wild gesticulation, dry humor, and highly accurate reporting. The station would wait to show their Ace until the storm was closer.

For now, Pete was stuck with the bit reporters. From what he gathered from the montage of reporters anxiously reporting from various beach spots and the angry red radar on the screen, Hurricane Al would hit with the most force around one in the morning. As much as Pete was dying to get to his coffee and the emails, he figured he should put up the hurricane shutters now while it was still possible.

Twenty minutes later, the house was eerily quiet and would be pitch black if not for the warm overhead lighting. Pete hated the claustrophobic feeling of being in the house with the shutters up, which might explain why he always procrastinated putting them up until the very last minute. He still wasn't used to riding out storms alone. He'd been through plenty of storms growing up, but he was always with his family. They'd play cards or board games and they were some of his best memories. One highly competitive game of Uno was still discussed at every family gathering to this day. Pete had stacked three skips in a row and triumphantly shouted, "UNO!" dancing The Dougie while both Thomas and Becky cried.

He must have known in theory that they were in danger, but his parents never let on because he'd never felt safer than he did tucked away from the world with his family. Later, he had traveled so much that he missed most of the storms. But now that he was well settled in his home, he had to ride out the smaller storms alone. He'd leave for the big ones—he wasn't crazy. But for the smaller ones, the hassle of getting in and out of the island over one of the bridges felt more dangerous than staying in his concrete home with all the latest hurricane updates. It could mean being cut off from services on the other side of the bridge, but that was part of the risk of life in Florida. Pete was prepared to 'hunker down.' The 'news' was showing a few kooks out trying to catch some waves in the ocean; Pete shook his head and turned it off. At least he had what he hoped was some interesting reading to keep him preoccupied.

He pulled out the giant stack of papers, feeling intimidated by the task of making sense of it all. He wondered if it might be like finding a needle in a haystack. Not like he had anywhere else to be, he sighed. After the first five emails, he realized he was in for trouble. They had the word *permit*, as in to allow. What a waste of time and money if this was going to be the case for the rest. Pete was discouraged, but plugged along. He decided to sort them into the verb and the noun *permit* instead of reading each email in full. Once he had sorted them, for better or for worse the *noun* permit pile was much smaller.

Pete realized he was hungry, so got up to make a quick salad and to check in on the storm. He sat on the couch, watching a young red-headed reporter (maybe an intern) struggle to take 30 seconds worth of news (a traffic light was already out) and drag it out into 15 minutes of coverage. Her wet hair was plastered along her face, and the hood of the rain jacket pulled tightly around it. Pete doubted this was the glamorous journalism life she'd had in mind.

These reporters had to keep the urgency mode on for another 10 hours minimum, but it was always tough in the beginning before the power was out and when it was only a few little branches blowing around. Pete raised his eyebrows as his lights gave a quick flicker. He wasn't too worried; he'd had a whole-house generator installed. Pete got caught up in the reporting when he realized over an hour had gone by. He should get back to the emails. He washed his dish and made his way over to the emails sitting on the coffee table when the house went pitch black.

"What the hell?" Pete tried to quell the panic as he waited for the generator to turn on. It had always been instantaneous in the past, but a full minute had now gone by as Pete sat in complete pitch black. Pete didn't even have a flashlight nearby; he'd been so dependent on the generator that he hadn't thought to prepare with a candle or a flashlight. Pete took a small step forward that reminded him of the 'stingray shuffle' he'd learned in St. Lucia. It was amazing how foreign your home—so familiar in the light—became when you couldn't see what was in front of you. After an agonizingly long time and a minor stubbed toe, Pete made his way over to the coffee table where he had left his cell phone. Pete shook the phone until the flashlight came on and headed out to the side of the house through the garage. He found his black Maglite and ventured out of the house to check on the generator.

Already, his palm trees were whipping wildly and the rain was pelting the house sideways. All the streetlights were now out, but the green-gray sky of the storm was still bright to Pete's eyes after being in the dark house. Pete shined his light on the generator case and read the error code: 'Battery too low.' "Are you kidding me?" Pete muttered in irritation. The generator was operated by a car battery and Pete had been so caught up in this whole PI thing that he hadn't bothered to check if the battery was working.

Thankfully, Pete had flipped so many cars that he had the equivalent of a small auto store in his garage. He found a new battery and a giant umbrella. He didn't love the idea of being outside in a hurricane with an umbrella like a human lightning rod but he also didn't love the idea of the rain pouring inside his $20,000 generator. Staying inside without the generator working didn't make it to the list of things he loved.

The panel was held in place by two screws, hard to get to from the small space between the generator and the hedges. It was only five minutes working at removing them but he was soaked and his umbrella had turned inside out. He knew he would likely have a massive crick in his neck from bending at such an awkward angle as he tried to get the battery in while keeping the generator dry. He ran back into the garage and flipped the reset switch. Pete saw the glorious green light. The choir of angels must have joined in as Pete yelled, "Hallelujah!" as the power kicked back on.

Back inside, after a hot shower and change of clothes, Pete finally sat down to finish the emails. Lots of boring reading after his burst of generator excitement, but Pete tried to focus. Suddenly, his attention and interest were piqued. An email about permits from Dave Carter read:

'Yes, code violations are generally under the purview of the city manager as they manage permits. However, if necessary, our office has the authority to become involved. Sounds like this might be a situation where it's necessary.'

A code violation the Sheriff felt warranted his involvement? Interesting. But what was more interesting to Pete was the recipient of the email: it was redacted.

Why would it be redacted? Pete flipped through and found a few other emails between Dave and this redacted and therefore anonymous person. He noticed the name was a specific length, but that wasn't much to go on. Pete wracked his brain, trying to figure out why these otherwise innocuous emails would be redacted. That's when it hit Pete: the other person wasn't part of the Florida government. If they were, they'd be part of the sunshine request. So, why was Dave emailing a civilian about getting the police involved with permits?

Pete stretched out on the couch to consider this question but with the lulling sound of the rain, he was fast asleep within minutes.

Pete rolled over, blinking and trying to make sense of where in the world he was. After a few blinks, his memory came into focus and he remembered he had fallen asleep during the storm. Without a view of the outside, he had no clue what time it was. He grabbed his phone. It was 6 a.m. and the storm had passed.

The alert at the top of his screen read, '*@trackamurder has made landfall in Florida but will be grounded until further notice due to Hurricane Al.*' The location was tagged at the major airport about an hour and a half away. Pete knew access to the island would be closed until officials inspected the bridges and storm damage. But a quick news search showed the storm had been fairly minor as far as damage was concerned. It wouldn't be long before the hosts of *Track a Murder* would be on his island and on his heels. Pete was running out of time. He needed to figure out what had happened before the hosts created their own justicetainment version of the facts. He went to the kitchen to splash water on his face and sat back down to make his plan of action.

Dry food rations and papers covered the island in his kitchen. Pete had spent most of the night trying to figure out how to find out who Dave had been emailing until the internet finally went out. He'd used the data plan on his phone to finally discover that his PI license would get him access to some research databases where he would be able to upload emails and supposedly get contact information on all the parties. There were several websites out there but Pete settled on the 'Spy Guy' website for no other reason than that he liked the name best. Pete hoped it was legit and not some kind of dark web sorta thing; he was running out of time and options.

Pete wanted to get Sarg ready for a trip to the Swamps, but he knew he needed to buckle down and get this course finished. First, he rolled up his shutters so as not to spend another second in his coffin house. As he walked back in through the garage, he sensed Sarg using his headlights to give Pete puppy dog eyes. It would likely be an entire year before another storm made landfall on the island. Pete was very, very tempted to jump in his truck. But then he remembered the Benson story and the haunting aftermath. Pete needed to focus.

Two hours later, Pete had finished the last of the courses and taken his test. It would be electronically submitted to the Florida Department of Professional Licensing and the license would come in the mail. All there was for Pete to do now was to wait. Pete thought back to Alexander's fourth commandment. He did have to wait on the emails, but maybe there were other things he could do in the meantime. He was stuck inside and he couldn't talk to anybody because everyone else would be trapped at home with hurricane cleanup, too. Who was available 24/7? Twitter.

Pete wanted to know more about this mystery poster who seemed to think (or know for sure?) Emily's death was a murder. He opened the app and searched for @bugcatcher. Not much was in the bio: a quote from Hitchhiker's Guide to the Galaxy and the avatar was a sepia-toned picture of Albert Einstein. Location was the Golden State.

Pete scanned the tweets. Most were about Emily, but Pete kept clicking *load more* until he hit the tweets just before Emily's death. They were sparser then, primarily arguing about the merits of various sports teams. A few retweets from @theworldofengineering. Pete was struggling to find a through-line from those earlier tweets and the person so actively blasting the island's handling of Emily's death.

Pete copied and pasted the @bugcatcher into Google and an Instagram account came up. Same bio as Twitter, so not a particularly creative person, Pete guessed. It was a private account, so Pete wasn't able to see any posts, but he saw it was only following one account: Emily Larson.

Pete clicked over to see that Emily was not following this person back. He was about to give up in frustration when he decided to Google one more time. This time, he searched and then clicked images instead of the web. Bingo! A cached picture of Emily and a guy with the caption:

'*"Never go on trips with anyone you do not love."*

– Ernest Hemingway

Love you Marc!'

Pete clicked on the picture and was taken to the login screen for Facebook. Pete would need the full name to see the original post. He skimmed Emily's Instagram again to make sure—no photos of this guy. So Pete had a new suspect on the list: Marc, possibly an ex-boyfriend. Marc, who Pete was guessing was an engineer, and very interested in saying Emily was murdered. Pete had a lot of questions about this guy, not the least of which was why he was so sure Emily was murdered and why he was keeping his identity private. Maybe he wanted to be caught?

The pressure of @trackamurder filled Pete with new boldness. He sent a DM to @bugcatcher: 'You seem to know a lot about Emily Larson. Can we talk?'

Pete was surprised to get an almost instantaneous reply.

'I've already told you I'm not looking to help you scumbags make a profit off my girlfriend's death. Go to hell. You keep making new accounts and I'll keep blocking.'

Girlfriend, not ex? Interesting. Also, Pete had clearly not been the first to reach out. He responded quickly, hoping it would be received before Marc had blocked him. Pete's mind raced for words that might catch Marc's attention. 'No profit. I'm a friend of Sam's and interested in helping.'

It wasn't strictly true, but he and Sam had been friendly enough that it wasn't a lie. He was guessing Marc must know about Sam if he'd been dating Emily. Five minutes ticked by. Pete sighed. Marc had probably blocked Pete before even reading the message. Oh well.

'Who are you?'

Pete cheered out loud when the message came in. It felt like winning the first heat. 'My name is Pete. I think you might be right that Emily didn't accidentally drown and I want to help.'

'What's in it for you?'

'My best friend is Shae Brunell and she is taking a lot of heat. So is my hometown. I think finding out the truth would be best for everyone. Plus, *Track a Murder* is on the way here.'

'I know. I thought you were another one of their producers. Okay, can you talk later? After 5? At work.'

Pete glanced at the clock. It was 7 a.m., too early for work. But then Pete remembered Marc was in California. He'd have to wait until about 8 p.m. his time to talk to him. He'd take the call at midnight if he had to. Pete confirmed and they set a time and exchanged numbers. More progress and yet still none at all. Pete went back to his list to see what was next. Pete took a breath, but he was done avoiding.

He sent a text: 'We need to talk.'

29

Despite his fear, Pete and Shae decided to meet out on the island again. Pete figured it had the benefit of being a familiar space while also giving him the chance to take another look around. Maybe the storm would turn up something new.

"Thanks for meeting me out here. How are you doing?" Pete wanted to establish some safety before getting to the hard questions.

Shae shrugged and that said enough. *Alive, but barely.* Pete nodded in understanding and moved on. "Shae, I think we need to talk about why you moved the body."

Shae started crying. "I've been asking myself the same thing over and over again. Like, how was I capable of something so awful? What kind of monster moves a dead body?"

Pete wanted to comfort her, but he also needed to let the moment be uncomfortable to make space for some answers.

"I also need to be sure she was dead when you found her. It's not that I doubt you but you need to be realistic about how it looks. Did you know *Track a Murder* is on its way?" Pete hoped he wasn't the breaker of bad news but the tense jaw and deep crease between her eyebrows confirmed she didn't know.

"What?" Shae jumped up in a panic, spraying sand behind her. "Oh my God, Pete. They're going to pin it on me and I'm going to go to prison." She bent over as if catching her breath after a run.

"They can't pin it on you if we can come up with some logical answers first. So we need to stay calm and think. I'm working on a few other things right now, but I also really need your help."

"Believe me, I know how it looks. First, we had the stupid argument on Instagram and everyone is reposting my comments out of context. Then Emily signed a brand deal with my competitor." She picked up a shell and threw it back down with force. "Then she shows up dead in a spot only I know about. It doesn't look good." Her face was grim.

Pete remembered the Instagram argument and then listened as Shae explained about how Glow Your Boat Tours had supposedly signed a brand deal with Emily before she died.

"It looks like a motive. And then I have the stupid ice cooler and gloves. And of course, I have no alibi because I was out here prepping for the tour. It looks bad, Pete. That's why we have to figure out the truth." Shae had stopped crying but her voice was hoarse.

"I know we already did this, but I think we need to walk through that night and search the island again. Can you think of any other details we might have missed?"

Shae stared up as if searching her brain. "She was lying over by there," Shae motioned to a tree near the site of the bonfire. "Her body was wet and she was curled up in a ball, like she had gone to sleep. I thought she was asleep at first. I had to unfold her to drag the body." Shae closed her eyes and put her head in her hands.

Pete needed Shae to stay with him. "Think back—did she have any marks on her?"

Shae nodded. "She had some scratches on her arms and legs. I think they were from the barnacles on the tree roots. So, I think she came in from the main canal," Shae motioned to the hidden entrance. "And she had some pink marks on her neck, but they didn't look like scratches. Like a bruise before it becomes a bruise."

"The bruise in the picture," Pete said, more to himself. "Did you see any kind of boat or paddleboard?" Pete wanted to know how Emily had made it to the island from the main canal. Someone could swim there from one of the houses, but why?

Shae shook her head. "No, nothing. And she was wearing a dress of some sort, so I don't think she was out swimming or anything." Shae paused as if searching her memory. "Her mascara was running, too. A girl doesn't put on mascara if she's planning on swimming."

Pete hadn't thought of that. So, Emily had likely been out on the main canal but wasn't planning on swimming. Pete felt it made it more likely that she had been in a motorboat versus something like a kayak, but he didn't have enough evidence to be sure yet. Questions about why she'd been in a boat and with whom flooded his brain. But first Pete needed to hear the rest, the part that made him feel sick.

"So, what did you do when you found her?" he asked quietly.

He could tell Shae was ashamed to tell the rest but was resigned to the fact that it was necessary.

"Well..." She paused. "I checked her pulse even though it was pretty clear she was dead. Then I was afraid, like what if someone had killed her and they were still there? So I sort of checked the island but I didn't see anyone. I guess I assumed she drowned or something. By then, I realized I was running behind schedule for the tour and I think that's when I panicked." Shae paused to look at the spot where Emily had died. A full breath and then Shae squared her shoulders. "I knew if I took her back in the boat, I would have to cancel the tour. And I'd have to paddle the whole way back with her basically in my lap because it's a one-seater. I got freaked out at that point and kind of shut down. So, I dragged her through the little clearing to the river side of the island. I was going to skip the part of the tour where we do a bonfire and call when I got back. I must have put her too close to the shoreline. Maybe the water rose. I don't know." Shae had rushed through the entire statement and now her jaw hung loosely, her lips slightly apart. The words had been said aloud and couldn't be taken back.

Pete would have to deal with his feelings about it later. He maintained a business-like tone. "Did you see any signs of alcohol? Bottles or cans or anything?" Pete was thinking back to Sam's comment about Emily being drunk.

Shae looked at him questioningly but searched her memory. "No, nothing like that at all. I saw her...her body...and nothing else."

They both knew the rest of the story, as did the entire internet. There wasn't much else to say. There would be no way to spin that part but it didn't warrant Shae going to prison for murder. They needed to figure out if Emily had left any clues behind that night. Pete was still struggling to make sense of Shae's actions, but they needed to move on and he said as much. "Okay. It could be worse."

She was visibly relieved. "What next, boss?"

Pete had an idea. He pulled up the photo where Emily had posted the word 'help.' After several minutes of trying to find the exact tree, they used the paddles and sticks to sift through the sand. They'd been in such a hurry last time that they hadn't dug very deep in this spot. They marked a wide circle around the tree and began their search. But 10 minutes in and they hadn't found anything. Pete struggled to hide his disappointment: another bust.

Just as they decided to move on, something caught Pete's eye. A little glitter of something was sticking out. Pete moved his fingers in the sand and pulled out a gold bracelet. The clasp was broken and it looked like maybe it had once contained some kind of stone that had since fallen out. Maybe it had fallen off Emily's wrist? Or was it from years ago and only a coincidence it was at the base of the tree where Emily had called for help? Maybe it didn't belong to Emily but instead to one of Shae's guests over the years. Pete tucked it in the pocket of his baggies; he wouldn't be finding out the answer now. But it was at least a good question.

They searched the island for another hour but didn't find anything else. "This is the first time I'm annoyed with myself that I'm so strict about picking up litter! I'm not finding anything," Shae said.

Pete had to agree, the island was spotless except for the bracelet. Pete craned his neck for a visual sweep of the island and then shrugged toward the boats. He hoped the bracelet would be helpful because they weren't going to find anything else on this trip.

***

"Hey man, listen. Thanks for getting on a call with me," Pete said as Marc answered the phone. "We're all on the same side here."

"If I'm going to be stuck in LA traffic, might as well make the most of it." Marc's voice sounded tinny through his car's Bluetooth speaker and more than a little guarded. "So, can you tell me again why you're doing this? You're a cop, right?"

How should Pete answer? He didn't want to seem like a CSI wannabe or a creep, so he went with the partial truth: "Something like that. I'm actually a private investigator. My client is Shae Brunell, owner of Island Guy Tours. As you probably know, she's taking a lot of heat online. We thought if we answered some of the false accusations with truth, people would back off. But the reality is, you raised some questions I'm having a hard time answering."

"Well, yeah, that's because the whole thing is bullshit. It's like they put the Mayberry police on this thing." Marc's California condescension was thick over the phone.

Pete felt defensive of his hometown but he couldn't argue that the police had done the best job. "That might be true but what makes you think it's murder? And why post it online?"

"I think I've put everything out there I could find. I figured if I made it public, the police would have to deal with it but clearly, that's not the case. The main thing is Emily was a very strong swimmer. Seems highly unlikely she'd drown in a few feet of freshwater," Marc said.

Pete fought the urge to correct him that it was brackish water. *Listen, don't speak.* "What about if she was drunk?" Pete thought back to Sam's comment about the police saying Emily had been drunk.

"I mean, sure, anything is a possibility. But Emily was very health-conscious and rarely drank alcohol. I don't think I ever saw her drink to the point of drunkenness." Marc sounded unconvinced but it wasn't enough to rule out the possibility alcohol contributed to Emily's death. "I don't know what else to say. Maybe I should go."

"If there's more, it's going to come out when *Track a Murder* starts looking, so might as well tell me now." Pete had no time to be equivocal.

Marc sighed. "It's not like it's a secret or anything, I haven't made it public knowledge. But I was in Florida the night they found Emily." His tone was guarded nearly to the point of aggression.

"So, you were here on business or..." Pete waited for Marc to explain.

"Sort of. I had a work trip to Florida, and so I decided to surprise Emily," Marc said.

"You decided to surprise your ex? Isn't that usually classified as stalking?" Pete was not getting a good feeling.

"Emily kept in touch with me. And she sounded lonely there in Florida, so I was worried about her. So, yeah. I figured I would stop by and see if we could hang out. I'm not going to lie—I hoped we would get back together, but my primary reason was to make sure she was doing okay." Marc was defensive.

"Did you guys get together?

There was a long pause before Marc responded. "No. She said she had a date." Another long pause came as the words sat heavy in the air.

"So, you flew down to 'surprise' your ex-girlfriend, found out she had a date with someone else, and then she was found dead." Pete let the words speak for themselves.

Marc let out a long sigh. "Look, I get it. It doesn't sound good. And everyone knows the ex-boyfriend is the first place to look. But the cops there—they didn't bother to talk to me. They have no idea I was even in Florida because they didn't bother to investigate this at all. So that's why I started posting. I know it puts me at risk, but finding out the truth about Emily is more important." Marc was indignant by the end of this statement.

Pete had to respect Marc's choice. It would be a genius way to throw Pete off, but then again, Marc didn't know about Pete when he first started posting. It didn't make any sense for someone to commit a murder and then bring attention to it when it was a closed case, so Pete had to move forward with the working assumption Marc was innocent. Pete was unhappy to hear once again the police hadn't done any kind of investigation, however.

The noise of the California freeway filled the line as Pete was processing. "Okay, I can respect that. So, do you have any ideas?" Pete finally responded.

"I know this will only add to the jealous ex-shtick, but I do think we need to find the guy who took her on a date. If nothing else, he might have been the last one to see her alive."

Pete nodded as though Marc was able to see him. "Good thinking. I'll see if I can find anything here locally and maybe you can reach out to some of her friends to see if they know anything?"

Marc agreed. "But let's be quick about it. Those *Track a Murder* leeches have been hounding me for weeks now and I can only keep them off for so long. No doubt they're gonna start plastering my face all over and putting this on me."

"We agree we need to move quickly and stay one step ahead of *Track a Murder*. So, let's keep in touch often, okay? This is my cell and you can call me or text me if you find anything and I'll do the same." Pete wasn't sure how they'd stay one step ahead of them, but he'd figure it out.

"Sounds like a plan. Look, thank you for reaching out. This means a lot to me and I think it would mean a lot to Emily." Marc's voice cracked at her name.

"It's best for all of us to find out the truth. Thanks for being open to talking to me." Pete said his goodbyes and they hung up.

30

'Please display conspicuously,' read Pete's Class CC Private Investigator license. "Right on," Pete said, smiling to himself. He had expected something more like his degree, not a tri-fold business letter. He tried to smooth out the folded paper as he walked into his office. He taped the permit up in between his favorite *Surfer* magazine cover and the *US Weekly* cover. The legal studies degree was still in a box somewhere; maybe he'd finally frame it and hang it next to the license.

But more exciting than thinking about redecorating his office was the fact that Pete could finally give Spy Guy the green light on decoding the redacted emails. Pete snapped a picture of the license and emailed his contact, Nikolai. Pete glanced at his phone; Nikolai was seven hours ahead, so it was pretty late there. The turnaround time was two days. Given it was Wednesday night there, Pete realized he probably wouldn't get an answer until Monday. Bummer. It frustrated Pete how it all seemed so hurry up and wait, but there wasn't much else to do at the moment.

Pete remembered how he'd had Frosted Flakes for dinner because his fridge was empty and decided to hit the store. It used to drive Jenna crazy when they lived together—how Pete would get so caught up in a project or in working on a new move he'd forget to shop or clean. His family of origin had become used to it, so Pete sort of took it as normal but Jenna would start in about how they both had a lot going on and it wasn't fair to stick her with all the domestic crap. What had she called it—the invisible mental load?

He'd been offended at the time, feeling like she was calling him a chauvinist when he believed he'd always been a supporter of women's equality. He'd argued instead of listening to what she was trying to tell him. Pete felt bad now; Jenna had been right. Pete had a tendency to be hyper-focused to the exclusion of the people he loved. Jenna took it to mean he thought his career was more important, but that wasn't it at all; Pete tuned everything else out. Pete had a lot of respect for Jenna and her career. She was—is—a hell of a surfer and he always knew she'd get her own yellow jersey. He wished he'd made it clearer when they were still together. Maybe he'd reach out to say sorry, at least.

For now, though, food. Pete headed out to the local supermarket. Pete never took a list; he ate mostly the same thing for breakfast and lunch. For dinners, he would stop by for whatever meat or seafood looked best that week. Pete was admiring the red snapper when Sam stopped her cart behind him. "We must be on the same schedule or something."

Pete gave a smile. "It must be the run-completely-out-of-food-and-scramble schedule."

Sam laughed loudly. "Actually, yes, then we are on *exactly* the same schedule!"

She had light skin and dark chestnut hair. Pete noticed how pretty Sam was. He hadn't noticed before because she was so different-looking from most of the women he thought of as pretty. But in this light, she was really something. She should be thought of as beautiful, not pretty he realized. And then, realizing he was looking at her too long, he asked, "How have you been?" Pete never asked the question lightly, and he wasn't asking it lightly of a woman who had lost her best friend.

Sam sighed and ran her hands through her hair. "I'm okay. I'm trying to get everything ready before heading back to Rhode Island for a bit. I'm like the opposite of a snowbird." She laughed her musical laugh and for a second, Pete wished he was a stand-up comedian.

"Where at in Rhode Island?" Pete was desperate to keep the conversation going.

"Just outside of Narragansett. You know it?" Sam winked. Narragansett Beach was the Mecca of the Northeast.

"Ahh, great spot. Maybe I can say hello next time I'm out there." Pete smiled.

"Uh yeah, maybe." Sam pushed a strand out of her eyes and her face was unreadable. "Anyway, I'm trying to get everything wrapped up here, but your friend is not making it easy on me." A dark look passed over her face.

"Shae is in a tough spot. She didn't do anything to cause this." Pete said. He was still analyzing the look on Sam's face and his words came out defensive.

"Who's Shae?" Sam gave a teasing smile. "I'm talking about Mizz Catherine Mellon." The last part dragged out in an imitation of the British aristocracy.

Pete didn't want to get in the middle of the Catherine-Sam situation. He was growing to like Sam but Catherine was a local and his loyalties were divided. He cleared his throat and gave a noncommittal nod while trying to change the subject. "Uh, can I ask you something? It's a difficult topic and I hate to hit you with it here in the middle of the grocery store but since you're leaving..." Pete's voice trailed off.

Sam looked a little alarmed, but then the tired look of someone who's had to face an unfair amount of difficulty settled on her face. She nodded for Pete to go on.

"I was just wondering. How did you know Emily was drunk that night?"

Sam looked surprised and had to think for a minute. Her face grew dark again. "Catherine told me. And not kindly, might I add. She was lecturing me about what a nasty person I was and that I was going to ruin the neighborhood by having a lot of party-goers at my house, like Emily. Said it was a family neighborhood. That bad accidents like that are bound to happen when people are drunk at my place. So, you know, basically blaming me for my best friend drowning."

"What a crappy way to find out," Pete said. He hoped Sam was exaggerating about how Catherine had talked to her but he wasn't so sure. Pete thought back to how Catherine had yelled at his dad after William's funeral, something about the flowers being wrong. He'd chalked it up to grief, but he hadn't been all that shocked by her behavior. There'd been stories. "So, you didn't talk to her that night?" Pete was trying to both clarify and change the subject.

Sam shook her head miserably. "I didn't even get to say goodbye. I don't know what she was thinking, getting drunk and going out in the water. She knew better than that!"

He shook his head as if in commiseration. "It's hard to watch someone you love struggle with alcohol."

He got the reaction he both wanted and didn't want: Sam looked at him in shock. "Oh, it wasn't like that. Emily rarely drank. That's what was the most frustrating part. Of all times to get drunk." Pete's heart almost broke at how sad her face was.

Sam seemed to sincerely think Emily's death was accidental. Pete hated to push on the wound, but he might not get another chance to talk to Sam. "What about Emily's ex? Marc? Any thoughts on him?"

Sam's face indicated slight surprise at the subject change but gave a slight shake to her head to clear her thoughts and keep up. "I never met him. I mean, Emily kind of made him out to be a stalker when they broke up, but honestly, she always thought guys were obsessed with her." Sam gave a light laugh. "And they probably were. She was beautiful and also very charismatic. So, yeah, guys tended to have a hard time letting go. But I was a little surprised when she dumped him because I thought she was happy with him. It sounded like it was getting serious. Though, thinking about it, that's probably exactly why she broke up with him. Not that I'm knocking her or anything. We're young and she wasn't ready to be settled down. I totally get it. I'm just saying."

They strolled their carts towards the produce section as an instrumental version of Blink-182 played on the overhead. Sam grabbed a papaya and moved to put it in her cart before Pete placed his hand gently on her arm. Electricity flooded his body and he quickly moved his hand.

"You want one with more yellow." He picked a papaya out of the bin and applied a slight pressure to the skin. "See how this one has a slight give? That's what you're looking for." He handed it to Sam.

She squeezed it lightly and gave an impressed nod to Pete, "Thanks for the tip."

"I grow them in my backyard if you ever want to—" Pete caught himself. "I grow them, so I know a lot about them."

Again, Pete struggled to read Sam's expression. Was it disappointment? He tried to focus on the conversation they'd been having before the explosion in his nerves.

"So, you didn't have any concerns about him or anything?" Again, Pete tried to clarify. If he was going to share any information with Marc in the future, he wanted to get a better feel on the guy.

Now Sam narrowed her eyes at Pete, possibly trying to figure out where this was coming from. She opened her mouth to say something but then closed it. She thought another moment more. "Like I said, I never met him. But from what Emily said about him, he sounded like a decent guy who treated her well when they were together."

"And after they split?"

Sam gave a slight frown as she tried to understand his questioning now. "If he said or did anything after they split, she never said anything to me. All I heard was he said he was willing to give her space and that he loved her." Sam shrugged. "Now it's my turn for a question. Why are you asking all of this?"

Pete debated sharing the truth but decided against it. He feigned a pitiful face. "I'm sorry. I'm kind of a *Track a Murder* superfan. I think I got a little caught up that they're coming here." Pete had to keep himself from puking after those words.

Clearly, Sam felt the same and he watched her entire opinion of him change in a millisecond. He was surprised at how desperate he was to regain her good opinion. She shook her head. "Can't say I'm a fan at all. I don't respect people who make entertainment out of other people's misery." Her words were pointed.

Pete didn't have to fake contrition. He felt awful lying to Sam and causing her more pain. "I'm sorry. That was insensitive of me. I hope you have a safe trip home."

Sam once again looked ready to say something but appeared to change her mind. "Take care of yourself, Pete." It was clear Sam was done with him. She turned and walked to the front of the store.

Pete thought about calling after her to ask for her number but decided against it after feeling the cold sting of her tone. Maybe in another lifetime. He walked back to the fishmonger and said, "I'll take the snapper."

31

Pete was in the middle of pan-searing the snapper when his phone dinged. 'Files are ready,' was the message from Nikolai at Spy Guy.

"Damn, that was fast," Pete muttered. He couldn't believe it was done in one day. Now, that was service. Pete was dying to read the results but he didn't want to overcook the fish. He finished up and did his best not to rush through eating his delicious Brown Butter and Herbs Red Snapper with grilled asparagus. It had won him first place at Bravo's Celebrity Cookoff two years earlier.

After thoroughly enjoying his meal and washing his single dish, Pete was ready to read through the emails. He had no idea what Nikolai's methods were but miraculously there it was: all of the email information was now visible.

The first email was between someone named Joe Kelly at Tropical Resorts and Dave Carter. Tropical Resorts was a huge international chain with a lot of skyrise hotels in Miami and some other smaller Florida cities like Daytona and Panama Beach. But they didn't have any properties on the island. As far as Pete knew, all of their resorts were well-above Beach Island's strict height restrictions. Joe was asking Dave about a police report on a code violation; Pete would have to see if he could get any records on the specific violation. Joe Kelly wrote that he was 'concerned' about the implications. Pete did a quick Google search and saw Joe was a VP of Legal based in Manhattan. Why would a VP of Legal in Manhattan be emailing a small town Sheriff about a code violation where they had no resorts?

The next email was from Brody Jackson. Pete was under the impression emails to and from commissioners would have fallen under the sunshine request, so Pete was surprised his was redacted. Maybe because Brody was sending from his business email at his brokerage and it got flagged as private? But still, Brody's name was well-known and it was hard to imagine the secretary wouldn't have known Brody was a city commissioner. Pete moved on to the content. *Huh.* Pete double-checked the last email to be sure. Brody had emailed Dave about the exact same code violation, asking if any progress had been made. What progress was to be made?

Pete skimmed the others. Nothing too interesting, a lot of people complaining to the Sheriff about how unfair the code enforcers had been and how they should go to jail. Or people wanting to press charges for the neighbor's 'criminally ugly' new roof. Another claiming a local shop owner had threatened her over a new sign she had installed, even though she had the correct permit. Apparently, the lady had said the sign was as ugly as this woman's face and both should be taken down. A bit of humor in Pete's day, but not too relevant from what he saw.

The emails from Joe and Brody were interesting, though Pete wasn't sure what the connection was. Emily was from California. He'd have to double-check, but Pete didn't remember seeing any brand deals with Tropical Resorts—that would have been a huge promotion for her, so Pete thought he'd remember. Emily didn't live here, so he also couldn't see how she'd be connected to a local code violation. It was interesting, but ultimately a bust. Oh well.

Pete looked at his original list of things to follow up on. He'd worked through most of his list and didn't feel he'd learned anything new. This was harder than he expected and Pete felt dejected. He remembered he had the date to try and track down, assuming Emily had gone out with someone. He also wanted to swing by Luke's place to see if Luke could tell him anything about the bracelet he had found. Pete's phone rang as he worked through his list. He didn't recognize the number and let it go to voicemail; the telemarketers were relentless these days. A few moments later, the transcribed voicemail showed up on his phone: it was Nate down at the station, hoping Pete would call him back. Pete didn't know how Nate had his number but rang him back right away.

"Hey Nate, it's Pete. Saw you called—what's up?" A cold fear gripped Pete; please don't let it be about my parents.

"Thanks for calling me back. Hang on a second while I walk outside." Pete heard the phone shuffling. Pete was still holding his breath. "Okay," said Nate. "I heard you were up here the other day, getting some records. So, you're doing the Sunshine thing?"

Pete's heart started beating again: nothing had happened to his parents. "Uh yeah, I did. And I just got my class CC license."

It sounded like Nate was relieved by his sigh. "Okay, cool. You didn't hear this from me, but I think we could use your help. I feel like the shit's about to hit the fan."

"I'm happy to do what I can." Pete was interested now that he was breathing again.

"Some reporters or something are doing a lot of digging around in the Larson case. And to be honest, it isn't looking good. The ex-boyfriend was in town and we didn't even know, let alone talk to him. Sounds like he might have been harassing the girl or something. They are going to run with that. Dave is having a shit fit but we don't have anything else."

It had to be the *Track a Murder* team. Just as Marc had said, they were going for the low-hanging fruit of the ex. It would be sensational, and since he had no alibi, pretty easy to blow up. It wouldn't matter if Marc was eventually found innocent: they'd blast his name everywhere and ruin his life. They claimed their show was about justice. It was really about telling an interesting story that would keep people hooked for five podcast episodes at a time. Pete felt sick. He'd need to give Marc a heads-up, though he guessed Marc already knew.

"I don't understand what you think I can do. If you guys haven't found anything, I'm pretty sure I won't." Pete was pacing the room.

The line was silent for so long Pete thought they had been disconnected. "Let's just say I'm not sure how hard we looked." Nate let the silence sit before adding, "Plus, you're the smartest dude I've ever met. Can you see if you can find anything?"

Pete agreed, not only for Nate but for Shae and Marc. And for Sam. Oh, and of course for Emily he added on in his mind guiltily. Pete hadn't even had his license for a week and he was now being asked by the police to help with an investigation. Pete turned his hat around and grabbed his keys. Shit just got real.

32

Pete went to the only place he thought to go when he was stuck. He'd texted his mom, Anna, to make sure his folks were home. She'd been ecstatic and insisted he come for dinner. His mom was of Italian heritage and loved nothing more than feeding her children. She'd made a giant pot of minestrone, which was Pete's favorite. Anna had her own competitive streak and her minestrone had won at the county fair for 15 years in a row. Everything his mom cooked was his favorite, but he loved her soups best of all.

"Who's this lucky lady?" Pete's dad asked as he walked out into the driveway. Pete laughed and shook his head. His dad walked around the driveway with an apprising look, nodding his head approvingly. "Very beautiful. So, what, what's her name? Where's this going?" Michael asked as he slapped the hood of a very rusty dull gray Hummer.

"Well, you know, found *him* on Facebook. So I'm gonna fix him up and flip him." Pete looked at Project Y and only saw the final vision in his mind's eye.

Pete's dad laughed. "You just can't stand to not have a project. So competitive, Petey. That is all from your mother, not me. It's good to see you. Come on in."

Pete walked into his childhood home; Pete's parents were creatures of habit and very little had changed in the almost 20 years since he had moved out. A Bob Dylan vinyl was even playing on the record player, the scent of sandalwood, sage, grapefruit, vanilla, and fig—the scents of each individual parent blending into a single unit—hung faintly in the air.

After fussing over him in the doorway for a few minutes, including pinching his hip bone and complaining he was too skinny, Anna returned to her soup in the kitchen. She was in there as so many other times throughout his childhood, singing Dean Martin with a glass of red wine while cooking. It was her happy place and he realized it was his too. Pete remembered how scared he had been when Nate called and walked in and gave her a big hug.

Her whole face glowed, "What was that for?"

"I love you, Mom." Pete smiled and walked back to the living room, where his dad was watching a documentary on mining.

He looked up at Pete with a smile and motioned for Pete to join him. After a little small talk about the neighbors and who had what damage from the storm, his dad crossed his arms as he did when he meant to get down to business. "So, how's everything with the friend?"

Pete appreciated how his dad hated small talk as much as he did. He thought about where to start. Pete hadn't even talked to his dad since deciding to get his PI license. He'd been so busy, as had Father Michael. Pete saw his parents more when he was busy touring because he'd made a point to come home for visits. It was terrible the way you could take family for granted when they only lived a few streets away. Pete made a mental note to visit more. Pete filled his dad in on the update of getting his PI license and on how *Track a Murder* was now in town.

His dad let out a slow whistle. "Wowza. That's a lot."

Pete hadn't even told his dad about Nate's call yet. He knew Nate likely meant it to be confidential, but this was one of the few perks of having a priest for a dad: they always kept your secrets, no matter how terrible.

Pete went on to explain the calls with Marc and Nate. "I feel out of my league, Dad. I was kind of doing this on a lark, like a favor or something. And now I might be responsible for someone's life? It feels like someone qualified should be doing this!"

"We don't get to pick the plan, God does. I mean, we can sometimes choose not to accept it but there's no reason to be afraid. God doesn't give us what we can't handle." Michael Brown appeared so confident in this, which Pete never understood. He couldn't begin to count the number of people his dad had buried as a priest, including children. It all seemed like more than someone should have to handle. But Pete wasn't here to argue theology—again.

His dad, sensing Pete's skepticism and looking to avoid a debate, continued, "Besides, you are a literal genius." Pete's parents never tired of reminding him of his IQ, no matter how uncomfortable it made him. "So, you are qualified. When you put your mind to something, I'd argue you're as qualified as anybody. Let's not forget you're a champion. That never goes away."

Pete had to stop from rolling his eyes; his parents thought he could do anything. He remembered the time he told his mom he had just returned from a run and she was convinced he should enter the Olympics for running. It was true Pete was good at a lot of stuff but they took it overboard. And he didn't feel like that guy anymore.

"Well, what do you think? Do you not think it was an accidental drowning as they reported? Do you think something else happened?" His dad asked the question Pete had been afraid to articulate for fear of needing to answer. He knew this was why he'd come to his dad: Michael was never afraid to ask the question, least of all when it came to finding out the truth.

Pete was quick and confident in his reply: "I don't think she drowned accidentally, no. At least, not the way they reported it. There are too many things that don't add up. And even if she did, they left too many stones unturned and I think someone should do her the justice of asking more questions." Damnit. Pete hated to know he felt so strongly about what he had just said.

His dad gave a knowing smile. "It sucks to have eyes to see. But be careful. If it wasn't accidental, either they were incompetent or someone had something to hide."

Pete hadn't thought about that. He noticed the knot in his stomach.

"An old military buddy of mine told me: 'A man who feels the need to tell the truth should always have his horse with a saddle outside.' Guess it's a Bedouin saying." His dad gave a short laugh, but Pete knew by the crease between his eyes that he was worried for him. He said, "Thursday is Eucharistic Adoration. I'll call in a favor."

Pete was about to reassure him, but he realized he couldn't be sure he was safe. He had never done anything like this.

Luckily, Anna came into the living room and called them to dinner. Pete's mom was no shrinking violet and had been through her share of challenges, but Pete still decided not to tell her about the license and the case. She was so full of joy and had enough stories of Pete's many nieces and nephews to fill the night with laughter that Pete decided to focus on being present. He'd have to save the worry for tomorrow.

33

Pete was stumped. He was inspired by his dad's words but inspiration wasn't going to cut it here. He needed some ideas of where to start. Suddenly, Pete realized he was urgently in need of putting a load of laundry in and rushed upstairs to his room. He took a lot of care in sorting colors, delicates, and whites. He had to get his anxiety under control.

Back in from the laundry room, Pete sat back down on the couch to think. He remembered his sister's birthday was coming up. He put in a call to Mary at Sea Grapes & Stems for a special order monstera; his sister had hopped on the latest plant craze. With that taken care of, he realized he was thirsty. He'd need to be hydrated to do any quality work. After a glass of coconut water, he realized he was now hungry. By the time he was done making and eating a turkey and avocado sandwich, he was due to put the next load of laundry in.

Pete tried to think of any other urgent chores to keep from the real task at hand but came up blank. Pete looked at his notebook again. He saw his notes on the permit emails. He should update Catherine. He felt bad that he had dropped the ball, even though she had more or less moved on. He'd feel better if he at least closed the loop on everything with the permits. He wasn't sure if the case in the emails was relevant, but figured he could at least ask. He shot over a text to Nate: 'Any chance you can tell me what case P6290 is about?'

Nate responded a few minutes later: 'Call me.'

Pete gave him a quick call.

"Hey man, I only have a few minutes." Pete heard the road noise through Nate's Bluetooth speaker. "I looked it up and it's a permit case. Looks like someone named Samantha Finnegan got a code violation and it got heated with the neighbor, none other than Catherine Mellon." Nate sucked his teeth. Catherine was beloved on the island, but no one wanted to mess with her either. "Kinda weird it's filed as a code violation case. Notes say it got violent so it should have been battery. Is this about the Larson case or..."

Pete was embarrassed to be caught avoiding working on the case. "No, just closing out something for a friend. Well, for Catherine to be honest." Pete was sheepish.

If Nate had judgment about Pete's lack of focus, he kept it to himself. "No worries. Hey, I'm running late to do a thing at the local high school. Talk to you later."

Pete was shocked. He hadn't thought of Sam as violent. Who would have a physical altercation with someone as old as Catherine? It disgusted him. She didn't seem so beautiful now. He thought back to their first interaction; she had been pretty rude, actually. Pete thought he was generally a good read of character: how did he overlook that she was capable of physical violence over something so ridiculous as a tiny house? He shook his head: the things people would do over money.

Suddenly, something clicked in Pete's brain. He ran to the counter to grab the emails and started frantically flipping through them. When he got to the one he was looking for, his blood ran cold.

It was from Brody Jackson to Sheriff Carter. The subject line referenced the case number and the body said, 'Thought you were handling this? Sounds like things got physical yesterday. We don't want any unnecessary attention on this or J might be out.' Although the meaning of the email took on a whole new tone now that Pete knew it was about Sam, it wasn't what had shocked him. It was the date: June 30.

Pete flipped open his notebook, using his finger to scan the notes. There it was. Sam had told Pete she had left for Rhode Island on June 29. Pete remembered because somehow it had come up that they shared a birthday and she said she celebrated by driving home from the airport to an empty house in Rhode Island. But there was no way she'd have been home in Rhode Island on June 29 if she was having an argument with Catherine on the island on June 30.

Why would she lie? Was she lying about being in Rhode Island the night of Emily's death? Was Sam capable of murder? Pete thought about how many of his 'friends' had turned against him when he became famous; jealousy can do crazy things to people. Plenty of people were comfortable hating on influencers—was it tough to be the best friend of one?

Pete was looking for more notes on Sam in the notebook when a page caught his attention. He remembered one of the case studies in Detective Alexander's course where Alexander had subpoenaed the body cam footage of an officer in a domestic dispute. If Pete secured the footage and proved Sam wasn't out of town, that might be a motive to investigate her further. In the meantime, he would also see what else he could dig up on her.

Pete was bummed to learn this about Sam, but he had to admit it was all kind of thrilling. He was pretty stoked that he had stumbled across this, even if it was because he was goofing off. He felt encouraged by this development. Like he was winning again.

34

Emily was enjoying lying out by the pool and dropped her joint when she heard a loud pounding on her front door. It was so intense Emily was afraid to get up and answer. She was alone at the house. But the pounding kept continuing and Emily reasoned that it was broad daylight in a neighborhood, so she would probably be fine. Emily was used to LA; she could handle anything this little island threw at her.

By the time she got to the door, she was pretty pissed off at whoever was on the other side. She threw open the door with an annoyed look on her face and promptly felt bad when she saw that it was an older woman on the other side. The feeling only lasted a moment when she saw the anger on the woman's face. Emily was immediately in defensive mode. "Can I help you?" she asked icily.

"I've been trying to get a hold of you for some time. I want to talk to you about this monstrosity in your backyard. I am quite unhappy." The woman huffed as if Emily should give a shit what she thought.

"Okay, well, sounds like your problem, not mine," Emily responded noncommittally, giving a lazy shrug she knew would make the other woman angrier. Emily was very good at the I-don't-give-a-shit surfer vibe when in conflict. She *had* spent her summers on Beach Island.

The woman put her hand to her throat like in the movies and gasped. "I think it's absolutely your problem. You are the one building this God-awful thing!"

Emily had to stop herself from laughing, but a smug smile still escaped.

This woman was so full of herself and Emily didn't mind going toe-to-toe. Emily didn't bother to correct her that she didn't live there. She was enjoying herself now. She knew Sam wouldn't stand up for herself. Again, Emily gave a lazy shrug—the kind that used to send Marc off the deep end. "It's my house and my backyard. I get to enjoy it how I please. How does it possibly affect you?"

"It's blocking my view," the woman spat out. "And you don't get to do whatever you want. You have to have the proper permits!" Her face was red with anger and a tiny dot of spit settled on her chin.

Emily was a bit out of her depth at this point but she knew Sam would have done things by the book. Sam was always the mom of the two, bringing a medical kit hiking, and actually studying before tests. She took a gamble and acted offended. "I have all the permits, obviously." She drew out the last word to make the woman feel stupid.

"You're a nasty little lying whore!" The woman was shouting now and gave Emily a hard shove on her shoulder. "You should watch your back. You have no idea who you're messing with."

"You're a fucking psycho!" Emily had lost her coolness and was both angry and a little bit afraid. "I'm calling the police." She pulled out her phone and dialed 911.

The woman looked triumphant for some bizarre reason. Her voice became smooth and in control. "Oh, please do." Now she was the one to smirk.

Emily felt a chill to her bones as she kept full eye contact with this woman while talking to the operator. "They're on their way." She meant it to be threatening to the woman but the lady only smiled.

A few minutes later, two officers pulled up. They immediately greeted the woman: "Well, hello Ms. Mellon! What seems to be the problem?"

Now Emily saw why the woman had looked so victorious. She was not prepared to cede any power. Emily cleared her voice angrily. "*I'm* the one who called. This woman pushed me and threatened me!"

The officer who had greeted Ms. Mellon creased his brow. "Hmm. And what's your name? Don't believe I've met you before." The implication that she was an outsider was clear as day. Emily stood straighter, suddenly fully aware she was standing there in a bikini while Mellon was in a Lily Pulitzer dress. "Sam Finnegan. I own this home," she lied, hoping home ownership would give her some credibility.

He turned again to Ms. Mellon. "What's going on here, Catherine?" So, they were on a first-name basis. Catherine went on to explain how 'Sam' was building an illegal structure in the backyard and she didn't have the proper permits.

"Do you have a copy of the permits, ma'am?"

Emily panicked a little. She had no idea where they would be. "They are at my main home in Rhode Island, but I can provide a copy. Are we going to ignore the fact that she assaulted me?" Emily was outraged.

The officers looked at each other and were trying not to laugh. They probably couldn't imagine this rich bitch attacking anyone. "Why don't you get a copy of your permits and bring them up to city hall? And let's just try to stay away from each other, okay?" The officer's voice was so condescending it took all of Emily's willpower not to smack his face.

Catherine gave a little demurring laugh and then a fake sigh. "I'll get back to my gardenias and let you two get back to *real* work. I'm sorry we had to keep you from the more important job of keeping people safe. We appreciate your service." The last part was solemn and overly flattering, her hands folded as if in prayer.

The officers gave a bow and went back to the cruiser. Catherine gave a tight smile to Emily. "I'd hoped we'd solve this as neighbors, but that doesn't seem to be the case."

"You'll need to accept the fact that I have the right to build in my backyard. I'm sorry it makes you unhappy, but it is what it is." Emily could tell this was the kind of woman used to getting her way. She'd bulldoze

Sam and Emily didn't want that for her best friend. She couldn't care less about the building, but she didn't want Sam to be bullied.

Catherine shrugged. "It is what it is," she repeated and walked back to her own house.

35

"We're reporting from America's self-proclaimed 'safest little cove.' But this cove appears to be harboring a very dark secret, right, Nancy?"

"That's right, John. We're on the island investigating the mysterious death of the beloved Instagram influencer, Emily Larson. Emily's body was found in the waters off the main island back in June and police ruled her death an accidental drowning. But we've uncovered some pretty interesting facts."

"Let's talk a little about how we got here. First of all, our friends out there—shout out to our TwitterTrackers—they knew something was wrong from the very beginning."

"We've got the best team of trackers out there. They sensed something was off right away and they were getting pretty annoyed at us for dragging our feet. We should have known to listen to them!" Nancy laughed.

"We admit we were wrong!" John feigned surrender in his voice. "But we're here now and that's what matters. Let's recap what we know so far. As always, we'll be recording and reporting real-time as we investigate this case."

"Exactly. We'll be recording daily and posting the episodes as soon as our producer, Kalie, works her magic. So, keep sending in your tips and feedback—we'll be working this case together in the search for justice for Emily Larson. Now, John, tell us what brought us here."

"Well, Nancy, our fans first took issue with the fact the police ruled this an accidental drowning even though Emily was a talented surfer as well as a stand-up paddle board instructor. In fact, her digital course was the best-selling of its kind."

"Mmhmm, that's right. They also pointed out Emily's last post appeared to be taken on the Endless Islands—a natural sanctuary right off the coast of the island—and had the caption, 'Help.' I mean, c'mon—how did the police overlook that?" They both laughed.

"So, that's what we knew coming into this, and after talking it over, we agreed this was a situation where we could bring our resources to help Emily's family."

"We've been here a few days now and have already found quite a few interesting things. First of all, we've discovered Emily was out on a date the night she died. So, this is where we need your help. Trackers, if you have any information on who Emily was going out with, please email us at justice@trackamurder.com."

"Exactly. We can't do this alone. Speaking of, we're going to take a quick break to thank our *Track a Murder* sponsors."

"We couldn't be here if it weren't for GoThere luggage. I am obsessed with their hard-cover carry-on. It's perfect for our equipment and *my make-up!*" Nancy laughed. "Get 10% off with our code 'trackers'."

"This mini-series is also made possible by the HearMe podcasting platform. Please be sure to thank our sponsor while also saving 15% off annual plans with the code 'onlytrackers.'"

"Okay, so back to our current case. We know Emily was on a date and we've got our national team of trackers working on that. We also received a tip that Emily's ex-boyfriend was actually in Florida the night of her death. We're still working on getting a few details on where in Florida, but this is not looking good."

"Hopefully, there aren't any other guys Emily was hiding out there—two ex-lovers is enough!" John laughed.

"Seriously! And we're working on a possible bombshell discovery about Island Guy Tours but we need to wait on that one. Remember, Island Guy Tours was leading the group of tourists who discovered Emily's body."

"Talk about needing a vacation from your vacation. Also, Island Guy is actually island gal Shae Brunell. Face of the now infamous noob meme."

Nancy snorted. "Oh my God, I love that one."

"Not me, my kids send it to me every time I try to tell them how to do something."

"I think that covers it for today. Not bad for a few days' work."

"More than the police were able to do in a few months!"

"Well, that's why we do this. America has become so dangerous and the police are either corrupt or overworked. It's up to regular citizens like us to make sure justice gets served."

"One hundred percent. After this next sponsor break, we'll be talking about a time when justice was not served. The Elizabeth Shore case of 1923."

"Yep, it's time for another *Track a Murder* historical case. These are always such a good reminder of how important this work is. Keeps me inspired."

"Exactly. Kind of like our next sponsor Pulp Art keeps me inspired. Have you seen their latest Knox prints? Too good!"

***

Third time's a charm, Pete thought to himself as he walked through the city hall doors. At this point, he wasn't too worried about seeing Dave. He refused to feel bad for following up where the police should have already looked. Besides, what was wrong with a little healthy competition?

"Hi, how are you today?" Pete flashed a smile at Secretary Standoffish. He didn't bother waiting for a response. "I'd like to request the bodycam footage from June 30 for case P6290. Here's my request form. Thank you." He flashed her another smile for good measure.

"Y'all are keeping me pretty busy today with all these record requests." The secretary (Pete would need to get her name if he was going to keep coming up here) looked highly annoyed, though it might be her normal face Pete realized.

Pete's interest was piqued. "You've had a lot of requests today? Hmm. Just in general?"

"No, not in general," she grumbled. "Specific to Miss Emily Larson."

Pete was uneasy. "Who was here requesting information on Emily Larson? Can you tell me?" Pete had an idea but wanted it confirmed.

"No, I can't tell you. But I'm going to anyway because I'm hoping you've got some kind of plan. I watched all seven WSLs that you won, by the way. It was a producer from *Track a Murder*." Her helpful response was at odds with her annoyed face; Pete decided it was just the way she looked.

Pete took a sharp inhale; it was as he suspected but that didn't mean he liked it. "Look, if you can get me the body-cam footage before you get them whatever they requested, I will work as hard as I can to figure something out. And I'm sorry, I didn't catch your name before."

"My name is Diana. Body cams usually take longer than the records they requested, but I will do my best to get you a head start on account of your bad ankle. Actually, they typically take three weeks, so it's going to be tough to do, if not impossible. I have no idea what is going on, but Dave is in rare form over all this. I heard him saying we could all lose our jobs if they report on this case." Diana said the last part in a hushed whisper. "Something about they were trying to make the island look bad for no other reason but to make money."

Pete shrugged. He tended to agree but he didn't know how to make sense of the situation yet. Plus, he wasn't ready to share his theories with anyone. "I don't know much but I can say I'm not a fan of how they pretend to solve crimes when they're making up a story they think will sell."

Diana looked over Pete's shoulder to see Dave walking down the hallway. "You should go. Like I said, Dave's in a mood and I don't think you want to talk to him today. I'll call you when the footage is ready. Do us proud."

Pete gave a grateful nod and prayer hands and hurried out to the parking lot. Pete hoped Diana got him the footage quickly. He had no idea what records *Track a Murder* was pulling or what story they would try and tell, but judging from the last episode they aired, it still looked like Marc was the main target. If Pete could show Sam had lied about being out of town, he'd at least be able to stall for more time. Of course, they were known for having a plot twist a few episodes in, so it might not be Marc they were after.

He wished he understood why and how the police had missed all this crucial information before things got so out of control. Why hadn't they done a basic investigation, particularly when it had gained steam online? Then they'd at least be putting that out there to offset some of the drama. Pete didn't doubt people would lose their jobs if Emily's death turned out to be a murder. Politicians were always making sure the lowest level people got fired to appease the public. Dave would be out of the reelection race, too. Pete needed a way to get the pressure off of Shae while not adding to public outrage on the case. If he couldn't get the body-cam footage, he was sunk. Three weeks was way too long. *Track a Murder* would likely be long gone before that time and the island would be ruined.

Pete sat in his truck wracking his brain for more ideas, but he was stumped. He was running out of time but he had to maintain calm. Just then, his phone buzzed; it was Shae. 'Nancy P came by my work. Said a source told them I always go out to my island before tours. Grilled me on whether I had been. Don't think I answered well. Freaking out.'

This was not good. Pete had been so sure they'd be following up on Marc he hadn't considered they'd think of Shae. 'Who was this source? How much did they know? Can u talk?'

'Not now, at work & am bartending later. Tomorrow?'

'Ok. Don't talk to anyone else before then.' Pete didn't want to scare Shae but he didn't want this getting any worse.

Shae liked the message and Pete put his phone back in the center console.

This was not good. If they somehow found out Shae had moved the body, then there was no doubt in Pete's mind she would become public enemy number one—not like she wasn't that already. Even if the body-cam footage proved helpful, it wouldn't be enough to stop that train.

36

Pete stared at the clenched jaw in his reflection. He hated to do it, but he was out of other ideas. The idea had come to him as he was stalking Nancy and John's social media profiles for hints on what they were researching. Nancy had tweeted something about how jealous her son was that she was on the island because he was really into surfing. Pete despised using his fame for anything—he never took free meals or free stuff unless it was from a sponsor. But he was desperate at this point. So he had logged into the blue check account and tagged Nancy, saying he'd be happy to give her a tour of the island and throw in an autographed poster for her son. Nancy had responded almost immediately and they had made plans to meet up via DM.

Pete hoped he could maintain basic civility; he was far from a fan. He'd agreed to pick her up from her rental condo and take her to Sun City for lunch. He'd point out a few surf spots on the way to help her win some credibility with her teenage son. He pulled Sarg into the driveway and sent a text, letting her know he had arrived.

A few minutes later, Nancy walked out with a huge, bright white smile. Her hair was platinum blonde and if Pete didn't know better, he'd assume she'd lived here all her life. She had on a Roxy sundress and a straw hat that somehow managed to look more local than touristy. She slid into the passenger seat and gushed when she shook his hand: "This is such a treat. Thank you so much for your time! My son is dying of jealousy. We haven't texted this much in months!"

Pete couldn't help but give a warm smile. A *real* smile. Nancy's bubbly energy was contagious. He remembered how hard it had been on his mom when his brother went through a sullen teenager stage. Pete wanted to be happy to help, although he felt like he was conspiring with the enemy. He managed to reply, "I'm glad this worked out. I love this island and I think you will, too."

Nancy was staying in a classic concrete block house, a single-lane road separating the property from the beach. A young family walked along the sidewalk behind them, pulling a wagon full of beach gear. By their red faces, Pete guessed they were on their way back to the safety of air-conditioning. He waited for them to pass and then backed out.

"So, you're out here recording episodes?" Pete acted aloof, trying to portray a surfer cool.

Nancy nodded and then squealed, "I just saw a dolphin! Oh my God, two!!"

Pete laughed. Dolphin pods were pretty common on the river. A set of fins rose slightly above the choppy water, probably a mother and baby. "No dolphins in New York?"

Now Nancy laughed and shook her head.

They cruised down A1A, each admiring the occasional view of the ocean peeking through the mass of palm trees and sea grape hedges. Pete pointed out a few of the main surfer spots like Monster Beach and Light's Out, narrating some history on the local surfing scene. Ever the reporter, Nancy took copious notes. Each site was a reminder to Pete that he was fighting for something bigger than himself, even as the enemy rode shotgun.

"Everyone calls themselves the local spot." Pete pointed to a crappy-looking pale pink building with a dilapidated sign that read: JACK's SHACK. "But that's *actually* where the locals go." At that moment, a red, single-engine plane pulled a banner in the sky above: SEA BREEZE BAR:

WHERE THE LOCALS GO. Pete motioned as if his point was proven and rolled his eyes.

Finally, the tires crunched on the coquina shell and dirt parking lot of Sun City. They grabbed a booth by the window and ordered. The rashguard he'd worn during his first championship hung above them.

Nancy raised her eyebrows towards the rashguard and Pete shrugged with a smile. After more small talk about the island, Nancy looked Pete right in the eyes: "So what's *your* story?"

Pete laughed uncomfortably. "Not sure what you mean. My life is a pretty open book, I think."

"Your surfing days, sure. But what about your new career? As an investigator? That's an interesting career move. Must have a reason." Nancy's face appeared unfazed as she stirred her drink with her straw. She held eye contact with Pete as he shifted in the booth. Her lips, shiny from lip gloss, curled in a slight smile.

Pete knew his face had turned bright red. He laughed uncomfortably again. He took a sip of his water. He'd forgotten to open his straw and the ice clumped at the edge of the cup, spilling water down Pete's chin and front of his shirt. He tried to stealthily dry his shirt, but Nancy was already laughing.

Pete grabbed his napkin and dabbed at his shirt. "What do you mean?"

"Well, you're a PI, right? So, I assume it's your new career? And that's why you reached out to me?"

The chatter of the restaurant receded into the background as Pete became hyperfocused. He'd let himself get too comfortable, but he was here for a purpose. How the hell did Nancy know all this? He recalled his training. Commandment number nine: *Thou shall be quiet.* The silence grew uncomfortable, at least for Pete.

Nancy kept plowing through the chips and salsa as if she was unbothered.

Pete was trying to think of a lie, but he was no good at lying. Even if he was good at lying, Nancy was a formidable opponent and he had no idea how much she knew. He thought of Alexander's second commandment and decided to go with the truth. He gave Nancy a brief overview of trying to help Shae, leaving out the part about moving the body to be safe. He stressed being a PI wasn't his job, it was just a means to an end.

Nancy nodded as if Pete was confirming what she already knew. "I looked you up after you DMed me. Famous or not, it's not my style to get into a car with men I don't know without researching them first. Goes with the job." She flashed another big smile.

The waiter delivered their food: tacos for Pete and a Monster Beach Burrito for Nancy. They took a few bites in silence.

Nancy paused, sipping her iced tea thoughtfully, and then appeared to decide something with a nod. "I think we should work together."

Pete was speechless, so Nancy continued. "This island is very tight-lipped. More than I have ever seen, between you and me. You seem to be trusted and well-loved around here. I can't drive two miles without seeing a statue of you." She tapped her manicured nails on the side of her cup. "If we combine our research resources with your connections, I think we can bring justice to Emily. Because we both know her death wasn't accidental." Another dead-in-the-eye stare followed.

"I can't say I know anything for sure. But I want to help Shae out. She's been through hell these last few months. But I don't want to throw someone innocent under the bus just to clear her name." Pete sensed the implication that Marc was heavy between them.

"Look. I know our haters say we do nothing but blast people, but it isn't true. We have an incredible track record of finding the information that led to the guilty person going to jail. I know we have a couple of cases where the charges ended up being thrown out. But if you look into them, both were due to inadmissible evidence, not that the accused were necessarily innocent. We are here for justice and we never want to bring harm to an innocent person." It was clear Nancy had given this schpiel before.

This was news to Pete and he decided to keep an open mind. He still thought she was being overly-kind to their methods but he also saw the possibility of them working together. *Another commandment: don't burn any sources.* If he could get access to their information, he might get somewhere.

"Okay, I'm down. But on one condition." Nancy raised her eyebrows and Pete continued, "You teach me your best investigation tips." Pete wanted to know how they had gotten to Shae so quickly.

Nancy cracked a wide smile and nodded. "Lovely. I'll have Kalie get you all the non-disclosure forms. And you can get me my signed poster." Nancy grinned and stuck out her hand for a fist-bump. Pete hoped this wasn't a huge mistake. Either way, *commandment number seven.*

37

Achime played as Pete opened the door, holding it and motioning for Nancy to go first.

"Hey Pete, long time no see!" Luke came out from behind the counter to hug Pete. He gave a questioning look to Nancy and she blushed. "Miss Blanston, was it not? How do you know my dear friend Pete?"

Pete looked to Nancy for an explanation. "Mr. Goldman, my name is Nancy Paulson and I'm an investigative journalist."

Pete thought this title was a bit over-formal for the work she did but he remained quiet. *Commandments three and nine.*

"I was in here trying to gather information about the town. I'm sorry for misleading you." Short and to the point. She was used to this.

Luke considered her words. "So, you won't be buying the tennis bracelet?" He looked put out.

Nancy confirmed the bad news with a shake of her head.

"You might have at least picked a charm or something smaller so as not to get my hopes up!" Luke pulled out a hankie and faux wept.

"I will keep that in mind for next time. Again, I am sorry. And I did so enjoy our conversation while I was here. I hope you know that." Nancy was genuine. It was impossible not to like Luke.

This pacified the jeweler. He had no patience for insincerity. "What brings you two here today?"

Pete pulled the bracelet out of his pocket. "Can you tell me anything about this?"

Luke pulled on his goldsmith's visor and looked over the piece. He glanced up. "You didn't find this on the marketplace, I hope?" Pete couldn't quite place the look on Luke's face—offended was the closest he could come. He shook his head no and Luke looked relieved. "Good! This is one of my pieces! I would be very upset if someone put one of my pieces on the marketplace like unwanted garbage." Luke frowned at the thought.

"What do you mean one of your pieces? You mean someone bought it here?" Nancy asked.

"No, I mean it is one I handcrafted myself." Luke then launched into the complete overview of his lost wax casting process, including a brief overview of how the practice originated with the ancient Egyptians. Any other day, Pete loved hearing Luke talk about the history of what Luke called the oldest art form in the world. But today he was impatient to hear more about the bracelet.

"What do you mean? How do you know?" Nancy appeared eager to cut to the chase as well. Pete let her be the one to bring them back on course; he'd rather not upset Luke by cutting him off from his favorite subject.

Luke walked over to Nancy, his eyes magnified into a comic hugeness by the visor. He handed a smaller loupe to Nancy. "See here, on the back of the bezel setting. Most jewelers stamp their pieces with a hallmark. See this lily—next to the 14K mark? That is my hallmark." He nodded approvingly.

"Do you remember who you made this for?" Pete groaned inwardly. Luke would be annoyed that she didn't ask about the meaning of his hallmark.

Sure enough, Luke creased his brow in annoyance. But he responded anyway, "I'm sorry, I don't know. This particular style, I have a mold of it so I have made it for many customers over the years. The stone would be a better clue but it is missing from this one."

"Did you ever make any custom jewelry for Emily Larson?" Pete asked. He remembered she had been in to sell some of her pieces; perhaps she had traded them for something new?

Luke shook his head. "Sadly, no. We talked about the possibility of a custom ring but that was it. But this bracelet couldn't have been hers."

"Why not?"

"The lobster clasp is getting a little loose." Luke used a pair of tweezers to point to the very small gap in the clasp. "That and the fact the hallmark is pretty worn tells me this is an older piece. At least a few years old, but I'd guess around five years old."

"How many bracelets like this do you think you've made over the last five years? And you don't have any idea what type of stone was in it? Do you think it was a birthstone?" Nancy was undeterred.

Luke considered the questions. "Not too many. I tend to do more pendants and rings than bracelets. And this has an oval bezel setting, so it was likely a cabochon stone." Nancy gave him a look like he was speaking another language and Luke was more than happy to explain more: "Your ring, you see you have prongs holding your stone. A bezel setting wraps around the stone like this." He pulled out a bezel-set red stone from the case. "It's named after Bezalel, a craftsman written about in the Torah." Luke couldn't help himself and Pete grinned. "And if we look at your stone again, you can see all the little cuts. It's called faceted. This stone..." Again, he held up the red stone and rubbed the pad of his finger along the top, "See, it's smooth. This is called a cabochon."

"Ok, got it. So, you're saying this bracelet originally had a cabochon. How many of those do you think you made over the last five years?" Pete was impressed by Nancy's complete focus on gleaning at least something from this visit.

"Yes, a cabochon or an opal. I'd guess I've made no more than one per year of this particular bracelet over the last five years. So, around five."

"Can you get us the names of the customers who ordered them?" Nancy was getting excited now. They'd gone from a meaningless piece of metal to the possibility of five names.

Luke looked extremely offended. "That's out of the question! Jewelry is private and my customers have a high degree of trust in me. I would never share their information."

Pete jumped in to smooth things over. This was an example of where Nancy didn't understand the private nature of the residents of the island. They might know each other's business but they didn't like to talk about it to strangers. "Luke, that's completely understandable. We don't want to invade anyone's privacy or put you in a bad situation." Luke looked mollified. "Do you think you can tell us what stones were in each of those five?" Pete figured maybe the stones would help them track down birth months or something. It was better than nothing, at least.

Luke considered and nodded. "Let me think. Last five years. I made this with a star sapphire for..." He laughed as he caught himself about to share the name. Nancy looked like a dog begging for scraps. "A star sapphire, an opal. Ooh, a gorgeous lapis lazuli a customer brought back raw from Iraq! I had it custom cut from the stone and we did a signet ring for him and a bracelet for his wife. Hmm, what else? A moonstone." Luke wrinkled his nose a bit; he had favorites among stones and this was not one. "Oh, and a gorgeous cabochon ruby. It looked like blood."

Nancy looked dubious. "You don't need to check your records?"

Again, Luke looked offended and he looked at Pete like 'Where did you find this woman?' His voice was a bit cold (but not enough to drive off a potential customer): "My pieces are like my babies. I remember them." He shrugged.

Just then, Pete's phone rang. It was the sheriff's department. "Hi, Pete. I wanted to let you know I pulled a lot of strings and got you the video footage early. I sent you a secure link to watch it—it should be in your inbox now. Don't go thinking that's the norm."

Pete sensed Diana needed some validation and he was happy to give it. This footage was huge and he couldn't wait to show it to Nancy. "You are amazing! Thank you, thank you. I owe you one!" Pete could have sworn he sensed a smile over the phone line, though he wasn't sure that was possible from Diana. Her response was as dry as ever, a curt thank you and good-bye.

"Thank you so much, man. This was very helpful and I appreciate you taking a look at this." Pete gave Luke a side five/handshake and then looked to Nancy: "Ready?"

Nancy smiled. "Almost. Luke, I did like the bracelet. Knock another $50 off and I'll take it."

"I knew it! I knew you really did love it—I saw it in your eyes! It's yours." Luke was beaming as he took the sparkling bracelet out of the case.

Pete looked at Nancy, who shrugged and said, "What? It's a business expense!"

Back in the car, Pete pulled out his phone. "I have something huge to show you." He gave a quick rundown of the officers visiting Sam to set the context.

Nancy whistled. "Wow, I am impressed. This could blow things wide open." She seemed genuinely interested and not jealous Pete had a scoop. "Well, let's see it!"

Pete clicked on the link and dragged it so the video filled the full screen of his phone. They huddled over, watching as the officer talked to Catherine. Lots of footage of the ground and people's feet.

Suddenly, they both said, "What the hell?" at the same moment. Nancy looked questioningly at Pete: "Zoom in." Pete was equally confused and pinched the screen to get a closer look. Sure enough, it was as they both thought. He hit pause.

"And you're absolutely sure Sam and Ms. Mellon had this dispute?" Nancy wanted to be sure. Pete scrambled to pull the paperwork out of his satchel to be sure. He showed her the documents and they both stared forward, processing what they had just seen.

After a few moments, he hit play again to be sure. Nothing had changed: it was still there, perfectly clear. The footage wasn't of Sam Finnegan and Catherine.

38

Catherine knocked on the door, her face ready in the friendliest smile she was able to manage. Emily peered through the side window and opened with a bored look on her face. "Come here to yell at me again?" Emily raised her eyebrows and stood, arms akimbo. Her lean, tanned body seemed to tower over the older woman.

Catherine let out a deep sigh and pulled out a vase with bright red oleanders, handing them to Emily. "I came to apologize. I am mortified about how I acted the other day. It's no excuse, but I find I have been losing my temper more quickly since William died. I shouldn't have taken it out on you." The corners of her lips were downturned and Catherine dropped her gaze to the ground.

Emily's expression softened. She felt bad this woman was a widow. "Thank you for saying that. I didn't handle things perfectly either. Let's just call it a truce." Emily put out her hand.

A huge smile broke out over Catherine's face and Emily thought she might have tears in her eyes. *Poor woman,* she thought. *She must be so lonely.*

"Oh, I'd love that!" Catherine shook Emily's hand enthusiastically. "I want to start over and welcome you properly like I should have from the beginning. Will you please join me for a splash tomorrow night? It's an island tradition and it would mean so much to me to be able to start over! I know you won't be here all the time, but we are neighbors after all." Catherine stared at Emily in earnest.

Emily didn't have the heart to tell her she wasn't the neighbor; Sam would sort that out later when Emily was back in California. It didn't sound like Emily's cup of tea but she had nothing else to do. Emily had toured the whole island twice over and she had to admit she was a little lonely, too. She'd even found herself tempted to text Marc. She smiled, "I'd love to. What time?"

Catherine gave a little delighted clap. "Wonderful! Oh, let's make it extra special and take the boat out! I haven't been on the canal in too long. A splash always starts at sundown, which should be around 7 p.m. I am so excited!"

Catherine's excitement was almost childlike and Emily gave a little laugh. "That sounds nice. Should I bring anything?" Emily panicked a little; she had no idea what women like this would eat.

Catherine waved away her question, "Absolutely not. This is my treat to have you over. See you tomorrow!" She flashed a smile and walked back over to her house, giving another wave over her shoulder.

Emily let her shoulders relax as she closed the door. She had felt guilty about the whole fight with the neighbor. She didn't want to put Sam in a bad position. Sam had been so kind to let Emily stay there and the last thing she wanted to do was add more stress to Sam's plate. Maybe by going to the splash, she'd smooth things over and help build a relationship with the neighbor. Emily could tell the neighbors all listened to Catherine, so it would go a long way to have her approval.

Maybe, after they had a nice night out, Emily would come clean and tell Catherine she was a friend of Sam's. If Emily could win Catherine over, she knew Catherine would love Sam. Sam was always the sweetest of Emily's friends. Emily pictured Catherine laughing over the mix-up. Maybe Emily could explain Sam's tiny house to Catherine and help her understand that Sam was just trying to fulfill the wishes of her grandfather.

Emily plopped back down to the leather couch to continue her binge-watching. She was getting pretty excited about being the middleman and getting the neighbors off to a better start. Just as she unpaused the show, her phone buzzed and Emily's mood went sour. It was Marc, again. Emily knew she should just block his number but couldn't bring herself to do it just yet.

She let out an annoyed sigh and opened her messages app. She read the message and was shocked to see he was trying to come see her! He had to be bluffing, trying to find out if she was seeing someone else. There was no way Marc was really on his way to Florida. Emily was surprised to find herself a little disappointed but quickly pushed the thought away. She typed off a quick response saying she already had plans, leaving it ambiguous on purpose.

She tried to concentrate on her show, but she was distracted. Finally, a little bit of action in this boring place. She clicked off the show and went to pick out an outfit. It would need to be sexy enough to make Marc jealous, but not too weird to wear around the neighbor.

She shuddered thinking of her last attempt at an outing here. She'd finally met up with the woman from the bar and it had been one of the most awkward nights of Emily's life. All night, Ali was pressing Emily for the latest make-up and skincare trends. It made Emily feel weird because she sensed Ali was jealous or something. Ali had drained her drinks early on and started crying, telling Emily she was worried Steve was going to leave her for someone younger.

Emily tried to comfort her but the night seemed to go on for ages. Of all places to be, she was going to be stuck on a pontoon boat that only went about 10 miles an hour. Emily hadn't bothered to ask about a brand deal. It would be all she could do to make it through the boat ride. God, she hoped tomorrow night wouldn't be like that. She opened her phone and swiped Marc's text into the archive. She stood to stretch and headed down the hallway to her guest room.

After sorting through all her clothes, Emily settled on a cute pink dress. The designer said it was crocheted and dyed by hand. The pink ties brought attention to her shoulders, one of her best features. The color brought out her skin tone and it was form-fitting without being too skimpy. Double bonus, it was from a brand deal that she needed to promote, so she could cross that off her list. She'd be waiting for the perfect outing to wear it and she finally had found it. Emily gave herself a satisfied smile in the mirror and hung the dress on the back of the door.

Her phone pinged again. Emily headed back to the living room for more drama, both on the show and in her texts.

39

Pete had brought Nancy to the Shabby Shiekh under the guise that they had tables across the water from the hidden island, but he just wanted some of their famous spicy sardines.

"I hate to admit it, but I am stumped." Nancy shifted the tasseled pillow beneath her and leaned back against the Oriental-carpeted wall. She took a long sip of her mint tea as she contemplated the notes in front of them. "And also, your notes look like gibberish."

Pete felt defensive. "I told you, it's the Alexander Algorithm. Commandment number 10! It's to keep your notes top secret." He pointed towards her lavender Moleskin journal. "What happens if you lose your notebook? It's full of confidential information!" he said accusingly.

Nancy conceded by raising her eyebrows and shrugging her shoulders. "Fair enough. But I still can't read it yet. Walk me through what you've got so far again. Let's start with our list of who."

"We've ruled out Sam. Kalie confirmed she was in fact out of town, right?" Nancy nodded affirmative so Pete continued, "So that leaves Emily herself as suicide or drunken accident, Marc the ex, Ali Murphy, and the mystery date who I think is the most obvious choice." Pete wasn't sure if he believed that or if he wanted to bring the focus off of Marc and Shae.

"Uh-uh. Don't do that." Nancy had a warning tone in her voice. Pete raised his eyebrows questioningly. "First and most important, you left off Shae and Catherine." Nancy put a hand up in response to Pete's incredulous eye roll. "I know, I know. But the footage is a big deal and you can't ignore it like that. If you want to solve this, you need to be more objective."

She tapped his notebook. "Speaking of, that's point two: you are way too tied to an outcome that doesn't include your friends. But I'm sorry to say you can't play favorites when justice is at stake. The truth is the truth, whether we like it or not. Hey, you asked me to teach you what I know! Don't shoot the messenger!" She put her hands up in mock surrender.

Pete thought of commandment three and gave a grim smile. Nancy was right. She was only repeating what both his dad and Detective Alexander had already told him in this process. He took a sharp inhale. "You're right. It's a blind spot of mine and I will work harder on being more objective. So then we add Catherine to the list." Nancy opened her mouth to object but Pete quickly added, "And Shae. Thanks for the feedback."

Nancy sat back, appeased for the moment.

Pete looked back at his open notebook. "But it doesn't change that we don't know enough about this mystery date. I think it's a bit crazy to start digging into all these other people without figuring out who she was with the night she died."

"Yeah, true. But we've asked her friends and family and we've pored through her social media. No clues on who this guy was. Whoever he was, she didn't meet him on the match app. So he was likely to be either visiting here or a local." Nancy doodled in her journal, trying to jumpstart her mind. "Let's move on to the how for now and see if it leads us anywhere."

The waiter came by with an iced mint tea refill and they ordered another round of lamb kabobs.

Nancy led this section. "Okay, so putting together our work, let's recap our working theory. Based on what my team has found and from

Emily's last post, we think someone choked her on the island and threw her body in the river." Nancy pulled out a glossy zoomed-in picture of the red marks on Emily's neck. "I'll admit we get stuck when trying to answer how she would get away for a minute and put up this post, though. We also have the issue that the island is almost impossible to find, so how did they even get out there?"

Pete took a deep breath. It was now or never and Pete would have to take a leap of faith in trusting Nancy. "Actually, there's more there. Shae found Emily's body on the island when she was prepping for her next tour. And then she moved it to the other side of the island, where we think the high tide washed it off the island and into the main canal. There was a fire lit when she found Emily's body. I believe Emily was alive when she got to the island." It all came out in a rapid jumble of words and Pete's heart raced.

Nancy choked on her tea. "Are you kidding me right now? When were you planning on telling me this?" Her face was red with anger and she started to pack her papers back in her Neverfull bag.

"I mean, I don't know. I wasn't planning on telling anyone until I figured out what happened. I know how bad it looks for Shae." Pete instantly regretted telling Nancy everything but there it was.

Nancy set the papers in her hand on the table. She looked to the ceiling and shook her head. She brought her gaze back to Pete. "Is there anything else?" she demanded.

Relief crept in; Nancy was talking to him at least. "Not really. That's the worst of it. But Shae did notice Emily had scratches on her arms. And it's hard to see in Emily's post, but look." Pete tapped Emily's arm in the enlarged photo. "I think she somehow swam to the island from the main canal and then had to push through the mangroves. It would make sense if she was trying to get away from someone because it's like a secret hideaway. It would make more sense for someone to swim to it than to be able to find it by boat. That leaves the question of who she was getting away from and how she died on the island."

From the main dining room inside came the faint sound of people singing Happy Birthday. It contrasted with the mournful sounds of a lute playing through the outdoor speaker.

Nancy stared off at the water. "Pete, I'm very concerned that you have a blind spot for Shae." She brought her gaze back to Pete and spoke slowly, "You could be charged as an accomplice to murder if you're wrong about her. Everything you've ever worked for would be gone. Your reputation ruined."

Pete held the eye contact. He'd already lived through that fear after the WSL Finals all those years ago. He was beginning to see that there was more to his life than surfing. Still, hearing his fears spoken out loud so clearly was difficult to sit through. He let a moment pass while he searched his heart and reviewed the facts in his mind. "I understand. It may not seem like I do, but I understand what's at risk for me. I'm willing to pay the price if I'm wrong about Shae," he leaned closer toward Nancy, "But I don't think I'm wrong. First of all, I don't think Shae had a motive. Second, Shae had her tour booked long in advance. Why would she murder Emily the night she would have to go back to the island with a group of witnesses?"

Nancy raised her eyebrows to indicate it was a good point. Pete continued, "I am willing to discuss it objectively if we find evidence. And I don't think Shae makes it to the top of the suspect list at the moment. I think we should stay focused on what the evidence tells us."

Nancy tapped her notebook with her pin. "Okay. So, she's out with someone on the main canal, they attack her, she jumps ship so to speak, and swims to the hidden island where she lights a fire, posts for help, and then dies." Nancy paused thoughtfully. "God, I wish we knew who she was out with! I can't believe it happened right there." Nancy grew quiet.

Pete stared out over the water. He tried to reconcile the beautiful islands, his haven, with Emily's senseless death. Pink light danced off the water and a giant pelican perched among the trees. He flipped back and forth through his notebook and sifted through the photos from Nancy. His frustration was mounting when something on the eave caught his eye.

Suddenly, Pete jumped up, almost knocking over his own mint tea. "I have an idea! I might have a way to see who she was with!"

40

Nancy started to stand up, "Fan-freaking-tastic. Let's go!"

"No, this is a job for a local. Hang tight, I'll be right back." Pete walked inside the restaurant.

Pete couldn't believe he hadn't thought of this before as he walked up to the center bar. "Hey Amar, how's it going? Can I talk to Uncle?"

The young bartender looked at Pete in concern. "Is something wrong? Did Adam fuck something up? God, I swear that kid is more trouble than he's worth." Amar was ready to curse out Pete's waiter.

"No, no—he's been great. I just need to ask Uncle about something. Is he around?"

Amar put down the glass and cloth and walked Pete to Uncle's office. Uncle stood to hug Pete, his silk kaftan shuffling as he moved his substantial body around the desk. "Pete, my friend, how can I help you?" His face darkened. "Is this about Adam? I swear, if he-"

Pete interrupted before Uncle got too carried away. "No, no, Adam has done a great job. I have a favor to ask." He turned and stared at Amar, not-too-subtly hinting it was a private ask. Amar threw his hands up and walked out of the office.

Uncle sat down behind his desk and motioned for Pete to take a seat. "How can I help you?"

"Can I review your dock footage from June 30?" Pete thought back to the time stamp on the post of the island. "From 7 p.m. to about 9 p.m.?" Pete had seen the camera on the eave over their table and knew Uncle had several cameras around the property. Pete remembered Uncle bragging about how the police often used their footage to catch drunken jet skiers on the big holidays. Busting jet skiers was a pastime for all locals.

Uncle flipped through the wall calendar next to him. "Hmm, a Monday, so we were closed." Then Uncle shook his head in disappointment. "But it only goes back 30 days."

Pete's heart sank. Again, his anger rose at the police. If they had looked into Emily's death more, they would have this footage. He thanked Uncle and walked back out to his table.

Moments before he pushed the double doors open to go to his table, Uncle came running breathlessly behind him. "Pete! I have it! I asked Junior about it just in case. He upgraded our systems and they go back six months! Come, come!" Uncle had a huge smile on his face.

They walked into the office and Junior was at the computer. The footage was up on the security screens. Uncle was beaming proudly at Junior as he pulled up the time and date Pete requested. After about 60 seconds of staring at the glittering water, Pete asked Junior to speed up the video. Pete figured seeing someone jump out of a boat would be hard to miss even at 10x speed. Four minutes in and there it was—a definite splash in the water. "Stop!" Pete yelled, startling both Uncle and Junior who had been lost in their thoughts. "Sorry, but can you rewind it and put it down to regular speed?"

Sure enough, Pete could make out a figure jumping off a boat and into the water. Pete got close to the screen, squinting to read the boat registration number or name but it was too dark. Pete had Amar Junior rewind and replay a few more times, but there was no way to read any of it. Pete had Junior freeze on a still of just the boat. Uncle and Junior exchanged confused glances but asked no questions, which was the unspoken policy of Shabby Shiekh.

Pete had an unsettled feeling in his chest he couldn't quite place. Pete stared and stared at the still until recollection began to take form in his mind. Dread filled Pete's entire body. This was impossible. Pete couldn't make sense of it but he would know that boat anywhere. How many times had its owner had him repaint the bottom stripes though the boat hadn't been in the water in years? Once he accepted the possibility, other facts began to click into place. Pete had to tell Nancy.

"Can you figure out a way to make another backup of this video? We must have a copy." Pete looked to Junior, who nodded. "Thank you both so much. I have to go but I'll be back."

Pete came back to the table to find Nancy almost dozing off on the cushions; Pete hated to wake her, but he couldn't wait to fill her in. He cleared his throat and she sat up straight, adjusting her clothes.

"I know who the mystery date was. And I can help you get an exclusive interview."

Nancy's mouth dropped open in disbelief and her eyes were now full of energy. "Okay, fill me in!" She packed her bag while mentally counting the bills Pete had thrown on the table. "Are you really leaving that big of a tip? That guy was the worst!"

Poor Adam. "Let's talk on the way there. But trust me, this is going to make up for the Shae thing." Pete extended his hand to help Nancy up and they went to catch a murderer.

41

"Okay, before we play today's episode, I do want to let our listeners know it's a bit different from our other episodes, right, Nancy?"

"That's right, John. The first part might be a bit confusing at first, but trust us and hang in there. I was taking my first stab at undercover work." She let out a light laugh. "You can let me know how I did when the episode is done."

"Oh, we always have people willing to share feedback!" They both laughed. "Okay, without further ado, here is Episode 3." The noir jazz intro song started playing.

Nancy walked into an immaculate house, admiring the original mid-century tiles and terrazzo floors. The home smelled like faint bleach and gardenias. She paused and admired the gorgeous view from the French doors. It truly was a killer view.

"Thank you again for having me. Pete here has told me so much about your history on the island but I thought it would be wonderful for our listeners to hear it from you." Nancy's voice strained as she tried to make her words reach her host in the kitchen.

Pete gave Nancy an encouraging smile. Guilt was creeping in but he thought of commandment eight and knew this was a time to be creative.

Catherine walked in with a tray holding three tumblers and a bottle of sparkling water. She set the tray on the coffee table and took a seat on the couch, motioning for Nancy to sit down next to her. She looked over at Pete with a smile, "Well, I've never done an interview like this. And I don't listen to podcasts, so I don't know how interesting this will be. But Pete insisted I talk to you and vouched for you, so I will do my best. Tell me again what this is for?"

"We're a traveling podcast and we like to highlight noteworthy people from the places we visit. Of course, Pete being Pete, we talked to him. And then he gave us some names of others we should talk to while we're here. And that's how you came up!"

Pete was impressed by Nancy's ability to tell half-lies with such ease. He was taking mental notes as he did his best to look relaxed.

Catherine gushed, "Oh my, I don't think I qualify to be on any list with someone like Pete! But my family *has* had this house for over 60 years, so I guess it does make me some kind of expert."

Pete moved to the edge of the room as one of the producers clipped a mic on Catherine's blouse. Nancy sat at the edge of the white fabric couch, managing her own mic. Her face was serious as she clicked through email on her laptop one last time. As if by a switch, Nancy turned on her bright smile and angled her body towards Catherine.

"Oh, don't be modest. Okay, I'm going to start recording now."

Catherine gave a nod of consent and Nancy continued, "First of all, the Mellon name is quite famous in American history. Tell me more."

Catherine took in a quick breath and smoothed out her purple skirt. She fixed the smile back on her face. "Oh, I come from the poor cousin's line. Andrew was my great-grandfather's cousin." Pete thought he detected bitterness in Catherine's eyes but she made sure her voice sounded proud.

Nancy nodded as if interested. "Mmm, that's right. And this home, it used to be your family's vacation home, am I right? And it's a beautiful home, I might add. How did you come to live here then?"

Pete was watching Catherine intently. He had never heard these stories. He hadn't connected Catherine to the famous Mellons, which he felt kind of bad about. But seeing the look in her eyes, Pete saw it wasn't a subject she enjoyed.

"Oh, it's quite boring. My parents moved my brother and me here full-time in the early 60s." Catherine took a sip of water.

"After the family had to sell off all the New York properties to pay off debt, correct?" Pete shot a look at Nancy, who was still smiling as if the question were run of the mill.

Catherine gave a hard stare at Nancy. Again, she pulled the tight smile on her face. "Yes, that's right. I told you, it's quite dull. I'm sure there are more interesting stories I could tell!"

"Oh, I don't doubt it! Tell me about the Big Dipper. You would have gone there in the glory days, right?" A softball question from Nancy to lower the tension. Catherine took the bait and shared several anecdotes of the infamous nightclub, like when astronaut John Woods drank so much after one of his missions he danced on the table. The shot of him mid-waltz was now an iconic photograph. Catherine relished the role of being one of the few people around who had been a local long enough to tell these stories. She had warmed back up to Nancy.

After a few of these stories, Nancy changed the subject. "I want to switch gears and talk about some of the other noteworthy islanders. It's my understanding you are a frequent patroness of another of the guests on this special episode, Luke Goldman."

"Oh, I adore Luke. I have several of his pieces! I wear them all the time." Catherine's face lit up and she instinctively put a hand on the custom opal necklace she was wearing. Pete noticed how bare her wrist looked with only a single bangle.

"So I hear! In fact, he made you a gorgeous custom opal bracelet a few years ago, isn't that right?" Nancy widened her eyes in innocence.

An almost imperceptible beat from Catherine. "Yes, it's lovely. I'm an October baby. He always calls me the Opal Queen." She laughed and looked to Pete for confirmation of her VIP status with Luke. Pete nodded in agreement.

"Oh, let's see it!" Nancy clapped her hands in delight.

"Oh goodness, it's all put away right now. And of course, it wouldn't do your listeners any good anyway!" Was it Pete's imagination or did Catherine seem nervous? Catherine's hand went to her wrist as if feeling for the missing bracelet.

"Too bad you don't have the bracelet to show us." Nancy pouted. "I also hear you are big on boating. Tell our listeners about that."

Catherine looked surprised and laughed. "I think you must be confused. My husband was big on boating but I haven't taken the boat out in ages. At least a year!"

"Are you sure? That is confusing. Hang on." Nancy fumbled to pull a video up on her phone. "This isn't your boat right here?" Nancy played the footage from Shabby Shiek for Catherine. Nancy motioned to the boat hanging on the dock out back. "Isn't that the same boat?"

Catherine glared at Pete and then at Nancy. "What is this?" Her voice dropped to a growl.

"Does the name Emily Larson ring a bell?" Nancy's voice dropped to her normal register as she stared Catherine dead in the eye, picking up a tumbler and sipping.

42

Catherine pulled her cardigan over her navy blue shift dress as she sat out by the water. The cranes flew in a V overhead and the reflection of the hull of her boat mixed in with the stunning mix of red and blue from the sunset created an abstract painting in the water. Catherine was unusually wistful; she used to love going out on the water with William. He would always wear his ridiculous captain's hat, even for a quick spin around the islands.

She laughed quietly at the memory. He'd be happily sitting behind the captain's wheel while she lounged on the front deck, waving at all the neighbors as they enjoyed their splashes on their decks. William and Catherine were the envy of the neighbors and Catherine relished the role while William aimed to live up to the expectation and image. He'd always been the better half. Catherine thought those days would go on forever, but of course nothing lasts. She raised her glass to the sky and took a sip of bourbon. To her last splash.

She wished she had been able to take the boat out after he died but it was too painful, more so now. She couldn't bear the thought of people pitying her as she drove the canals alone. She envisioned the smug smiles from the neighbors, glad something bad had finally happened to the untouchable Catherine Mellon. If only they knew the pain under the fake smiles. But people loved to create a villain they could hate—a scapegoat for their own self-loathing.

Over the last few years, Catherine enjoyed her splash from the deck. It wasn't quite the same, but sitting there waving at the boaters every evening was a ritual that helped her feel connected to her husband and her parents. The deck was her connection to the generations of the past. Her daughters were always so busy that she felt like she was the one tasked with maintaining this generational connection. The house was her refuge.

She glanced over at Sam's house and let the anger pass over her. Catherine had no fight in her at the moment and soon her body felt weak. Oh, how this woman had created such a mess. All over a stupid tiny house in her backyard. Over something so base as money. She had no idea what she was taking from Catherine when so much had already been taken.

Catherine had been surprised when the woman first showed up. She'd assumed that perhaps it was a renter but Peggy told her it was Sam Finnegan, the owner of the house. Peggy was rattling on about Bob's doctor's appointments and medical ailments but Catherine only heard the sound of the blood rushing in her ears. *There must be some mistake,* she thought as she fought to maintain her composure.

She'd asked Peggy how she knew it was Sam. Peggy said she had met her earlier that morning. Said the girl was nice enough and she remembered her as a little girl visiting. Catherine's fury mounted as Peggy droned on and on. As soon as Peggy left, Catherine went over in a rage and laid into Sam. Sam had been crying and muttered something about her best friend just dying.

Now Catherine only felt numb. What kind of people were these young kids today? Why had Emily lied to Catherine? Now look what it got her. Catherine raised a glass as the Morgans passed by in their pontoon.

The sky was turning fuchsia now. Catherine thought she'd been in the clear when the commission voted to rule Emily's death an accidental drowning. Dave had been only too happy to go along. Murder would look bad for his reelection. Even when people started talking about it online, she knew he wouldn't cave to pressure from outsiders. It wasn't how things were done here.

Predictably, he'd changed his tune now. She took another deep swig, this time, emptying her glass in one sip. As far as she knew, no autopsy was done, so at least, they wouldn't have found the oleander sap in her system—not that they would have looked. She had banked on the local coroner not having the tools necessary nor the dedication to find the oleander when the blood alcohol levels were so high.

Unfortunately, no autopsy also meant they didn't find the alcohol and so no one had seen it as a case of a drunken tourist like Catherine had planned. The locals were always so concerned about the town going the way of Panama City of Daytona Beach. Oh well. Catherine refilled her cup.

If it weren't for that trashy girl from the trailer park, the body probably wouldn't have even been discovered. Catherine reflected on the stories from her youth of all the 'loose' women that went missing. She'd thought it was the kind of local myth meant to keep débutantes in check when the astronauts were in town. Men away from their wives and reckless from the thought of being shot into space. But a few years ago, Catherine had come across a documentary about five waitresses who went missing back in the 60s. The director implied that they'd been dumped in the Endless Islands, but no bodies had ever been found. If only Catherine had been that lucky.

Much had gone to plan, but it had been foolish and impulsive for Catherine to try to strangle her. She had been so overcome with her anger that she attacked. She should have known she was no physical match for a girl in her prime, though she was pretty sure she had broken her windpipe before being pushed off. Catherine was amazed by what her body had been capable of when fueled by anger. Still, it was a mistake to leave any kind of physical mark on her. Catherine wished she had let the poison take its toll like she planned but it was done now.

All that effort and Sam was still alive and moving forward with her building. Catherine was leaving for her daughter's house in the morning.

She'd have to rent out the house to pay the legal bills. It was that or sell it. The temptation to give up was almost enough to pull Catherine under.

Just then, Sam stepped out into her yard to put something away. The women made eye contact, each icy and cold. Catherine held firm; she would not be the one to look away. Sam was weak, and after only a brief moment, she cast her eyes back to the ground and went inside. A small triumph for Catherine and enough to remind her of her own strength. Catherine had come this far—she'd have to figure out something else. She was a survivor, after all.

43

"I mean, I knew you liked to go big but this is on a whole 'nother level." Nate laughed as he took a sip of his coffee. He gave Pete a fist bump that exploded into an open hand and then looked around for anyone from the force. "You probably want to lay low for a little bit and not come by the office anytime soon."

Pete shrugged. It was fine by him. He'd only set out to help with a little online image management, not to solve a murder or to ruin anyone's life. But now Catherine Mellon had been arrested and Dave had been put on a leave of absence. He was proud he had helped in getting justice for Emily, but it was bittersweet. He struggled with feeling like he had betrayed his friends.

"What do you think will happen to Catherine?" It was hard to replace all those years of knowing her as a family friend with this woman who had murdered an innocent young woman. He hated that he still cared about her, but he did.

It was Nate's turn to shrug. "She lawyered up pretty quickly and she spared no expense on getting a good one. And with no autopsy, it's going to be tough to prove she committed murder. Forensics was able to get footage of Catherine attacking Emily on the video from the Shabby

Shiekh. It also showed Emily jumping into the water. The raid turned up some kind of homemade poison. But will it lead to a murder conviction? I doubt it. It's all pretty circumstantial. Best case would be some kind of manslaughter charge."

"I was surprised to see Dave take such heat when he was coming out so strong on prosecuting her. And between you and me, I was surprised to see him pushing on prosecuting for murder. It was a different vibe than I was picking up from him the entire time." Pete wasn't sure how far he could push Nate for details; Nate was still a cop when it was all said and done.

Nate either didn't know what Pete was talking about or he was playing dumb. "What do you mean?"

Pete went on, choosing his words carefully, "Well, I felt pretty shut down when I brought up the Emily situation with Dave. And he got extra weird when I requested records. So, I was kinda wondering how much he knew about the whole thing. But now he seems pretty full force on Catherine, so I don't know what to think."

"Maybe you misread him," Nate said, holding eye contact in a way Pete thought he was trying to say more.

Pete leaned back in the booth and considered. "I misread him." He repeated, more to himself than to anyone.

"Well, you know. When we're focused on one thing, we can get tunnel vision. We think everything is about The One Thing and miss other stuff." Again, Pete had the feeling Nate was trying to tell him a lot more. Why didn't he just come out and say it? Pete didn't know but he didn't want to push too hard. Pete would have to reflect on this later. For now, he wanted to enjoy his coffee and the sense of accomplishment. Even if Catherine didn't get the full murder charge, he knew Shae and Marc were cleared. And Emily had more justice than she had before. It wasn't perfect and Pete was going to have to learn to accept that.

"How's Shae?" Nate's voice interrupted Pete's thoughts.

"Shae? Good, man. Google did take the negative reviews down and she's become kind of a cult hero. I think Nancy and John did a good job painting her as a decent person in a bad situation, and so people love her now. She even got a couple of talk shows booked to talk about her story and her conservation work." Pete had to laugh. It had been a different, more convoluted path but ultimately he had achieved his goal of helping Shae with the reviews. Of course, now Shae had been flooded with false positive reviews from people who'd never set foot on Beach Island but no one was complaining. The irony was not lost on Pete.

"I can't believe you talked to those guys after they took all the credit. They never would have put together all the pieces if you hadn't found the video and pulled the body-cam footage." Nate shook his head in disgust.

"I wanted no part of that circus. It might have been my idea, but I've had my share of fame and I didn't need any credit. I'm very happy for my name to be nowhere near this mess." Nancy and John hadn't needed much convincing when Pete broached the idea of giving all the credit to the *Track a Murder* team in exchange for ending the mini-series on a high note that made the island seem safe. They'd even included a plug for the Brunell Grant, a privately funded grant for local nonprofits to plant new Mangrove nurseries.

Track a Murder had still brought massive attention to Beach Island. There was no way to avoid that after the story broke. But for the most part, it led to a surge of interest in the ecology of the Endless Islands as well as unprecedented Google searches on the history of the early days of Beach Island. The tourist board confirmed a strong uptick in visitors but they seemed to be interested mostly in history, not murder.

Nancy had been more than happy to comply with Pete's minor requests. After the series dropped, she admitted this had been one of the few cases she'd thought would end up unsolved. Pete wasn't sure whether he should be proud or afraid that the locals had been so tight-lipped and unhelpful. Pete knew he was facing a rare opportunity to get the word out and he'd also probably change his mind if he didn't just jump into it immediately.

"Well, it was cool to hear that you're finally doing the surf competition thing. We've all been waiting!" Nate gave a soft punch to Pete's arm.

Pete's feelings were still mixed but he knew he'd be promoting it nonstop and he'd have to learn to grin and bear it. "It was a long time coming. Greg's been bugging me since I retired. This feels like the right time."

Next spring, Pete would host Beach Island's one and only surf competition. The proceeds would benefit local preservation efforts. The contest was full within an hour of Pete launching the registration site. *Track a Murder* had brought fame to Beach Island but Pete was determined to use it for good. What Pete hadn't admitted to anyone—not even really to himself—was that he was considering competing in the event.

"So what's on the agenda for today?" Nate asked, as he took the last sip of his coffee and scooted to the edge of the seat.

Pete looked at his watch. "It's the second Monday of the month, so it's station day. I have a call with Brody and then I'm heading downtown to hand out flyers. Actually, he's gonna call any minute, so I better run. It was good seeing you." They both slid out of the booth and took a quick stretch of their legs.

"It was good seeing you, too. But don't tell anyone else I said that!" Nate joked as they walked out to the parking lot.

44

Just as Pete pulled into his front seat, his phone buzzed; it was Brody from the commission. "Hey man, what's up?" Pete hadn't talked to Brody in ages, so he had no idea why Brody had reached out and asked to talk over the phone.

"Thanks for taking my call, Pete." Brody had always sounded like a newscaster to Pete, even back in high school. "I wanted to thank you."

Pete gave a confused laugh, "O-kay. For what?" Only a few people were supposed to know anything about Pete helping with the Larson case. Nate had implied some people at the force were pretty unhappy with him; he hoped they weren't spreading the news.

"For bringing down Catherine, first of all. That woman was a menace. And Dave told me you got the permit files and I wanted to say thanks for keeping everything on the DL until the new seats were filled. I was freaking out, to be honest, but Dave said you were a chill guy. At this point, I think we're in the clear."

"I'm sorry, I am not tracking." Pete had no idea what Brody was on about.

"You know, the code expiration Sam used on her building. The case files you requested. Catherine was fighting that and was even trying to

"

buy a seat for Brendan on the commission. I thought you knew all this…" Brody's voice now trailed off.

Pete had an uneasy feeling. Pete had agreed to talk to Justin for Catherine but that was it. He vaguely remembered her saying it was bigger but he'd been focused on other things. Suddenly, Nate's words came into his head and he became alert. "Oh, you're talking about Justin." Pete tested the waters cautiously. He had no idea what he was saying but his intuition told him something was up.

Brody let out an exhale of relief. "Yes! Exactly. The guy has been holding up permits because I guess he's some kind of vigilante. I think he hoped some like-minded commissioner would get voted in and they could reinstate the expired permit code. But that did not happen. It's kind of funny that Catherine was willing to do anything to prevent new permits from coming through but she's the reason it slipped through the vote. Everybody was focused on Emily Larson and nothing else." Brody gave an obnoxious laugh. It was like a wood chopper grinding tree limbs.

Pete gave a noncommittal laugh. He'd also been so focused on Emily's case that he hadn't paid much attention to the city commissioners' vote, either. "Well, I can't take any credit." That much was true.

"Whatever you say, man. But this is going to be huge for the island. Let's just say a certain resort brand with very deep pockets has been dying to get here for ages and can finally break ground here. Justin had been dragging his feet on their permits too but now he's got no excuse. This is going to bring in a lot of extra money for the island. They are very appreciative, if you know what I mean." Pete didn't know what Brody meant, but it didn't sound very legal. "It's good to know you've got good people on your side. This might get very ugly. Now we've just got to be sure the right guy gets on the commissioner board and we're golden."

Pete gave a vague, "Hmm."

Brody continued, "Anyway, I just wanted to touch base. Let me know if you have any ideas for the commissioner seat." Pete felt like Brody was dropping a hint but he didn't bite. "And I'm sure the resort would love to sponsor your surf contest. Do you want me to put you guys in touch?" That was another hint.

Pete suspected Brody was referring to Tropical Resorts and he wanted nothing from them. But he knew it would be better to keep the peace for now. "Yeah, sure, feel free to give them my number. Thanks, man."

They hung up and Pete immediately went to his main source for island information: the locals' Facebook group. The commissioner vote was now the talk of the group. How had he missed this? Just as Nate said, Pete had suffered from tunnel vision. But he guessed they all had; Brody was right that a lot of focus had been on Emily Larson over the last few months.

From what Pete gathered by reading through the flurry of posts, a 20-year-old building code policy had expired right before elections. Locals were complaining Tropical Resorts now had the legal right to build a massive family waterpark resort that was well over the current height limits. Some were going too far as to say the resort had several commissioners in their pocket and that was how the whole thing had been missed in the first place.

A handful of people were defending the new building but the vast majority were against it. People were calling for the item to be put to a vote as soon as possible so the code could be reinstated. It was unclear whether a vote was legally required before Tropical started building. It would all be discussed and decided at the commissioners' first meeting in January. Now that Catherine had been arrested, there were two seats open, which was adding to the confusion about a vote. Locals were crying for a re-vote.

Pete's mind was spinning as he tried to make sense of Brody's call. So, Justin had been slow in approving Sam's permit request because he knew it would set a precedent for Tropical. And Catherine was using her money to run a campaign for Brendan's city commissioner seat in an attempt to influence his vote. If the plan had been successful, Justin could have delayed any approvals until the new seats were filled with people more likely to vote in favor of renewing the expired codes.

But Brody was in favor of letting the code expire and, therefore, disappear. And from the call, it seemed he was working with Dave. That was why Dave was so weird when Pete asked about those particular files and permits; he thought Pete was investigating the codes. Why would he be so nervous if he wasn't doing anything wrong?

Pete shook the thoughts out of his head and put Sarg into gear. He had advertising goals to hit today and he didn't need any more distractions. He'd already spent enough time on the Larson case and he was ready to get back to his life. He turned the bill of his hat backward and headed for the Swamps.

45

Pete tried to focus on writing the new ads for his new fishing charter service (one of the station's new sponsors, courtesy of Pete), but he was too distracted by anger. The last thing Pete wanted to see on his island was a tacky giant waterpark and hotel. He'd spent the last week researching more about the possible Tropical deal and it wasn't good. Sure, it might bring some revenue to the locals through the occupancy tax, but from what he could tell, the tax was more than wiped out by the debt that the city was taking on to give Tropical the land. The city was proposing $15 million in tax credits in exchange for access to a special events space at the mega hotel. It was a stupid deal and Pete had no idea why it was even under discussion.

They'd destroy so much land to make space for the waterpark and the massive parking lot that would be needed to hold all the visitors. Not to mention the pollution impact on the waterways from the chemicals needed to keep the waterpark hyper-chlorinated. And above all, Pete thought it was just plain tacky!

He looked at his phone. Two hours and he had written five words. He couldn't get his brain to stop thinking about the resort and what roles Dave and Brody might have played. Pete and his neighbors couldn't all just sit back and let this mega-corporation take over their island. Maybe he should write down his thoughts.

Before he realized what he was doing, Pete found his first five words exploding into a powerful manifesto of his love for the island and how the codes were an essential part of keeping their island special. He briefly hesitated, but then figured lots of people were posting their thoughts on the issue. Maybe he'd feel better getting it all out of his system; he hit post and closed out of Facebook.

He was right. It had helped him to get his thoughts out and he wrote three versions of his ad in 90 minutes. It had flown by and he was happy with the content. He was about to close his computer down for the day when he decided to click back over to Facebook to see if anyone had commented on his post. The little bell had a red bubble with the number 82. Twenty-five people had commented and another 57 had liked his post. Pete had posted a few times in the group but never had a reaction like this. His profile used his middle name because he only used it for marketplace deals and he didn't need people to know the famous Pete Brown was coming to buy their rusty car or ATV. He read through the comments, a little worried about how people might have taken his passionate post.

Hell yes! Paul, you nailed it. You need to speak at the commissioners' meeting in January.

Thank you for saying what we are all feeling. We appreciate you!

Paul for president! Or at least city commissioner!

Agree with @Michele Stefano – you need to say all this at the meeting. We need someone to fight on behalf of the residents.

Pete felt encouraged that his words had resonated with so many people. He was relieved to know most people were against the idea of the Tropical deal. But then again, Tropical had made it this far in their deal. Pete wasn't naive enough to believe a few angry residents were a match for the smooth-talking lawyers from Tropical Resort. What if democracy didn't succeed in this situation? Or what if no one else spoke up? Pete had no idea what he was going to do, but just in case, he penciled in the date of the commissioner meeting in his journal.

Pete stood and stretched. Hopefully, his post had been enough and others would get motivated to take a stand. Pete wanted to get back to his own life. He needed a break after the last few months. He flipped his journal back to the current week and saw he had two yacht bookings later in the week. Perfect. And he'd be heading out on his Rincon trip soon, too. Pete's stomach rumbled at the thought of a week of eating and surfing in PR. His food fantasies were interrupted by his phone ringing. According to the caller ID, it was Diana from the local police station.

"Hello?"

"Pete, it's Major." Pete's gruff jiu-jitsu instructor sounded tired and scared over the line. "I need help."

Pete's brain strained to keep up; he'd been expecting Diana's sarcastic tone and was having a hard time making sense of hearing Major's voice. They'd never even talked on the phone before.

"Major? Where are you? What's going on?" Was Major calling him from the police station?

"One of the guys here said to call you, said you could help me. Pete, we found a dead guy at my gym this morning."

"Don't say another word." Pete turned his hat forward, grabbed his notebook, and hopped into Sarg for another heat.

GENE ALEXANDER'S 10 COMMANDMENTS OF CHASE

1. Thou shall not play God. Your job is to remain objective and consider all facts equally. As soon as you think you know everything, you will lose the chase.

2. Thou shall not place anyone or anything before the truth. Your job is to seek the truth, not play loyalties or please your clients. Review everyone and every fact with open eyes. You may upset a client here or there, but in the end, your reputation will win you more business than you can handle.

3. Thou shall love your neighbor. Keep your enemies close, but your friends closer. Remember, you are playing the long game in this career. Don't burn your sources and don't burn any friends that would help you move a body. You're going to need good friends often in this career.

4. Thou shall not covet information you don't have. Don't waste time thinking about what information you wish you had. Squeeze every last drop out of the information you do have and the rest will come.

5. Thou shall not become a criminal. You're going to find yourself among a lot of nefarious people with a level of access that will be overwhelming at first. Never forget, you are a fighter of the truth

and light. Know your values and stick to them. Check-in with those who keep you honest.

6. Thou shall rest. Rest is essential for the investigative mind. You'll be tempted by deadlines, money, and ego to keep pushing, but that's when your work gets messy. Take regular rest to allow the facts to percolate in your mind.

7. Thou shall do your job. Your job is to investigate, not wait around for a stroke of good luck. You will know the best tricks of the trade: use the tools at your disposal to win the chase.

8. Thou shall be free. You are not the police. They are limited by a political and bureaucratic system while you can roam free. Be creative and shrewd (but also, see #5).

9. Thou shall be quiet. Loose lips sink ships. Your job is to ask questions and allow silence. Most people hate silence and will overshare to fill the void. Don't be one of those people, and others will solve your cases for you. Talk too much and it will inevitably get back to your target.

10. Thou shall be organized, but cryptic. Keep notes, but keep everything secure using either encrypted technology or the Alexander Algorithm. By keeping notes and referring to them often, the patterns will show themselves.

ACKNOWLEDGMENTS

First and foremost: thank you to my best friend and husband, Jesse. You've probably read this book more times than even I have. Thank you for your thoughtful feedback and your endless encouragement, including carrying a heavier load so I could write. You're the very best example of what it means to be a partner and my life is infinitely better because of you. I love you more than you know.

To Sofia, Vivian, Henry, and Charles: thank you for putting me on the best adventure of my life. You're each my favorite.

To my family and friends: thank you for the support and encouragement along the way.

Kathy Andrew and John Piowaty: words cannot express my gratitude for the gift of your time and keen eye in reading my early draft. Not to mention the kind words that gave me the courage to keep moving forward.

ABOUT THE AUTHOR

As a Florida native and lifelong resident, Angie Ross has no shortage of inspiration from the unusual and mysterious ways of her beloved Sunshine State. She earned her master's from Harvard University and has several non-fiction publications. By day, Angie is a small business owner and lives beachside with her family. This is her first fiction novel.

www.ingramcontent.com/pod-product-compliance
Lightning Source LLC
Chambersburg PA
CBHW070502300726
48975CB00007B/2294